Christmas and a Snowfall of Blessings

STAND-ALONE BOOK

A Christian Historical Romance Book

by

Olivia Haywood

Disclaimer & Copyright

This is a work of fiction. Names, characters, places and incidents either are products of the author's imagination or are used fictitiously. Any resemblance to actual events or locales or persons, living or dead, is entirely coincidental.

Table of Contents

Prologue

Copper Mountain, Colorado, 1885

Noelle Foster lay on the kitchen floor, grasping at her bleeding temple, trying her best not to lose consciousness. Her husband, Henry, had returned just past midnight, as he always did, drunk from his hours spent at the saloon.

As per usual, he'd burst into the room, rousing her from sleep, and demanded a *hot* meal. Not the cold dinner she'd left covered on the stove; the same dinner he'd been too late to eat, and she'd been left to eat alone with only the fruit flies as company.

Of course, when she'd taken too long to heat the potatoes and chicken, she'd spent hours preparing that afternoon, he'd gotten angry. Angry enough to shove her down to the floor, causing her to hit her head hard enough that a faint trickle of blood now stained the collar of her white sleeping gown.

After taking a few moments to recollect herself, Noelle mustered enough strength to lift herself off the ground, rinse her face, and tumble into bed. Leaving a feasting husband downstairs, she stared at the ceiling for a while, listening to the clanking of pots and plates. Tears rolled down her cheeks into her neck, washing away the dreams she'd once had for herself, and left her with nothing but a wet hem and a broken heart.

***

The next morning, tendrils of sunlight danced upon the white ceiling, like beautiful ballerinas come to remind her that she would be okay. Noelle lay in bed, tightly wrapped within her white linens, her copper hair strewn about the pillows. She rose, a sad smile on her face as she let her fingers dance in the light, as if she could take some of the sun's warmth into her soul.

The house was silent save for the calm buzz of insects in the garden outside—no breaking glass, no shattering bones, no sounds of her body hitting the wood floors. Noelle made her way to the kitchen, ignoring the exact spot where droplets of her blood had been. Henry was seated at the breakfast table, thumbing through the newspaper, smoking a pipe. His wrinkled face was pulled into a scowl, displaying his displeasure and usual broodiness. He said nothing, not that he ever did after a... *scene.*

"I need to speak with you about something," she said, her voice timid and awfully soft. "It is rather important. And I think it would please you."

He snorted. "A man cannot even eat breakfast before being bombarded with a woman's relentless cries. What is it?"

Noelle kept her back to him as she mixed the pancake batter, the eggs already sizzling in the pan. "Well, last Sunday in church, Pastor Hastings told me about an orphanage nearby. You see, I'd told him about our—" He cleared his throat, interrupting her sentence and making his point clear. She hurriedly added, "*my* inability to have a child. And he was gracious enough to offer a kind word about us to the Sister in charge of the orphanage."

"Does this story have an end in sight, Noelle?"

"Well, I made a stop there, with no real intent. But I had the thought—to give a child a family, as we have waited so long to have." It had been her life-long dream, and even though she could not manage to carry a baby to term, that didn't mean she couldn't be a mother at all.

"So you have found us a son?" He interrupted, belching in her face as she hunched over to pour him a glass of milk. She did not want to be bothered with his cries of heartburn again.

"Her name is Carol," Noelle said carefully. "Her parents died tragically in a fire, and she's been left without a family or a home."

"I want a son, Noelle. Daughters cannot carry my name and continue my bloodline. Nor can they inherit this ranch," he said, shaking the newspaper upright. "I did not spend my life working this ranch to see it be given to another man's son."

"I understand, Henry. But—"

A plate whizzed by her head, smashing into the cupboard above her. The scrape of the chair was all she heard before he roughly grabbed her by the arm, surely leaving bruises behind.

"Forget that child, Noelle. I am old and I cannot wait any longer than you have forced me to."

With that, he departed, grabbing his coat and hat from the hanger at the front of the house. Noelle was praying by the time the door slammed, asking The Lord for strength.

Chapter One

Copper Mountain, Colorado, 1885

One Month Later

The choir had once again outdone themselves, leaving Noelle to wipe salty tears from her cheeks as she made to file out of the church. Their symphonies had spoken to her soul, making her raise her arms in worship as she felt the warm embrace of the Holy Spirit. She smiled at passing people, laughing when some of them shot her knowing looks. Noelle had a habit of crying in church, much to the adoration and amusement of the people around her.

The sermon had been just what she needed today, a little pick-me-up after the horrid week she'd had. Henry had absolutely forbidden her to speak of Carol or the orphanage again, and had threatened more violence should she not heed his command. There were no more talks of adoption unless she mentioned a son, which she wished were the case, but she had no connection to another child like the one she had with Carol.

The boys at the orphanage were all uninterested and cold, indifferent towards her when she tried her best to form a connection. It was cruel of her to say, but she'd rather not have a child than adopt a child that she did not have a connection with. Was she horrible to say that?

It felt like it. Although if she was being honest, it had more to do with not being able to adopt Carol than it did with not wanting a child at all. Noelle had prayed every morning and night, and even sometimes in the afternoon that week, for strength and the ability to persuade her husband.

He hadn't even considered going with her to the orphanage, nor had he softened in his resolve to have a son. She tried her best, the bruises on her arms, legs, and torso were proof of that; but he didn't relent. Henry Foster wanted a son. And nothing else. No matter what destiny or God might have to do with it.

Henry had once again not joined her, claiming a badly sprained ankle from the night before. But she knew better than to believe the ankle part—she'd bet her prized chickens he had a headache and was packing away her specialty grilled chicken. Possibly also chugging an obscene amount of water to flush his liver and rid himself of the ever-persistent thirst he no-doubt also had. She shook her head, not too upset that he'd been unable to join. She wanted the day to herself, to think and to mourn the family that could have been. She needed that Sunday to reflect and regain her composure.

Noelle dodged puddles as she made her way over to the small white building off the left of the church, lifting her baby-blue skirt and smiling to herself as she spotted tiny little humans running around and enjoying themselves.

They all greeted her with smiles and shouts of joy, overwhelming her with laughter and hugs until she had to clutch onto the building to stay upright. She'd been helping Pastor Sam at the Sunday school since two winters passed, and she loved every second of it. It was a way for her to connect fully to her own inner child and also to surround herself with the childlike innocence adults seemed to lose in their lifetimes.

It was also a way for her to do good, sharing the tales of God and Jesus with young minds so that they might become wonderful young adults who lived for the word of God. However, it was bittersweet.

Pastor Sam joined soon after, laughing and shooing away the hordes of children until they were all seated in a little circle, intent on listening to the tales of their Lord and Savior. Their eyes were wide with wonder as Pastor Sam told them about Noah and the Ark, and how he'd been instructed by God himself.

So many hands raised with questions once he was done, and the kind-hearted man answered every single curious mind's question, until they could no longer contain their restlessness. Afterward, when Noelle was on her way to the small little horse-pulled wagon, she felt the all-too familiar pang of longing and sadness return, making her shoulders feel packed with weight and her heart ache with pain. She loved interacting with the children, and she loved even more to help Pastor Sam with the Sunday school sessions.

But she would be lying if she didn't feel envy at every mother catching their running child into their arms, or every child that received a kiss from their parents. Noelle's face contorted in a pained smile, her heart cracking and soaring at the same time. She was happy for the mothers that had children to hold, but she could not escape the small part of her heart that hurt whenever she saw their moments.

"What troubles you, friend?" Pastor Sam's smooth voice sounded behind her, greeting her with a warm smile as he fell in step beside her. "You are not yourself today."

Noelle smiled, fidgeting with the ruffles on her gloves as they walked. His presence was calming, his unrelenting kindness a safe space for so many to talk about their troubles and heartaches. Pastor Sam always had wisdom to share and advice to give to the downtrodden souls that sought his help, and he was usually right.

"I visited the orphanage that you told me of last week." Noelle started, her voice wobbling with sadness already. "And I met a young girl—her name was Carol—who'd lost her family in a tragic fire."

Pastor Sam inclined his head supportively, prompting her to continue. His black robes dragged through the mud and dirt as they walked, but he didn't seem too bothered about it. He never seemed bothered by anything.

"I fell in love with her instantly—I felt a deep connection to her, like she was meant to be my daughter, and I her mother," Noelle said, but added hurriedly, "I do not want to sound insensitive toward her situation or offend her own mother. But we are connected somehow, Carol and I." Her voice was desperate, her hands clutching at each other as she talked. She was visibly frustrated with the whole situation, and the utter desperation in her voice was saddening.

"I cannot explain it, but I just *know* that God intended for me to adopt Carol."

"Why don't you join my family for lunch," he said, placing a supportive hand on her upper back, "then we can talk on the way."

"Will I not be intruding?" She sounded uncertain even to her own ears.

"A friend in need never intrudes." Crinkles appeared around his eyes as he smiled reassuringly. Noelle relented, following him as he led her to his home. She knew his wife and kids well, as they were friends outside of church. They were wonderful and warm people, and it was at his home that he'd told her about the orphanage, using his very cute children as persuasion for Noelle to give it a try.

"Forgive me, friend, but I do not see what troubles you so," Pastor Sam said carefully. "Are you not happy to have found a child?"

They passed rows and rows of trees lining the sidewalks along either side of the road, fallen leaves decorating the concrete with orange and brown. The air was crisp with winter, their breaths puffing with each word that was spoken.

She shook her head, eyes glued to the sidewalk as she spoke. "It is not the child that troubles me. My husband... he does not want a daughter. He wishes for a son that can carry his name, and inherit the ranch when he has gone. He insists that he is old, and that he cannot wait any longer for risk of passing on without a legacy to leave behind."

Pastor Sam was quiet as she spoke, allowing her to get it all out. "He has forbidden me from speaking of it entirely, claiming that I would not leave it alone if he did otherwise. But I do not understand, Pastor, why did God bring me to this child, why did He lead me to her if I am to be denied? When she is now also denied a mother that would love her dearly? Why do I suffer so?"

Before he could answer, Noelle started crying. "I am a Godly woman. I am a good wife, a whole-hearted Christian, and yet I still seem to struggle more than some of the people I know. Do I not do enough? Must I prove myself worthy of His blessing?"

Pastor Sam looked sympathetically at his friend, smiling softly as she tried to wipe the tears before he could see. "I understand you are struggling now. And I can understand why you might feel like you are being punished, or that you must somehow prove yourself worthy of our Lord's blessing. But I can assure you that if anyone is receiving it, it is you, Noelle."

"It does not feel that way, forgive me for saying."

"The Lord has his own plan for our lives, his own ways that he ensures we live the most wonderful lives we can. And in doing so, sometimes we wait a bit longer than we wished. But I can assure you, friend, that God has a plan for you.

And I am sorry, but He will make your dreams come true when He wishes it, and when He believes is the best time to make them happen." His words calmed her, his voice kind and patient as he encouraged her. He spoke like a father motivating his disheartened child; she'd never felt more disheartened than she had before their talk.

They rounded another corner that would lead them to the front of his home, Noelle could already hear the hordes of children playing. The grass was covered in snow, their footsteps crunching as they went, the scent of pine and snow assaulting her senses. She was suddenly very thankful for the boots she had on beneath her dress.

The home that stretched before them was wonderfully built with a wrap-around white porch, decorated with porch swings and a seating arrangement. It stretched far above them, the second-story home she knew had more than enough rooms for all eight of the kids that now ran rampant in the front yard, chasing each other and dirtying their church clothes, throwing snowballs that would most likely take out one of the large windows that lined the house.

They stopped before the porch, turning towards each other as Sam smiled warmly again.

"Do not lose faith and do not become discouraged. There is a bigger plan at play here, bigger than any of us can see. It will happen for you, friend. I have no doubt about it."

"I was wondering when you were going to saunter back here." Pastor Sam's wife greeted, throwing the dish rag over her shoulder as she did. Her smile was warm, her soft brown eyes awfully kind. She was right on time, as their conversation had ended. Noelle wished she felt better about it all, and she did, ever so slightly. But she still felt the ache in her chest, the impatience in her mind, when she saw their children running about. When she heard their unchecked laughter.

"Please come in, I just finished up with lunch." His wife welcomed, sweeping an arm at the entrance to their home.

Noelle followed them inside, sighing at the blissful aroma of a well-cooked meal. Sam's wife had always been the best cook, and had been someone Noelle looked up to. She still was, especially with the way she handled all eight of their children with ease, while cooking and cleaning. She never complained about it either, or rather, not to Noelle. But she supposed Sam got an earful whenever he didn't do his part. As it should be, Noelle supposed. She wouldn't know what it was to talk back to your husband; she was too afraid.

They led her to the dining room, a large wood oak table in the center of it, already bedecked with a centerpiece, loads of dishes and a plate at each chair. There was even a plate for her, as if they had planned on inviting her all along.

Her heart warmed, Sam's wife imploring her to take a seat beside her so that they might converse. Soon after she yelled outside, bounties of children came running through the den, almost tipping over the chairs in their haste to stuff their tiny little mouths. Sam and his wife did not find it amusing, but not having to be the parent in this scenario, Noelle laughed softly as she watched them sternly control their children's energy.

The afternoon was absolutely marvelous, and the food was delicious. More so, the company she shared was even more wonderful than the big meal they had prepared. Noelle spoke with Pastor Sam and Katherine, his wife, and their children—the latter telling her tall tales of all the dragons they'd slayed that day, and how good they were doing in school. By the time Pastor Sam had walked her to her wagon, her tummy, and her heart, were full. The latter incredibly filled with love and warmth, her belly aching with all the laughter, and her eyes once again alight with joy.

***

Noelle was barely through the door when her husband's grumble reached her, distaste and irritation making the hordes of wrinkles in his face even deeper. He was seated in the living room before he came to meet her at the door, disgruntled and upset that she had not made him lunch.

"I'm sorry, I was at Sunday school, and it ran late." Noelle blushed at her lie, which Henry took immediate notice of. "I'll make something to eat."

"You smell like roast beef. Where were you after church?" He accused, pointed at her with a meaty finger.

"I was at Sunday school, and then Pastor Sam invited me to join his family for lunch."

"So you leave me here to starve so you can eat at another man's house?"

She knew that tone. Noelle had first heard it years ago when they'd first married, and he'd hit her for the first, but not the last, time.

She flinched again, as she always did, when the first slap landed, stinging her cheek. However, she was grateful. This attack didn't last as long as the rest did, and she escaped with barely a scratch aside for the bruise she'd have on her cheek. She wasn't always so fortunate.

That night, in bed, Noelle lay awake as her older husband snored next to her. She had never wanted to marry him in the first place, but her father had insisted, like she was some cattle to be sold and not his own daughter. She listened to his rumbling as she prayed, wishing to God that he would remove her from this childless life. Remove her from this abusive man and the life she had not chosen for herself.

Tears stained her pillow when she fell asleep, wetting her copper hair, and washing away her will to live.

Chapter Two

Copper Mountain, Colorado, 1885

Seated in his office, hard at work, Nicholas Birch was a sight to behold. Immersed in what seemed like mountains of paperwork, his face was pulled into a concentrated frown, slight lines appearing between his brows and beside his eyes. The office around him was deathly quiet, no sound beside the men working and shouting outside, and the sound of chatter in one of the other offices.

He was never one that could work in too much noise. Seated at a large wooden desk, swaying his large body this way and that on his pivotal wheel desk chair, Nicholas just stared at the work before him. The mounds of paperwork in front of him blur together as the hours droned by without end.

His men were deep underground today, his most trusted managers all assigned to this specific project to make sure everyone remained safe and alive. He would never forgive himself if something were to happen under his watch. But it seemed God had other plans for Nicholas.

The door to his office door burst open, Callum, one of his best workers, was absolutely red in the face and hyperventilating where he stood. The young man was leaning against the doorway, carrying the weight of the world on his shoulders. His eyes were panicked, and his face was ghostly white.

Nicholas rose from his chair, dropping the pen on the papers he's just been working on.

"There's been an accident," the boy gasped out. "An avalanche—it's flooded the whole mine."

Nicholas sped around the desk, the young boy jogging to keep up with his long-legged pace as they moved through the various hallways to the entrance of the mine. His heart was beating a mile a minute, his breath coming in short bursts as his world crumbled.

"They're dispatching a rescue team now, but it's likely we won't be able to do much. There's too much snow."

Nicholas said nothing for the whole time it took for them to get to the scene, and he didn't say anything after that either. Mounds and mounds of snow covered the entrance of the mine, and according to other workers, had completely filled the mine as well. They estimated that every single worker in the mine that he'd assigned, was either deceased or about to suffocate.

Survival rate was close to none. And Nicholas had the shameful job of having to inform their families. His heart broke into a million tiny pieces, guilt threatening to choke him to death as he stood there, staring at the natural disaster that had just placed a weight on his shoulders. All of the men he'd promised safety to, each and every man, husband, and father—they were all dead because of his incompetence to protect his men against these things.

If he was being fair, he'd say that it wasn't his fault as he could not predict a natural disaster. But he had known the risks, had assessed them with his team and still decided to send them down. He would never forgive himself, and neither would the families. *But then again, why should they?*

***

The dirt road led to a sprawling ranch home with a wrap-around porch and wonderfully painted wood porch furniture. A porch swing played in the wind, covered potted plants and flowers decorating either side of the wood oak front door. Trees swayed lazily in the wind, covered in pockets of snow. His wagon rolled to a stop, the horse at the front huffing in annoyance and hoofing at the ground.

His boots crunched in the snow, echoing off the wooden boards when he made his way to the front door. This was his last family of the day, then he would return home and take a hot bath until the skin melted from his bones—though he doubted he'd have the hot water to do it. Nicholas was in no mood to haul buckets of water to and fro, just to wallow in sadness.

He had spent all day today visiting the families of the fallen men, taking tear after tear, shouldering insult after insult, and kept every single broken-hearted face in his memory. He did not know how he had gone through the day without breaking down in tears himself, but he steeled himself once more. Last one, and then he'd be done.

Nicholas rapped his knuckles on the door twice, the sound echoing off the wood and summoning the next heart to be broken by his words and decisions.

The door swung open, some of the snow entering the foyer and being captured by the rug thrown a few feet from the door. He almost gasped at the woman that stood there, magnificent in her being.

The woman had copper hair and dark blue eyes, her cheekbones were sharp, and her eyes held intelligence and kindness in them. Her hair was done in an elaborate twist, tiny wisps escaping the overall updo and framing her beautiful face perfectly. Her lips were full and pouty, but not too full to look out of proportion.

Nicholas could simply stare at her beauty, but then remembered why he was there and immediately felt guilty. He had just been ogling a dead man's wife, while there to inform said wife of her husband's tragic death. What kind of man did that make him?

"Good day, Ma'am" Nicholas started, pausing to clear his throat. "You may not know me, but I am one of your husband's employers at the mine. My name is Nicholas Birch."

The woman stared at him a moment, throwing a rag over her shoulder as she stepped away from the door, opening the doorway for him to enter. "Please come in, Mr. Birch."

They were soon seated on the plush couch in the living room, the space decorated with muted shades of green and cream. Mrs. Foster, Noelle, she'd informed him; offered him a cup of tea which he politely refused, wringing his cold hands nervously.

"How may I help you, Mr. Birch?"

He almost corrected her, insisting that she call him Nicholas. But the setting didn't demand it. Deciding not to delay the inevitable, he cut to the horrible chase.

"I am sorry to inform you, Mrs. Foster, but your husband, Henry, has passed away. There was a mining accident, and we were unable to rescue any survivors."

He waited for the wail, or even a shout of agony. But the woman was silent, sitting still as a statue across from him. Her face was stoic, pale as a ghost, and her delicate hands were clutching the rag in her hands until the knuckles were white. Her eyes held no emotion but shock; no tears or remorse, and definitely no grief.

It was like he'd chased the wind from her sails, and she had no idea how to react. Conflicting feelings made her mouth tighten into a tight line. He almost felt awkward, staring at her as she tried to process his news. Was he dumb to say she didn't look all that devastated?

Suddenly she spoke. "Thank you for taking the time to inform me yourself, Mr. Birch. I hope you do not think me rude, but I must ask you to leave now."

He immediately shot up from his seat, almost knocking over the small coffee table she'd placed specially for him and his items. Nicholas nodded. "I am sorry for your loss, Mrs. Foster. Please let me know if there is anything I can help with."

He didn't know why he said it, because he hadn't with the other families, but the words tumbled unguarded out of his mouth. Noelle nodded, making her copper bun bounce, and followed him promptly to the door. She barely gave him another look before she shut the door at his back, leaving him stranded in the cold. He stared at the closed oak door, not really knowing what to do with the lack of reaction from the wife of the man he'd involuntarily killed.

He had grown accustomed to screaming and wailing, some women even throwing valuable stuff around in their house. This lack of remorse was something he was not accustomed to, and definitely not something he expected. So Nicholas wordlessly walked to his wagon, trying his best not to picture that beautiful face, and especially not trying to picture it smiling or laughing at his jokes.

It was utterly disrespectful, to fantasize about a dead man's wife, whom he had just informed of her husband's death. For that, he felt even more guilt and shame.

With flaming cheeks and all, Nicholas sat for a moment, trying to gather his thoughts, and stifle the guilt that once again threatened to choke the life from him. He had a knot in his stomach since this morning, and it had persisted until now. Now it flared, making him nauseous and having to lean off the side of his wagon to empty the contents of stomach. It was nothing but bile since he had not even had the stomach to eat.

Nicholas wiped his mouth, glancing at the house once more before he sat back up, and nudged the horse into motion. On his way home, he thought of the men he'd lost and what their families might be experiencing now. How many of them would be suffering from poverty now that the only means for money was unavailable to them.

Of course, it was cruel to think that way, but it was the reality of this cruel world. Some of the families he'd visited had had more than one child, some of them even having what he would consider hordes. He wondered how they would make do now, he knew the women were out of options. Someone had to stay home and look after the children. Those that had older sons were better off than the women with infant children. He wished there was more that he could do, but he could not care for hordes of children and their mothers. Nicholas simply did not have the time, nor did he have the funds.

His mind ran wild with all of the stress they might now have on them, and he wondered if they would even have a meal to eat come month end and there was no fund to cover the cost of food. Sure, they would each receive a sum, but he doubted it was enough for the size of some of the families.

Nicholas was never one for catastrophizing, but he felt immense guilt at the suffering these people would now endure not only emotionally but physically as well. He knew some of them might have fathers and uncles that could help, but it did not ease the guilt. It was his fault those men had died, and it remained his fault alone. If he had not pressed for them to finish in the mine, if he had indeed listened to his advisors and allowed the men to take one day off, they might be alive.

Even though he knew deep down that the avalanche could have happened on any other day as well. His heart was broken, and he was sick with the thought of all of the suffering the men had gone through–suffocating under mounds of snow as their life slowly drained away and they either froze to death or suffocated. Nicholas was sick as he stumbled into his home, not bothering to eat or lock the door as he bounded for the bath—which was nothing more than a slightly oversized bucket held in his washroom.

However, as soon as the heat from the water hit his head, he was up and out; getting dressed like his behind was on fire. He felt horrible, and for some reason, he'd forgotten to inform Mrs. Foster of the most important fact. He *needed* to return to her home, if only to offer that small mercy to a woman he was certain needed a small miracle.

Chapter Three

Bile rose in her throat like an impending natural disaster, swelling and growing until Noelle was rushing towards the washroom, desperately clutching at her mouth to keep her breakfast down. The wood boards beneath her feet creaked and groaned, a dull thud echoing through the enormous house as she fell to her knees, head buried in a bucket. She still clutched at the cloth she'd held all through her conversation with Mr. Birch, as if it could ground her and keep her from going off the deep end.

Warring feelings fought inside her, relief and grief, worry and happiness, sadness, and guilt—she felt like she was on a rollercoaster of emotions that had no end in sight. When he had spoken those words... she had felt relief. Soul-damning and guilt-causing relief, that she would no longer have to bow to a cruel man like Henry. Like the world had been lifted from her shoulders, Noelle had smiled at the thud of that oak door closing.

As if she had closed the door on Henry and his memory, left buried beneath mounds of snow that suffocated him as he had suffocated her all these years—as he had suffocated her dreams, smothering any joy she might have felt in her miserable life with him. But then, horror had clouded that sunny conclusion, bringing with it the rain of dread and the storm of absolute uncertainty.

A woman in this age was nothing without her husband— she had no 'heir' of Henry to secure the ranch for her, and she had no rights to the money he had left behind. She had nothing but the right to hand over the ranch to whomever might claim it, and say goodbye to her life here—and the life she'd wanted to build for herself and Carol.

It had been her first thought after Mr. Birch had spoken those words—and she didn't know what that made her. Was she horrible for thinking of a future without her husband, so soon after his death? Was she heartless for not crying her eyes out and wailing like the widow she now was? She had prayed for her life to change, and this was the result. Was she directly responsible? Was she to blame for his death because she'd so desperately wanted to escape him?

Lifting her head from the bucket, Noelle stared at the portrait situated above the small washbasin. Her gaze traveled from the picture to the metal bath, and settled on the large white button-up shirt that hung from a hanger hooked on a boudoir-like cabinet she used to store extra towels and linens. The washroom was withered and somewhat neglected, with the varnish from the wood chipped and starting to fade. The ceiling was stained from the steam of the bath, or so she presumed, making it look like mold—which didn't sit right with her. How was she to raise a child in a home like this? Not that she had any reason to fix it up, seeing as she would lose it anyway.

Her knees protested as she rose from her perch, making her wince and hiss. She'd take a sore knee over vomit-clean-up-duty anytime. Just as she steadily rose to her feet, a groan escaping her dry lips, another knock sounded at the front door. Noelle frowned, glancing at the granny clock in her passing by the living room.

It was late to have company, but she wondered if news of Henry's death had reached some of their friends—which would explain the late company. They were probably here to offer their condolences to a heartbroken widow. She snorted at the irony.

The wind bit at her face as the door swung open, revealing a half-frozen Mr. Birch standing on her porch once again, looking even more stricken than he had. For some reason, she was pleased. As if grateful for company she hadn't wanted in the first place.

"Mr. Birch, how can I help you?" She asked, glancing towards her living room. "Did you forget something?"

He nodded, grasping his jacket tightly around him, trying to shelter himself from the cold wind that seemed to blow right through him. She noticed his hair was wet, which would explain all his shivering and the tiny bits of ice forming on the tips of the strands of dark hair. Without waiting for his answer, she stepped aside, motioning for him to enter. Mr. Birch did so without hesitation, following her eagerly as she led him to the fireplace in the main living room. It was bedecked in a horrible orange color-scheme Henry had insisted on, which was why she hardly ever used it.

"You get yourself warm, I'll make us some tea," she said, moving towards the kitchen without waiting for his reply. Her heart was racing for some reason, which was strange since she really had no reason to feel this nervous. He had probably forgotten something, and she would be a horrible human to just send him on his way without a cup of warm tea to lessen the cold on the way home.

Noelle's mind raced as she filled the metal kettle with water, hanging it in the small fireplace in the kitchen. It would take a few moments to boil, so she decided to warm some biscuits for them as well. She'd baked them this morning, per Henry's request, and she had no idea if it would be disrespectful to offer them to another man the day of his death. Did she really even care? She wouldn't know. She didn't know a lot of things right now. Glancing into the living room adjacent to the kitchen, Noelle stared at Mr. Birch's back, wondering what might have prompted him to come back this way, especially in the freezing cold—and with his hair wet. She supposed she'd find out soon enough.

Noelle removed the biscuits from the oven, carefully placing them on the same scorch marks on her wooden counters she'd made the first time she ever cooked in her kitchen. Then, she removed the kettle from its hanging, the steady flow of steam from the nozzle informing her that it was indeed time for that long-awaited-for cup of tea. Her mouth was practically watering.

She'd have indulged in a cup of coffee, were she alone, but Mr. Birch had ruined those plans for her. Goodness knew what society thought of a woman drinking coffee. Quickly tucking the strands of stray copper hair behind her ears, she smoothed down her apron before grasping both handles of the tray, and made her way to the main living room.

Their furniture had never been too fancy; in fact, the frayed seats had all seen their fair share of better days. But they were comfortable and whole enough to sit on, and that was more than most had those days. Besides, the torn fabric and worn wood was easy enough to cover up with a few woven throws.

"Please help yourself to some biscuits as well. They're freshly baked this morning." Noelle said warmly, placing the cup and saucer right in front of Mr. Birch, on the coffee table set there just for him. He seemed warmer now, the shivers having died off, and the ice in his hair melted to wet the strands once again.

"Thank you for your kindness," he said, his voice gruff and slightly wobbly with nerves.

She smiled, sipping from her cup.

"I apologize for disturbing you in this eve of mourning, but I had forgotten to inform you of your compensation upon my haste to leave."

Noelle's eyebrows rose, which prompted him to add. "Not haste to leave, apologies. But haste to leave you with your grief. To not disturb."

Mr. Birch was starting to stumble over his words, his grip turning white-knuckled on the small teacup he held. She swore he'd be able to break it if he squeezed hard enough. She put him out of his misery with a kind smile. "I know what you meant, sir. However, I do not know what you mean by compensation?"

Mr. Birch scooted forward, "Well, we are willing to compensate you a certain amount for the death of your husband. He had been nominated for an extremely dangerous project, with the surety that they would be paid handsomely upon its success. As a result of the incident, the families of the men that perished will now receive the amount as compensation to keep them fed until they can make other arrangements."

Noelle's eyes almost bugged out of her head. "That is very kind of you. But I would much rather offer my share to a family with children—I am alone now, I don't have use for that much money. Especially not when another family might need it more. Besides, my husband has some funds he's put away."

"It's not a large sum, ma'am." He said ashamedly. "But it will be enough to help you during the months you need until you can make an arrangement."

She stared at him, her mind struggling to conjure any thought. So Noelle just nodded, sipping from her tea. "Thank you for your generosity."

"It is our pleasure, ma'am. And I thank you for the tea and biscuits, but I believe I have to go now." Mr. Birch replied, as if hasty to leave. He rose from his seat, long legs stretching as he did. He was a tall, lean man, she just noticed. His length putting him a whole head and shoulders taller than her. And he was muscular, but not brawny, the kind of muscular that was beautiful instead of brutal. He caught her gaping though, resulting in her lowering her eyes so fast she was sure they were spinning in their sockets.

They walked to the front door in comfortable silence, not bothered to rush or to speak, and came to an abrupt stand still when they saw the heaps of snow that had not been there an hour earlier. His wagon stood in the middle of the snow-covered dirt road, the wheels trapped with mounds of snow that'd take at least half-an-hour to shovel. The horse he'd safely tucked in the barn would stand no chance against this weather, which meant he'd have to stay the night.

Judging by their nervous glances, they both reached the conclusion at the same time, and were definitely not keen on the idea. However, there was no other option—he had his fair share of choices to sleep; namely the guest bedroom or the barn; but he was here for the night.

"You can sleep in the barn," Noelle hastily said, deciding for the both of them. "There's a small cot that's usually used by the ranch hand we hire in the summertime. I'll bring you some blankets and a pillow."

She left before he could answer, disappearing into the heart of the house, in search of thicker blankets that would keep the frost of the night from him. The barn was warm enough, and might be slightly warmer because of the horses keeping him company—if not smellier as well.

By the time they'd finished setting him up for the night, and bidding each other a good night, Noelle was exhausted. However, she slept fitfully, expecting a drunk Henry to come stumbling home as if the day had just been a big joke to make a fool of her. But he did not return, and she did not have to warm food in the middle of the night. Neither did she have to clean up her own blood for a change.

In the morning, when the sun awoke a still-tired Noelle, she made her way to the barn, boots squelching in the mud that was a result of the melted snow. Mr. Birch and his wagon were gone, the blankets neatly tidied up and set at the foot of the small cot. But not only had he tidied up, he'd also taken the liberty to fix the hole in the roof at the far-left corner of the barn—something Henry had never gotten to, because of his inability to safely climb a ladder without drunkenly breaking one of his bones. Noelle smiled slightly, the sun warm on her face, and the sight of that fixed roof warm on her heart.

Chapter Four

Monday, the day after his impromptu sleepover in Noelle Foster's barn, Nicholas spent his time seeing the men's families that were left behind. His decision to fix the hole in the roof of the barn had awoken some sense of *"Good Samaritan"* within him, making him realize that he could help in more ways than just shoving money in their pockets.

He could help by fulfilling the smallest part of the role their husband's had unwillingly left behind—by helping around their homes and doing the things that only a man could. Sure, some of them had sons old enough to do the heavy lifting around the home, but not all of them had enough experience to completely take the lead in their household. And to think, it had simply come from a restless night in a semi-cold barn, staring at a hole in the roof and trying to forget about the newly-single woman in the house only a few yards away.

However, with every broken fence or roof he fixed, with every wagon wheel bolt he tightened, and every horse he tamed; he had one thing on his mind—Noelle Foster. She stayed within the corners of his mind like a phantom, refusing to leave until he was almost mad.

He saw her face, the absence of grief in it; he saw the delicate hands with which she handed him the tea, saw her smile when she'd thanked him for his kindness. Her very essence haunted him, chasing away the thoughts of these men that had haunted him before her. It was like she was taking over his body, hijacking his senses until he was nothing but a lost puppy vying for her affections—not that he was. It worsened as the week went by, her memory haunting him at every funeral he attended, her face appearing within every widow he faced.

Hours and hours spent fixing whatever needed fixing in whoever's house—some of them even going far enough to request daunting tasks like installing an outhouse, and even helping them move furniture when they moved away to some distant family member of theirs. And through all of it, his thoughts remained on the tall redheaded woman who'd offered him a cup of tea on a cold day, when she'd been the one that needed to be taken care of.

At the end of the week, on Friday, at Henry Foster's funeral, Nicholas was ready to shame himself for the way he was constantly staring at the man's widow. He was at his funeral, for darned sake's, and he could look at nothing and no-one else but Noelle Foster. She was radiant, even dressed in black, and wore the expression of someone who had just received a new lease on life, not someone who had lost a loved one.

Her hair was pulled back from her face, held in a twist at the back of her head with a needle-like stick she'd stuck into the middle of it. A net of black hung over her face, obscuring those beautiful features, and tormenting him with the urge to lift it and gaze into those dark blue eyes that had captured him from the first moment she'd opened the door.

The church around him was buzzing with people, some wiping tears, some comforting others, and some staring blankly at the floor beneath them. And even though it felt wrong, and it *was* wrong; Nicholas could not keep his eyes off of Noelle, not for one second during the very long funeral. Her back was straight, arms pinned stiffly to her side, as if she were more uncomfortable, than saddened, by the death of her husband.

The weather was suited for a funeral, the clouds dark and gloomy, and shutting out any evidence of the sun. The snow came down in soft flutters, not as heavy as it had been the night he'd spent at Mrs. Foster's home. The ground beneath them was a soggy mess combined with snow and sprouts of green here and there.

Ice cold wind wrapped around them like a cloth, threatening to chase away any warmth, just like death did. He pulled that cold air right into his lungs, holding it there as if it might burn the shame from him, as if it might clear his mind of the woman and redirect his thoughts.

The pine trees around them made the air rich with the smell of nature, representing the parallel of death—life. Nicholas had always loved winter. Perhaps it was his cold heart that called to its like, or maybe it was the stark beauty of nature and its ever-changing seasons that had him in its grasp.

Right after the church service, when everyone was gathered in the courtyard, Nicholas tracked her down, concerned for her well-being in this difficult time. She was surrounded by friends and neighbors, all of them touching her arm sympathetically, smiling sadly, and speaking to her in hushed tones as if she were a small animal one loud word away from breaking. He waited patiently until the last of them had departed, stopping beside her as she was turning from another.

"Good day, ma'am. I just wanted to offer my condolences once again, and see how you were doing." He tried to steady his voice, but nerves were making him stutter like a broken phonograph. Noelle smiled slightly, lacing her fingers together as they spoke. Her hands were covered in black gloves, her long black dress soaking wet at the bottom as a result of the snow they trudged through.

"I am... adjusting." Noelle said, her eyes flashing as if she hid something. "I must thank you for the barn roof you fixed, it has solved a lot of problems for me. When it would snow that heavily, the feed would get wet and rot because of the excess water leaking into the barn during the warmer days. Now I no longer have that problem—thank you."

He nodded, his heart soaring at the thought of having helped her. "Please do not hesitate to let me know if there is anything else—I wouldn't want you to struggle."

Nicholas realized his words, hastily recovering. "I wouldn't want any woman to struggle—with you being alone and all." He almost cringed when the words left his mouth, realizing that he'd only worsened the conversation with his addition to the first sentence he'd uttered. A blush crept along his scruff-covered cheeks, making Noelle smile slightly.

As he tried to compose himself, more groups of people exited the church, making their way to her. Her eyes grew wide as saucers, gloved fingers squeezing each other hard enough to strain the material.

"Please excuse me, Mr. Birch," she said hurriedly, then rushed, moving with a speed he'd never seen before, right to her wagon. She almost whipped the skin from the horse's back as she urged it to move, frantically eyeing every couple that sought her attention. Nicholas watched the road she disappeared down, only returning to himself when he felt a presence behind him.

Pastor Sam greeted him with his signature warm and welcoming smile, the skin around his eyes crinkling. Nicholas stuck his hand out, firmly squeezing the man's hand, "Pastor Sam, how have you been?"

The man shrugged, his robe rippling with the motion. "I have been good. Better than most of our community this past week."

"So you heard, huh?" Nicholas was not doing his best today, the words were like vomit flowing out of his mouth, with no floodgates to stop them. Of course the man had heard, he'd been preparing the sermon's for every funeral that had been held since the accident. How insensitive of him.

As if reading his mind, Pastor Sam inclined his head, motioning for Nicholas to follow. He cast one last look down the drive she had disappeared, trying to mask his curiosity and disappointment. But his friend knew him too well.

"Ask what you want to ask, Nicholas. Speak freely." Pastor Sam said, shoes squelching in the mud as they made their way over to the other side of the church, where he'd left his wagon only an hour before.

"I don't know how to ask what I want to ask, that's the problem." Nicholas responded, playing with a piece of lint in his coat pockets. "I have the tendency to be insensitive and slightly judgmental about some things."

"Slightly?" Pastor Sam teased.

Nicholas only scoffed, but added seriously, "I don't know how to say this without sounding heartless—but she doesn't look or act like someone's widow. She acts like an inmate just set free for the first time in years. She doesn't cry, she doesn't stare at the empty coffin like I've seen most of them do—she doesn't..."

"Mourn?" He supplied, eyes traveling over the courtyard and the people around them.

Nicholas nodded, shame coating his cheeks in red. "It sounds horrible, but it's an observation."

"I understand, Nicholas. There is no need to explain yourself to me." Pastor Sam looked thoughtful. "But if I may give you some advice... do not judge too quickly when it comes to Noelle Foster. You might find yourself judging wrongly."

"How's that?" Nicholas wished for anything to take this hollow feeling from his stomach, anything to erase her from his mind entirely. He felt horrible, pining after a dead man's wife—*discussing* her at his *funeral*. How was he to be redeemed when his actions were less than pure?

He was about to ask, but immediately shut his mouth when Pastor Sam finally answered what he didn't have the courage to ask. "Without betraying Noelle's confidence—she has not had the easiest life. There is more to her story than what is witnessed, and what she has allowed to be witnessed by outsiders such as yourself."

"She seemed like one of those," Nicholas said in answer, thinking back to the moment he'd revealed her husband had passed. The way the wail of heartbreak had never come, those sad and empty eyes that plagued so many of these other wives had never made an appearance on her gorgeous face, and while she'd worn black, her sunny disposition had made it seem like more of an outfit choice than a real mourning of a lost loved one. He didn't know if that made him the biggest jerk on earth, or if he was simply making observations that held a pinch of truth. He decided it was the latter.

"That does not mean she does not feel the pain of his loss, Nicholas. Even though she might seem in better spirits than the others, it doesn't mean she does not experience her own heartbreak."

"She doesn't show it at all, Sam," He added, making sure to remind the Pastor that even though he might know of Noelle's situation, and even though her lack of feelings might be justified, she was still married to the man for years—surely that must strike some sort of feeling in her. "And that is something to watch out for. The whole town can see it, see the absence of grief in her eyes. Goodness knows we've all been around enough widows to notice the absence of their heartbrokenness."

"You are not in a position to make such an observation," Pastor Sam said slightly agitated, "You do not know the woman. But all I shall say is that you would feel the same if you had spent even a sliver of the time she spent with the man."

Somehow, even though he had not intentionally done so, being scolded by Pastor Sam is what made Nicholas take a step back and reassess his approach towards this whole situation. Why did it bother him anyway? He had no business with these people besides compensating them for their husbands' sacrifices, and making sure they were fine. He had no business shoving his blood-red, cold-frosted nose into their affairs.

Nicholas nodded his defeat, clasping Pastor Sam's hand again as he left to mount his wagon. On his way home, with the wind threatening to make his ears and nose frost-bitten, he thought of the forbidden-not-what-she-seems Noelle Foster, and wondered—why was he so attracted to her? What was it that drew him to her so fiercely?

Chapter Five

Two weeks later, Noelle was still fretting over the fact that she wasn't heartbroken over the death of her husband. Dust clung to her every pore as she swept the wrap-around porch of her sprawling home. Her gray dress now had patches of brown and red dust clinging to it, the hem absolutely covered with what she considered heaps of dust bunnies.

The snow had finally stopped enough for her to be able to clean without leaving streaks of mud, and a soggy mess of a broom to contend with. Her mind was always silent during cleaning days, preoccupied with what she was doing and not with what she was so desperately trying to avoid—why she wasn't the least bit concerned about her husband's death.

Guilt as heavy as a wagon crushed her chest every moment of every day and night. Thoughts and memories of her prayer haunted her, her desire for Henry to be gone sticking to her subconscious like a rat to a piece of food. It ate her alive, those thoughts.

The fact that she'd wanted him gone, and now barely acknowledged his absence, made her feel like the worst person on this earth. Was she? Was she truly so horrible for not missing the man who had made her life hell all these years? And did she well and truly bring forth the man's death via her wishes and prayers?

The familiar rattling of a wagon on the drive echoed up the dirt and snow road, the latter crunching as the wheels came to a stop a few feet from the porch. Nicholas sat on the buckboard, a long black coat obscuring those strong arms of his. She knew if he came closer, he'd have a smatter of stubble on his jaw and chin, accentuating his handsome features.

She hadn't seen a lot of him in the last few weeks, as a result of his being busy and herself being too caught up in guilt to consider seeing anybody. Noelle suspected he'd brought the money today, as he had promised the week before the funeral, even though she'd insisted he give it to another family. At first, she had not considered him as someone she'd call handsome, but seeing him now, after seeing him so often, had expanded her mind—making her see beyond guilt and the years of training she'd undergone under Henry's watchful eye and fists.

It made her notice what she'd never noticed before; namely, how handsome he was.

Nicholas jumped from the wagon in one smooth move, patting the horse's neck before dutifully crunching through the snow to meet her on the porch. He smiled warmly, those whiskey brown eyes twinkling as he did. She had not noticed it before, but his eyes held such kindness in them—the type you would read about in the romance books she'd been told to stay away from. Although she'd known he was kind from his actions, it was an entirely different experience to see it in someone's eyes.

"Mornin', ma'am." Nicholas drawled, fake-tipping his hat. Noelle smirked, his humor infectious.

"Good morning, kind sir. How can I help you? Do you want to come in for some tea?" She placed the broom against the porch set, a wooden chair-and-table set Henry had built for her on one of his sober days. It was a bitter-sweet memory now.

Nicholas nodded. "Sure. But I can't stay long—I actually just came by to drop off the money."

They made their way to the front door, just as the distant clamoring of a buggy sounded. Noelle frowned, not expecting company, and gazed into the distance. However, when she saw Beatrice at the front of it, a smile made her face light up like a candle. Nicholas suddenly went very still, but she paid him no mind, leaving him gaping as she rushed—through the mud and dirt, to meet Sister Beatrice, from the orphanage, along with her aide, Sister Margaret and one of the orphanage patrons, Mr. Bartholomew Banks.

She just remembered that she'd signed up for a home visit at the orphanage, and never canceled it in hope of Henry changing his mind about the adoption. She had totally forgotten about it during those last few weeks, and she thanked the Lord that she'd chosen that day to clean.

Noelle smoother her hands down her gray dress, cursing herself for choosing this plain color. Her stained white apron was no better, and barely helped her look better. No-one ever said copper red hair and gray looked good together, but there she was, clad in the worst attire she owned. But she supposed it was better than wearing something rattier.

The buggy came to a stop right next to Nicholas' wagon, Sister Beatrice barely giving Noelle a glance as she openly surveyed and judged her home. Sister Margaret gave her a slight smile, filing out of the buggy in quick fashion. It felt like Beatrice was performing an autopsy on the house, trying to find any fault or flaw, any crack in its foundation, and possibly anything that would scream *"This is not a suitable house."* Noelle didn't know if it was such a good thing for her, but at least she knew this woman was passionate about what she did—no child under her care would be sacrificed to a disorderly house.

She waited at the front of her buggy, offering a friendly smile. It dawned on her that she should have had some beverages or snacks in hand, seeing as there was never any harm done in making a good first impression. The woman also clearly thought so, seeing as she scowled at Noelle's empty hands. The other two guests suddenly felt very uncomfortable, shifting on their feet.

"Good day, Sister. I hope the road was not too tricky, may I carry your things for you?" Noelle reached to take Beatrice's things, retreated a step when the woman grunted and ripped her things back. Stunned, but not entirely discouraged just yet, Noelle simply smiled and ushered them to the front door.

Nicholas was standing right where she left him, a questioning look making lines appear between and above his eyebrows. It made him look slightly animated. She swallowed a laugh as Sister Beatrice walked right past him, not bothering with a greeting, and marched right through the open door.

He exchanged greetings with Sister Margaret and Mr. Banks, motioning for them to enter. Beatrice's chunky heeled boots clunked off the wooden floor as she made her way through the home, stopping in every room, taking in every piece of furniture, and every single flaw or perfection. Meanwhile, Noelle returned to the kitchen to boil the kettle, hanging it above the trusty fireplace. She cursed herself for not baking today, but thought the tea would have to be enough.

Trying her best not to follow Sister Beatrice around the house like a child, she kept herself busy in the kitchen, quickly and efficiently wiping off the expensive tea set Henry had bought for her one summer, after she'd seated the rest in the living room. Nicholas came waltzing in, still wearing his look of confusion, and took a stance by the doorway. He looked her up and down, noticed her smoothing her hands down her dress for the millionth time, and scoffed.

"You look fine, Noelle." He moved closer, slapping an envelope on the breakfast table as he did. "Mind if I ask what this is about? Who are these people, and who is that woman exploring your house like it's an unmarked cave of riches?"

"Well," she said, smiling slightly. "Henry and I had been talking about adopting for quite a while, and I made an appointment for a house visit."

He frowned. "Didn't you think to cancel it? Seeing as the circumstances have changed?"

Was that judgment she was detecting in his tone? It couldn't be. So she ignored it, still polishing her tea set and putting her best apron on, and grabbing her best set of rags to use in case of a spill.

"I forgot about the appointment, initially," she said, lowering her voice to a whisper. "So it must be fate, then."

Noelle could've sworn she heard a scoff from his side of the room, but she ignored it once again. She was focused on other things now, not the reaction of a man that had nothing to do with this in any case. As soon as the clacking of Beatrice's heavy boots sounded in the hall, she rushed out with a tray in hand, and led the woman to the second living room, the one she favored and where she'd seated her companions.

Beatrice was a bigger, taller woman, with a behind that was slightly too big for the couch Noelle had navigated her toward at first, so she redirected her to the two-seater wooden bench couch with the pretty yellow and white flower pillows. Placing one of the wood coffee tables in front of her, she placed a teacup and saucer down for her, pouring it to the brim.

The woman watched on in silence, listening to Noelle's chatter but not deigning to answer—not even a grunt or a nod. Mr. Banks took his tea immediately, sipping carefully at the hot beverage before he set it down. Sister Margaret barely touched her tea, simply setting it down to be forgotten.

Nicholas stayed in the kitchen before she motioned him over, having him take a seat on the small wooden rocking chair beside hers. She was too excited to notice the picture it painted, but judging by Beatrice's assessing eyes, she noticed it immediately.

"You're Mrs. Foster—correct?" Beatrice asked gruffly. Noelle nodded. "Then you must be Mr. Foster?"

Both Nicholas and Noelle stay silent for a moment, the latter answering before either of them could even exchange a look, much rather leave space for Nicholas to correct the woman. Her thoughts had rushed in at a mile a minute—if she didn't have a husband to care for them or to keep this ranch in her hands, she stood no chance in adopting Carol. Women couldn't work, and there was no way she'd find a husband in the short time it would take to foster Carol and then adopt her. And if Beatrice knew all of this, she'd *never* even consider Noelle as a possible parent. So she did all she could do, the only option she had left, and the thing that she hoped wouldn't damn her soul. For the first time since her childhood, Noelle Foster lied.

"Yes, he is." Noelle said, making Nicholas's eyes stretch wide as the saucers they placed their white and pink rose teacups on. Her own heart stopped in her chest, ceasing to beat, as if she was just as afraid of a lightning bolt striking her down for the lie as she was. She could feel its rot settle into her soul, like the lie was ink bleeding on the paper of her innocence and righteousness.

The grip he had on his knee turned white-knuckled, Beatrice hardly noticing as she jotted down whatever notes she made during her short time there. She went through her questions, giving Noelle just enough time to get half of her sentences out before she moved on. She was not an easy woman, and she was one not so easily impressed. However, Noelle would do whatever it took to get Carol there—to take her daughter and give her a home.

During their whole exchange, Nicholas never said a word. All he did was grasp onto his knee with a white-knuckled grip, his eyes settled onto Beatrice and jumping between the two of them as Noelle answered question after question. At some point, she even heard him excuse himself to use the washroom.

She hoped Beatrice and the others wrote his strange behavior off as nerves and not lies she'd dragged him into. It was the first thing they taught you in childhood, and in Sunday school as children—never lie. Big lies, small lies; it was of no consequence. A lie was a lie no matter how big or how small. And it was the thing that was used the most by sinners, every day.

Sure, everyone was a sinner in their daily lives, but she felt like she had *chosen* this sin, instead of letting it happen subconsciously like it did most of the time. No Christian was perfect—but it was one thing to sin unintentionally as was their nature, and quite another to sin intentionally in order to gain something. Suddenly, Noelle felt queasy, like her tea had turned sour in her stomach.

Chapter Six

Nicholas swore his heart was beating in his throat, going a mile a minute, and threatening to burst out of his chest. He splashed the cold water from the bucket on the floor in his face, trying his best to recompose himself before he went back to the conversation being held in the second living room. He had no idea why Noelle had said yes, or even why she'd lie about it in the first place.

However, when he brought into consideration what she was trying to accomplish, and what society demands, then he could slightly understand. Even though he wanted nothing to do with this whole arrangement he'd gotten himself into. Or rather, the one he'd been dragged into, unwillingly and unwittingly. Not to mention the whole act of lying, and how he felt about it.

He'd been told, since he was a boy, that lying was wrong— no matter how big or how small. A lie was a lie. He could have sworn Noelle would be the type of woman who knew that, and tried her best—just like he did, to keep to the traditional values they so struggled to uphold sometimes.

But apparently, he was wrong. And that meant Pastor Sam was wrong about his friend, and that this woman was not who she came forth to be. Without further delay, Nicholas wiped his face on the small white towel hung on the edge of the metal bath and exited the washroom. Praying for forgiveness and patience, or he might lose his mind with this woman.

Why had she even agreed to this visit in the first place? She was without a husband, she could not work, and she had an enormous ranch to run. Where would she find the funds for the ranch, let alone to look after herself and a child. Sure, the money he'd given her might keep them up and running for a few months if she pinched her pennies—but it was so utterly irresponsible of her, he wondered if she was even fit to be a mother.

Immediately, he scolded himself for the thought. Of course she was, he suspected any child on this earth lucky enough to have her as a mother would be so well taken care of, others would think them the most blessed child out there.

When he returned, the conversation was still ongoing; Noelle answering their questions with finesse and class that did not agree with the sin she was committing. She told them tall tales of their *marriage*; how they'd met, how he'd inherited the farm, how he looked after their family, and even went as far as to put her hand on his arm.

And although his morals did not agree with what she was doing, the thump in his chest and the warm feeling in his stomach definitely agreed with her tactics. Her delicate, pale hand wrapped around a quarter of his bicep, resting there as if it was made specially for this purpose, as if his muscle were a cushion for those hard-working hands to rest on.

Before Nicholas could catch himself, he was staring, placing his own hand on hers, making her gasp quietly as the woman—he'd forgotten her name—jotted down whatever answer Noelle had just given them. He'd honestly not been listening, instead staring at that hand touching him and trying his best to calm the raging emotions in his body.

The people in the room noticed him staring, soft smiles appearing on the other two's faces, as if they were a couple in love and being admired. The stern-faced Sister didn't smile though, she just watched him watch Noelle, and wrote down what she saw. He'd be lying if he said it was an act. She was just that beautiful, like a painting in need of admiration for it to be fully understood and adored. Noelle was his own art gallery, and he wanted to get lost in the halls of her soul.

"Henry," Noelle said, the name like ice water flowing down his back and snapping him out of whatever haze he'd been. "Would you please assist me in the kitchen? These lovely guests would like some more tea and I need some help carrying it all."

"Sure," He said gruffly, following her to the kitchen dutifully, and rightfully very angry. She seemed to sense his irritation, because those dark blue eyes were wide and apologetic as they met his, her mouth set in a tight line. He stared at her pointedly as she filled the kettle almost to the brim, and hung it to boil over the fireplace. She put one slender finger over her mouth, threatening him with her eyes, should he be too loud.

"I'm sorry," she pleaded, her voice barely above a whisper. "I panicked, they'll never let me adopt if they know I'm a widow."

"That's ridiculous—"

"I know, Nicholas. But I don't have another choice, do I? I can't work, I won't find a husband within the few months it will take me to adopt, and I just know they won't let me adopt if they think I can't look after a child."

"You can't, Noelle." Nicholas whispered angrily. Was this woman delusional? "You just said it yourself; you can't work, that means you won't have money after the money you do have has run out—which, judging by the size of this ranch, means it's going to be soon. How can you assure a better life for a child if you don't have a means for income?"

She opened her mouth to continue, but he cut her off. "Not to mention that you have now dragged me into this, via *lies*. And what do you plan on doing when they find his death certificate, Noelle? This is not something you have thought through correctly and with the attention it requires."

"I know" Noelle whisper-shouted, making his brows slam down and annoyance flare in his gut. Anger made his face turn red, irritation for this *annoying* woman making him mad. He was just about to spark the argument again, when she whirled, removing the kettle from the fire, and setting it down on the same scorch mark she did every time.

Pouring the boiling water in the white and pink flower teapot, she gave him a pointed look and exited the room with him in tow, carrying the teacups and saucers on a tray. His feet felt heavy, like he'd poured cement into his boots before placing his feet in them and tying the laces. He couldn't exactly describe why he felt that way—besides carrying the weight of sin on his back. It wasn't like he was going to look after Noelle and the child, he'd simply stand in for now until she figured it out. He wasn't tied down to this place, to her. And he could not explain the disappointment that came with that realization.

Noelle poured all of them another cup of tea each, glancing out the bay windows at the back of the couch Beatrice—he finally remembered—sat on. She moved the white curtains, heaps of snow once again coming down on them. He'd seen storms like that, and the last time he'd been stuck on that very ranch as a result of it. It was not looking good for

Nicholas, or the orphanage visitors. Which meant, they'd have to keep this charade up for another while.

Noelle cleared her throat. "I'm sorry Sisters, Mr. Banks—but it seems your window of opportunity to leave has passed. The snow is too thick for you to be able to get through it with the buggy."

Beatrice almost had a heart attack. She sat up abruptly, almost spilling the tea all over herself. "We cannot stay the night, we need to get back to the children."

Nicholas rose from his seat, stretching his long legs as he did. He moved over to Noelle, peering out through the window, his face only inches from hers. His heart stopped dead in his chest, and judging by her slightly parted lips, so did hers. Nicholas risked placing a hand on her upper back,

"I'm afraid my wife is right." He turned back to the guests, looking somber. "You're not gonna get far in that much snow—not with the buggy."

Beatrice's face grew sour, deep lines appearing at the corners of her eyes, mouth, and along her cheeks. The woman was not happy at all, however, the others did not seem so disappointed. He suspected they were happy for the quick break from the orphanage, he imagined it was not easy taking care of so many children—even though he knew they did it out of love and kindness. He could not fault them for seeking a brief reprieve from the ever-busy halls of the orphanage.

"Very well then." Nicholas' eyebrows shot up at the woman's sour tone, but he returned to his seat, ever the relaxed husband. Well, make-believe husband.

Noelle smiled warmly. "I have a wonderful guest bedroom that will suit the ladies perfectly, as for Mr. Banks, however—I'm afraid you'll have to sleep in the barn."

Red coated her cheeks at the declaration, shame possibly leaving a hollow feeling in her stomach. Nicholas knew what she might be thinking, and even though it was utter nonsense, he could still see the gears in her pretty head turning.

She probably thought having one of the orphanage patrons sleep in the barn would reflect poorly on her, and her manners. But he thought differently—Mr. Banks was still a man, orphanage patron or no, so he would be the one to sleep in the barn. That was simply just the way the world worked. Women before men, children before spouses, and God before all else. He just wondered where he would be sleeping, since his barn-bed had been so graciously offered to Mr. Banks.

"I apologize, Mr. Banks. But that is the only bed I have left to offer—I hope I don't offend you?"

The man smiled, warmly and kindly. "Not at all, Mrs. Foster. The barn shall be just fine."

Noelle hurriedly added, moving closer. "The barn is quite warm, and my husband kindly fixed the hole in the roof—so there should be no problem. I shall leave some extra blankets for you as well."

"It is truly no problem, my dear." Mr. Banks said, utterly unfazed that he would be spending his night in a barn. For a filthy rich man, he wasn't too bad, upon Nicholas's observation. He had none of the qualms the rest of the wealthy man usually had. He didn't lift his nose at the torn furniture pillows, he didn't sniff at the tea before drinking it, and he didn't throw a tantrum or find any displeasure with spending his evening sleeping in a barn with horses. He was the first ordinary rich man Nicholas had encountered, and he wondered if it was a blessing or if he should be saddened by the thought.

"Very well. Then it's settled, you're staying for dinner." Noelle's smile stretched over her entire face, her hands clasped together in childlike excitement. Nicholas found himself smothering a smile in turn, despite still being angry with her. She was a radiant human being, oozing kindness and excitement wherever she went and no matter with whom she conversed. Even at the height of her grieving, she'd been smiling kindly at the people who'd come to pay their respects to Henry, and even comforted some of them when she was the one that needed comforting. Not to mention her graciousness in offering these people dinner, tea, and a place to sleep.

Noelle scurried off to get some linens and start with cooking, he followed her around the house like a lost puppy, not daring to strike up the conversation he so desperately wanted to have—not now, when one of them could easily be lurking around one of the many corners of this sprawling ranch house.

So he followed her dutifully, taking the linens she piled in his arms, watching carefully as she motioned for him to be quiet and that they would speak later. He'd assure her they would, giving her a stern and pointed look. He would bargain, was he able to see them now, that he'd burst out laughing. She was a strange one indeed; strong and soft at the same time, intelligent and foolish, humorous and serious—she was both sides of a coin. And he suspected he was still far from having figured her out.

Chapter Seven

Nicholas helped her with dinner, cutting the vegetables as she prepared some boiling water for broth in the small fireplace across from the stove. She set the kettle boiling again as well, making sure to keep the people fed and without thirst. He kept throwing her meaningful glances, stern and unforgiving, but most importantly—with intent that they need to talk, and soon.

The kitchen around them grew heated, both from the cooking pots and pans, but also from their anger. She supposed she had no real reason to be angry with him, and that he was entitled to his anger. But could he not understand how desperately she wanted this? Could he not understand that she was desperate enough to risk a lie or two to get Carol here and in her arms? But then again, she had not yet taken the time to explain to him. All in good time.

Her apron was stained and dirty from the food already, her gray dress still covered with mud at the bottom; and her hair was now starting its usual nonsense. Stray copper strands fell into her face as she worked, frequently wiping sweat from her brow and tucking those hairs behind her ears. She felt like she'd been awake for days, the excitement of the visit finally dwindling down to a light simmer of joy. It drained the last of her strength, leaving her sweaty and tired in the middle of the kitchen still having to cook a meal.

This was nothing compared to the torture of warming food in the middle of the night though, so she supposed she had no reason to complain. However, with memories of her past few years came the memory of Henry and the guilt she'd so easily forgotten about. Nausea made her throat close up, made her place a hand against her stomach as if it would settle that roiling feeling.

Distantly, she heard Nicholas still chopping vegetables, trying his best to catch her attention by *psst*-ing. She ignored him, trying to calm her mind and herself. Why was she like this? Did she truly care so little about the man she'd spent most of her life with? Sure, he hadn't been the best husband, but hadn't there been some moment in her life where she might've grown attached in some way?

Why was there this hollow emptiness inside of her where heartbreak and despair should have been? Why was she unable to feel any feelings about the entire situation besides the guilt of having *wished* him removed from her life—even if it meant death.

She remembered her prayer from that night, how she'd begged the Lord to grant her a better life, where he was nothing and no one to her. She remembered distinctly getting the fleeting thought of his death, before banishing it entirely. However, it seems the recipient had gotten the message.

Finally, banishing all thoughts of her guilt, and of Henry, to face when she was alone, she turned to Nicholas just as he was staring at her again, his eyes threatening to bug out of his head. She swore he could stare holes in her head with those whiskey eyes. Noelle almost snorted, but immediately sobered up when she saw the seriousness in his face.

"I know this is wrong, Nicholas. I have the same thoughts as you, we share the same beliefs. We had the same religious upbringing. You do not have to lecture me on what is wrong and what is right." Her face was tight with anger, but he was unfazed.

"It seems to me like you do need a lesson—what are you going to do months from now when all of this is aired out? How will you look after the child? What will you do when they see me walking in the street and hear someone call me by my true name?" His hands were now aggressively cutting the vegetables, the knife thudding off the wooden cutting board like a guillotine. He was whisper-shouting in response to hers, their voices hushed but laced with anger potent enough to shatter the usually calm atmosphere of the house. She wondered if the guests could hear them, or possibly feel the shift in the home.

"I don't know, Nicholas. But I will sort it out for myself—after tonight, I don't need your help."

Her voice cracked, making his eyes lift abruptly from the cutting board and to her face. They scanned whatever lay there, softening at whatever it was he saw.

"Why are you doing this, Noelle?" He asked, no anger or negative emotions. Purely confusion and maybe a bit of curiosity in his tone. "Why not wait until you can find a husband who will provide for you?"

"Because there will never be another child like Carol, and I am afraid someone will take her if I do not do it now." Her voice was soft, but he heard her clearly. She made sure of it, willed the strength and determination into her voice. "I have a deep connection with this child, Nicholas. One that has been nurtured since that first day in the orphanage, where we had one conversation and I had finally felt like a mother. And then it was ripped away from me, by my husband, claiming he wanted nothing but a son. You have to understand…"

The sound of cutting died off, but she never once looked him in the eye as she spoke. "I was expected to say goodbye to a dream that I already had a taste of—I had *felt* that dream coming true. And he ripped it away from me. It was like he'd dangled a bucket of water in front of a thirsty horse, taking it away just as it dipped its snout in it. He allowed me to fall in love with the idea of a family, let me begin to love that child— then told me that I could not bring her home."

Tears were starting to spill down her cheek, salty and warm against the cold flesh of her face. Out of the corner of her eye, she saw Nicholas set the knife down, reaching out as if to touch her, and then lowered his hand again. She ignored the disappointment, ignored the phantom touch and her suddenly tingling skin.

"But now… I don't have to worry about that. I don't have to ask his permission for anything anymore, and I finally have an opportunity to bring Carol home. To bring *my child* home." She struggled to catch the desperation from leaking into her voice as she spoke. Because that's what she was—so utterly and hopelessly desperate.

She'd bring Carol home, without even having a real plan. And then what? What would she do then? She didn't have any means for income to ensure they had money to put food on the table—not to mention enough money to buy clothes for Carol that weren't hand-me-downs and too big for her.

Tears welled in her eyes, making the wood beneath her blur. "It's all I've ever wanted in my whole life. The one selfish thing I want more than anything in this world—to be a mother. But not just to any child, only to Carol. And I need this home visitation to go well for that to happen, Nicholas. And yes, I'm willing to do anything to make that happen—even lie, as horrible as that may sound."

Noelle stopped talking, her heart shredding with every word she'd just uttered. She feared it might perish completely if she spoke more about this. Nicholas seemed to understand, staying with her in comfortable silence until the stew was ready and she was on her way to set the big oak dining table in the dining room parallel to the kitchen.

She went through the motions, listening intently to the conversation going on in the other room, hoping and praying to God that he would bless her with the opportunity to finally have a child. Perhaps the blizzard was a sign, a blessing in disguise to grant her more time with them; more time to convince them of her ability to take care of Carol.

They could now see the home during the evening, sense its peace as it was surrounded by pine, animals, and snow. See her cooking and know that Carol would have a warm plate of food every night. Indeed, this was a blessing from a forgiving and loving God who had seen Noelle's heartache and decided to apply a balm, granting her this opportunity to make her dream-life a reality.

She tried her best to hear what they were saying, but could not, much to her disappointment.

When she returned to the kitchen, after setting up the jade dining set she'd kept all of these years, she found Nicholas waiting for her. She knew he was waiting, because he was actively staring at her and tapping his finger in rhythm with the ticking of the grandfather clock in the other room.

Nicholas nodded. "I understand."

She released a breath at his words, a weight lifting from her shoulders. She had no idea why she'd been stressed in the first place. His opinion didn't matter, did it? She had no reason to put so much value in his words, so much weight in his actions. He was nothing to her, he was the employer of her now-dead husband.

And that was all. What type of woman was she in any way, to even look at a man in that way so soon after her husband's death. What was wrong with her? Why was she acting so unseemly? So immaturely? So immorally? She wanted to shake herself, snap herself out of this emotionally distant haze.

"I'll help you with this, and then it's done. I'm no liar, and I feel horribly uncomfortable with being asked to be one. But I'll not ruin this for you. You don't have to worry about that," he continued, squeezing the lip of the counter. His rolled-up sleeves revealed muscular forearms, the muscles shifting when he moved ever so slightly. Her eyes were suddenly drawn to them, no longer looking at his face.

They snapped back to his face, his eyes meeting hers in a star that set her on fire. She'd just had this talk with herself, was she seriously going down that road again? Those whiskey brown eyes bore into hers, holding kindness and warmth, and maybe a bit of hesitation.

Did she also detect some distrust there as well? Before she could dissect it even further, Nicholas shifted in place once again, her eyes getting trapped on those muscles again. However, Noelle quickly snapped out of it when he stood, moving past her.

Henry had never been this muscular, and had never held the same kindness in his eyes that Nicholas did. It was like the man was strong and soft at the same time, like that tenderness was a strength in itself. At one point, she'd hated strength—because of what she'd experienced it could do. But now, she wondered if what she had experienced was the opposite of what true strength truly was.

"Thank you," she whispered, not knowing any other words that could express the sudden relief and gratitude she felt in that moment. She knew she'd feel horrible about it later, forcing this man into something he'd never wanted to be a part of. He'd only come to drop some money off, for goodness sake.

But at that moment, she was nothing but grateful. It reflected in the smile she wore all the way to the living room, informing their guests of dinner and taking her seat at the sprawling table. It was the first time it had been so full, the only two chairs that had ever been used being the head of the table and the one right next to it. Her heart soared at the scrape of more than one chair being pulled out, smiling as everyone dug in and grabbed some stew before conversation started.

They prayed before eating, Nicholas-slash-Henry taking on the honor of the prayer, and they all dug in. It was the perfect night, especially considering it was a home visit—the first one. Despite the lying, and the fighting, Noelle was sure she was on the fast-track to bringing her daughter home.

Chapter Eight

The food felt ashen on Nicholas' tongue, his mind wandering as the conversation flowed easily. Noelle was seated next to him, with him at the head of the table—where the husband usually sat—and the rest scattered along the table. Beatrice was seated next to Noelle, eating delicately like a small bird, and asking whatever questions she deemed necessary, which were many.

Nicholas had hoped she would run out of questions, but sadly she did not. The woman talked for what seemed like hours, Noelle answering her questions gleefully and leaving him out of the conversation entirely, which he was thankful for. What he was not thankful for, however, is that she brushed her hands against his arm every now and then.

Like a loving wife would do to her faithful husband. She'd placed her fingers on his forearm or shoulder as she spoke about their apparently very happy marriage. And not because he didn't like it, but because it made his heart race, made blood pump in his ears, and made his throat close up. Apparently, they'd met when she was eighteen, and spent the summer together courting each other. After that, he'd proposed, and inherited this ranch from his parents—they were deceased, fortunately or unfortunately for him—and they were planning on building a family together.

"What made a young couple such as yourself decide to adopt, Henry?"

He was lost in his own thoughts, chewing the pieces of meat from the stew over and over as he simmered on the fact that he was lying and being dragged into a mess he most certainly did not want to be a part of. And though he could blame his lack of response on the fact that he was not listening to half of the things being said, he could also blame it on the fact that his name was not *Henry*. Noelle kicked him in the shin underneath the table, stirring him from his thoughts. When he stared blankly at all of them, she sighed, like an exasperated wife, and spoke for him.

"Well, we have been trying to conceive for the past few years," Noelle said, meeting his eyes. Those dark blue depths held a sorrow in them, an open wound that had yet to heal. His heart tightened, that sadness somehow reached inside his chest to pull at his heart strings. "Sadly—due to no shortcoming of Henry's, but rather my own—I have been unable to carry a child to term."

He started to frown, properly confused at why she would feel the need to give herself the fault. And why she felt the need to protect his masculinity? He wondered why she had glanced at him then, her eyes searching his face in an attempt to find... approval? But before he could go too deeply into it, she looked away, Sister Beatrice already steering the conversation away again.

The dinner felt like it lasted for ages, even though he enjoyed the stew Noelle had made. The snow outside kept coming, winds he was sure could blow the roof off making the doors on the home and barn rattle. Glancing at the storm outside, he was thankful the guests had decided to spend the night, otherwise they might have fallen victim to the cold. However, that made him wonder how he was going to get home. His wagon wasn't much better equipped for the blizzard either. It seemed he was out of options.

After dinner, Nicholas helped Noelle gather some warm blankets for Mr. Banks, and he insisted he be the one to take it out to the man so that she wouldn't have to. The woman was a hurricane, always busy with something, and never standing still in the same place for too long. That was evident when he returned from the barn, covered in snow, and shivering like a madman, to find her cleaning the kitchen, as if she wasn't already exhausted from being on her feet all day. The other guests had already retired for the night, locked in their guest room and possibly already asleep.

"I should probably get going," he announced, blowing hot air into his hands to chase away the cold. His fingers were numb, and his body was one more shiver away from cracking like a glass. Noelle turned abruptly, almost dropping the pot she held in her hands. She glanced out of the window behind him, the curtains leaving a big enough sliver for her to see the raging blizzard outside.

"What are you talking about? You can't leave now—and especially not in that storm." Noelle said, moving towards him.

"Then what do you suggest I do?" He said, agitated. He was tired, and he wanted to sleep. He didn't have the energy or the time to waste arguing with her right now. "The barn is taken, the guestroom is taken—there really isn't any place for me to spend the night."

"You can sleep in my room," she said, making him stop dead in his tracks. Nicholas was unsure if he'd heard correctly, and he hoped he hadn't because that would mean a great deal of trouble for him. First the lying, and now sharing a bed with a woman before marriage? A *widow*, nonetheless. Not to mention that her husband had only passed a week before, and here he was, expected to sleep in her room—possibly her bed. How did he find himself in this situation? And why was she leading him on this path? Most importantly, why hadn't he uttered the word *no*, yet?

Before his thoughts could drown him in shame and guilt, Noelle continued, as if she could sense his spiraling and was trying to stabilize him. "You can sleep on the floor—but you must sleep in my room. What married couple doesn't sleep in the same room?"

Nicholas supposed she was right; how were they going to sell themselves as a married couple if he was sleeping in another room, let alone in his own home so far away from his apparently inherited ranch. He felt immensely uncomfortable with this situation, his skin feeling like it was crawling underneath his clothes.

His clothes felt like they fit too tight, the collar of his shirt seemingly growing smaller and smaller, threatening to choke the life out of him. Noelle stood eerily still, watching his internal struggle. He was silent for a good long moment, the two of them just watching each other and weighing the cons of what they were about to do.

It wasn't so much the act of sleeping in the same room—though a part of him was ashamed of that as well—but more so what it would mean should others in the community find out a newly widowed woman was sleeping in the same place as the employer responsible for her husband's death.

Not everyone was under the impression that the Sisters and Mr. Banks were; and not everyone would know that they had truly just slept. If this got out, it would mean social suicide for Noelle, and an undesirable reputation for him.

This was not a thing to take lightly—even if he did sleep on the floor.

Noelle turned back to the kitchen, her back towards him as he tried to master his emotions. In just two weeks of meeting this woman, he's already been roped into something he didn't want to be a part of. But she needed his help, and he had set out to help in the first place—though he never would have thought it might lead to this mess.

Sighing, Nicholas went to go help her clean up, neatly folding the cloth placemats up and placing them in the drawer of the beautiful china cabinet against the wall right by the window. It was delicately crafted, with swirls and whirls engraved into the wood to make it look even more beautiful. It was a chestnut color, a deep brown-red varnish shining and making the things inside look even more expensive.

Such expensive things in some parts of the house, and neglected things in others. How could a woman with such wealth have any reason to be unhappy, when there were so many others who did not have nearly as much. A china cabinet, this sprawling house, the yards of land she had no use for now, and the clothes she had. From what he'd seen, she wore expensive dresses made with quality material—none of the raggedy material some of the other wives wore.

But then he thought back to what Pastor Sam had said, about Noelle being able to hide her unhappiness away, and that there was more to the story than he had first let on. He thought back to the moment at the dining table earlier, how she'd taken the blame for something nature had caused, and how she'd felt the need to protect his masculinity by emphasizing that their inability to have children was far from his fault.

None of them had eluded to it, or even thought about it, but she'd added it anyway. Made a point of making sure they knew that the fault was entirely hers. Strange, Nicholas thought, strange to add something so inconsequential to the conversation.

After they cleaned up, and Nicholas' thoughts finally left him alone, they made their way upstairs, quietly climbing the creaking steps so as not to wake the guests. Judging by the amount of snoring coming from the door to their left, however, he'd say they were deep enough in their sleep to not notice anything short of a bomb going off.

Her room was the door to the right, adjacent to the washroom in the upstairs part of the home. He was once again baffled by her wealth, having two washrooms to accommodate both guests and herself. But it was nothing compared to her bedroom.

It wasn't big, per se, but it was more spacious than the average bedroom. It was bedecked in chestnut furniture; a dresser, vanity, and four-poster bed furnishing the white-bedecked room. Her linens, pure white to match the walls, were spotless, and had frills at the bottom of the duvet.

Small decorative dots of yarn bedecked the corners of the duvet, complementing the matching pillows and decorative pillows thrown on top. The true wealth was not in her home, but in the very obviously expensive sheets she had on her bed. He now understood why she'd insisted he give the money to other families, seeing as she had no need for it herself—especially not since she could splurge on unnecessarily pretty linens.

"I hope you don't mind sleeping on the floor. I'll give you some blankets to soften the floor a bit," she rushed out, the creaking of the hallway linen closet reaching his ears. Nicholas stood still for a moment, and then silently freaked out. He mouthed horrible curse words, looking around the outrageous room, and abruptly returned to his sullen state when she entered the room again, linens in hand.

There were two sheep-wool blankets that would do well as a makeshift mattress to soften his lay on this hardwood floor, and two wool blankets he would use for what they were. Noelle silently handed him a pillow as he made his bed, waving him off when he made sure she was okay with the white-covered pillow on the dirty floor. Of course she wouldn't be worried, she probably had a stack saved up somewhere she could use to buy another pillowcase just like it—for an outrageous amount of money.

Later that night, close to midnight, Nicholas was awoken by a frantically crying Noelle. She was thrashing at the blankets from what he could see, and there were hoarse cries leaving her lips. He sat up, throwing the blankets off of him as he rose to rush to her side. She was fast asleep, sweat glistening on her moon-white skin as she fought whatever nightmare she was stuck in. Fear twisted her beautiful face, her copper hair damp with sweat and tears, every tight line in her face illuminated by the silver light of the moon shining through her bedroom window.

Nicholas grasped at her arms, gently shaking her awake so that he wouldn't startle her. After a few shakes, her deep blue eyes finally fluttered open, a fear so primal shining in them, that he almost lost control over his own legs.

Noelle was sobbing now, falling into his arms as he sat on the edge of the bed, cradling her as if she were a baby. Rib-shaking, back-breaking sobs shook her whole body, a broken noise escaping every now and then as she worked through the horror she must have experienced just now.

He smoothed his hand over her hair, making soothing noises as she cried every ounce of heartbreak out of her system. Somehow, he knew it was not heartbreak for Henry, but because of him. She sobbed for hours, cradled in his arms, clutching at him like he was a life-raft, and she was stuck at sea.

He let her, holding her while she broke apart, keeping pieces of her together so that one might not get lost. She clung to him like that all night, even after he got into bed beside her, with her cradled on his lap and still hysterical. They slept like that until morning, Noelle didn't stir again. Not once.

Chapter Nine

Noelle, Sister Beatrice, *Sister* Margaret, and Mr. Banks stood at the front of the buggy, bidding their farewells. They thanked her for her hospitality, catastrophizing what might have happened had they daunted the storm of the previous night.

Some of the pine trees surrounding her home had been bent or broken, leaning against each other in seek of support to recover from the raging storm that had so easily broken their stumps. One could say it *stumped* them. Noelle snorted at her joke, earning strange looks from both Mr. Banks and Sister Margaret. Beatrice simply ignored her and continued with the conversation.

"Well, Mrs. Foster. It is with great pleasure that I admit the home visitation had gone extremely well. You should be able to continue with the adoption of little miss Carol." Sister Beatrice hid a ghost of a smile, glancing at the sprawling ranch home behind Noelle. Nicholas stood on the porch, looking sour and honestly like a problem she did not want to deal with at this moment.

She felt joy and excitement stretch a smile across her face, free and without limitation. Her heart soared as high as the eagle that screeched above them, singing as sweetly as the wind that blew leaves and dust against them. The sun was out today, warming her face as Beatrice's news warmed her heart. Composing herself, she straightened her spine in an attempt to look as much the elegant mother-to-be as she could.

"That is such wonderful news, Sister. I thank you for your generosity, and for trusting me. I hope you have safe travels." Noelle said in her most sophisticated tone. She waved them off as they mounted the buggy, trailing off down the road and disappeared from view. She kept waving until she was certain they were gone, and only then did she turn to acknowledge the six-foot-one sourpuss standing on the porch behind her. They still hadn't spoken about last night and she had—quite frankly—refused to even acknowledge what had happened.

It had been the first time in a long time that she'd had the nightmare, one so intense she'd been sobbing in his arms for most of the night until she drifted off to peaceful sleep. It wasn't because of the embarrassment that she didn't want to talk about it—it was about the fact that she had never slept so soundly in her life. In his arms, the person she'd least expected, she had found such profound peace that she was as rested as she'd been when she was a child without fear.

Nicholas had not only calmed her mind, but also her soul, making her sleep like the dead. She felt *safe* in his arms, which scared her far more than her hysterics embarrassed her.

Noelle approached him, if not carefully. His arms were folded as he leaned against one of the beams that held up the porch roof. His posture was relaxed, if not slightly stiff, but his eyes were like a storm. A hurricane waiting to lay waste to everything around it. She cleared her throat, struggling to contain the beaming smile on her face. Nicholas stared down at her, eyes trailing over her face, and then the pale green dress she wore today—with a green petticoat to match and defend against the cold.

It was Nicholas who spoke first, his voice gruff and stern. "I understand your desire to have a child, Noelle. And I understand that you have a soul connection to Carol—but you must realize that you have convinced these people that she will grow up in a household with a mother and father. You deceived them into believing it when you have no way to really take care of her now that Henry has passed."

Noelle opened her mouth to object, her heart suddenly aching from his words. He did not give her the chance, instead opting to speak over her. He took a step down from the porch as he spoke, anger lining his body.

"How will you work, Noelle? How will you take care of this ranch and work when you have a child?" He was a foot away from her, staring her down with those beautiful eyes.

Noelle knew he was right, knew she had been thinking impractically. She knew that she'd just made her life a whole lot more difficult than it had been. She had been lying awake thinking about it last night, right before her nightmare came to rob her of the peace she had. There was no excuse really, and nerves were causing a whirlwind in her belly. She had just been so excited to adopt Carol, had seen her dream within her grasp, and leaned in to snatch it up before it could escape or be blown away once again.

"I know, Nicholas. You don't have to remind me. I am a grown woman, you know." She snapped at him, lifting her chin in defiance. Something twinkled in those brown eyes before he leaned closer, their lips barely a hairsbreadth from each other.

"It's a shame you don't act like it." And then he moved away, taking a long-legged stride towards his waiting wagon.

Noelle scoffed, sticking her tongue out at his back. She kicked the dirt on her way to the house, covering her pretty green suede boots in dust. What an insufferable man. What a horribly arrogant, insufferable, rude, and condescending man. She watched him leave for work through the small windows in the door, the colored glass painting him in a more colorful fashion than he was.

Still angry and irritated even an hour later, Noelle started to get ready for her volunteering at the church this afternoon. She chose her best dress, but also the darkest, in case it required getting dirty. She'd hate for her lighter dresses to become stained. Even though they were only putting together Christmas boxes for the orphanage, she thought it was better safe than sorry.

Maybe there was some crafting to be done. The ride on the way to church was bumpier than usual, courtesy of the melted snow leaving welts in the dirt road leading from the ranch to the town. She thought as she rode, her mind so incredibly busy she almost missed the turn that would take her right to the front entrance to the church.

What she'd done—and what she'd forced Nicholas to do the night before—weighed heavily on her, making her question her morality and the type of person she was. It also made her doubt her faith, and how much of a Christian she truly was if she managed to lie so easily. Guilt made her nauseous, causing her to almost hurl her guts out as she came to a stop over a bumpy patch of semi-dead grass in the middle of the rest of the wagons.

As Noelle walked to the church, she felt as if all eyes were on her, as if the unsuspecting people surrounding her had somehow become privy to what she'd done. It felt to her like she was under scrutiny, like she had *"liar"* written on her forehead. She grabbed her coat closer to her, as if it would shield her from being judged, or keep the truth from coming out. It was like that during the entire day she volunteered.

Every leering eye felt like it penetrated her skin, seeing right into her soul. Every giggle emitted by someone felt like it was directed at her, centered around her downfall because of lies. Every pointing hand and every frowning face felt like they were directed right at her, judging and shaming her for poor decisions, lies, and utterly shameful behavior.

By the afternoon, she had had enough, and went seeking Pastor Sam's guidance. She found him where he usually was, at the playground, speaking blessings out over the hordes of children that could—because of their innocent ignorance— not care less. Screeches of delight and joy made her smile, his welcoming one making the heavy weight on her chest seem like a feather.

Her friend had always been a steady force, immovable, and aiding all of them in the same. He seemed able to steady even the most nervous of them, like a source of strength planted specifically here for this purpose, to aid and guide the rest of them. She supposed that was the purpose of a Pastor; to spread the word of God and guide the masses.

"Noelle, how have you been?" He asked, his eyes regarding her with platonic love and respect.

"If I may be frank, I have not been good." Tears suddenly welled in her eyes, making her lower her face in case someone was looking. "I have not been good at all."

Pastor Sam put a hand on her upper back, guiding her away from the masses. "Walk with me."

He waited until they were out of earshot of others, before turning to her. Noelle sniffled, rubbing underneath her eyes, and wiping her nose with a cloth handkerchief.

"How can that be? Sister Beatrice informed me that she approved your application to adopt. I thought you would be overjoyed?"

Noelle nodded, sniffling. "I am—I was, I mean. But you don't understand; it was the way I obtained the approval. What I did to get approved. I am a horrible human being, Pastor."

He placed a hand on her shoulder. "Slow down, and take a deep breath."

"I came to ask for your forgiveness. Last night, I lied to them—to Sister Beatrice and Mr. Banks and the other *sister*. I told them that my friend was Henry, and that we'd been married for years." It all came spilling from her tear-soaked, lie-telling mouth. "I had booked an appointment a long time ago, and it seemed to have slipped my mind. Beatrice asked about Henry, and in a moment of pure panic I told them that my friend who'd been visiting me was him. I told them he was my husband."

"Forgive me if I sound a bit brash, but why would you do that, dear child?"

"Because I am desperate; I am so desperate to have a child, to adopt Carol, that I panicked and lied to be able to make that happen. They would never let me adopt her if they knew I was without a husband, Pastor. You know how this society is, how harsh it becomes toward unmarried women. How would I ever have gotten that chance to adopt her if I hadn't lied about it?" She looked at him, clutching at his arm as the desperation to make him understand took over.

"I have no means of work, no income, I have a ranch that needs running, and I have no husband to provide solutions for any of those problems. Tell me how that would've convinced Beatrice of my ability to care for Carol? Because I cannot. All I see is a woman who has once again been thrown into the deep end, and in her attempt to claw herself out, was desperate enough to *sin* to achieve what she needed. I feel like a failure, like a horrible and immoral person."

Pastor Sam made soothing noises as she broke down, rubbing her upper back in an attempt to stave off the sadness making a mess of her. He looked at her with pity, making that guilt swell like a balloon having air constantly added to it until it finally popped.

"I do not agree with what you have done, my friend. But I also do not forsake or judge you for it—just as God does not forsake you for it. We are all sinners, and we all have moments of weakness where sin might seem like the easier and faster route to getting what we want." His voice was soothing, calm, and collected. "It is nothing but a weak moment you've had, and there is no shame in having a weakness. My advice to you, my friend, is to pray for forgiveness and guidance in this trying time. The forgiveness for your soul, and the guidance for what it is you need to do about the situation you have put yourself in."

"What if God does not forgive me? What if this is my punishment? What if he takes Carol away from me completely as a lesson for my greed and deceit?" Noelle was distraught, her blue eyes devoid of any of the joy she'd expressed just this morning. Before Nicholas had come charging in with reality and ruined it for her. Well, not ruined, but made her realize just what exactly she'd done and made her wonder how she was going to fix it.

"Our God is not without forgiveness, Noelle. He understands us better than we will ever be able to grasp—he is our creator after all. He does not punish, he redirects you onto the path he has set out for you. And I am sorry, my friend, but if that means that Carol is to be taken away then you have to trust Him. This is all hard to hear, I know," he continued, placing a hand on her arm in tender support and consolation. "But you have to believe that He has a plan that stretches far above our comprehension. You also have to believe in His ability to forgive, and that forgiveness starts within yourself. He knew what you were going to do before you did it, which means that you have been forgiven far before you ever contemplated sinning. But you will only start to feel the relief that comes with forgiveness once *you* extend that forgiveness to yourself."

While she was a tad bit hysterical, Noelle thought she understood what he meant. She always knew to count on him, that he would provide comfort and guidance when someone needed it most, especially in their darkest moment when they needed the reassurance of God's love for them to keep them going—no matter what matter of sin they might have indulged in. She wiped her tears, walking beside Pastor Sam as he guided her back to her wagon.

"All will be well, Noelle. Pray about this and have faith. God is never absent from your life, so do not be absent from Him."

Chapter Ten

For the next week, Nicholas decided to busy himself with work and nothing else—or rather, *no one* else. The mound of paperwork before him was enough to keep him busy for sure, but his mind still wandered. It still made rounds checking in on the thought of her, as if to reassure him that she was still ever-present and making a quick appearance through the sea of words.

The days passed slowly, at a pace that was both agonizingly slow and too fast to really grasp the significance of every moment. He was stuck in some time loop since he'd left her sprawling ranch home.

Ever since the accident, things around the mine had been extremely quiet, the usual drone of laughter and good-natured teasing reduced to the occasional attempt at a joke, and the usual work-place conversation needed to keep the place running. He was the one doing most of the talking, being one of the main employers, and somehow it made him feel dirty.

As if this mine had become a graveyard and he was soiling its sacred grounds by speaking aloud. He supposed it was a graveyard, if the men still buried under slowly melting mounds of snow had anything to say about it.

That prompted Nicholas' next thought; how they would remove the bodies of the men once the snow fully melted. Would his superiors even allow them to enter the mine to accomplish that task? How would their bodies look? He couldn't imagine it being a pretty sight. Would their families even want to see them, claim their decomposed bodies? Go through that heartbreak all over again? Or would his superiors seal the mine completely and leave them there for eternity?

Both of those options troubled him, made his jaw tighten and his brows draw together. He felt a pit in his stomach, growing worse each day, and tried his best to focus on his work again.

But his mind wandered back to her, to that night they'd shared a room. The night she'd awoken in terror, and he'd needed to hold her for her screams to quiet down. He knew, just as he had known that night, that the subject of those night terrors was none other than Henry Foster—if the sobs and whimpers she'd emitted were any indication.

It had sounded close to begging at one point, almost causing his heart to break into a million tiny pieces. When she'd sobbed in his arms that night, he'd realized what Pastor Sam had meant when he said there was more to the story that was Noelle's marriage and her lack of sadness regarding her husband's death. He could still hear her screams, still feel the shaking of her body against his as she sobbed. It haunted him, that awful sadness that plagued her. It made him mad with the memory of it.

It was almost an hour later, and he was still on the same page as before. Somehow, no matter how much progress he made with the paperwork, there seemed to be another page waiting to replace the other. As if they duplicated every time he completed a sheet, specifically designed to age him before his time.

When he could no longer concentrate through the blurry vision of exhaustion, Nicholas stood, taking to pacing around his office to clear his mind of the fog hovering there. His boots thudded on the wood, his steps growing wearier as he paced and paced. He had a small fireplace in his office used to warm the space during the winter months, so he decided to heat a cup of tea in the meanwhile. He sincerely hoped it rid him of this lingering tiredness.

His mind wandered again as the water boiled; flashing blue eyes and curling red hair appearing at the forefront of his thoughts, and especially what she'd made him do. Nicholas would be lying if he said he wasn't still angry with her. He was *very* angry with her, and the fact that she'd made him lie for personal gain. Not to mention what conflicting feelings she caused within him, even among her very strange, and very sinful, ways.

Nicholas wondered what she was doing, if she had the little girl she'd dreamed about tucked against her side this evening. Was that possible? He did not know the adoption process so well, but—even though he still felt uncomfortable—he hoped she had the little girl in her arms already. He had a soft spot for the woman, for some reason.

Just as he poured a steaming cup of tea, a knock sounded at the door. Nicholas frowned, glancing out the window at the sky dotted with falling snowflakes. It was still within acceptable visiting hours, and very obviously working hours, but it was strange to have someone knocking at his door—his workers were usually bursting into the room in a panic. However, he was grateful and excited when he was greeted with Pastor Sam's smile—shining and bright despite the cold seeping into his bones.

Nicholas ushered his friend inside, taking the man's coat eagerly. Pastor Sam cupped his hands before him, blowing hot air into them and rubbed them together profusely, forcing the joints to warm up. He glanced around, suddenly feeling slightly self-conscious about the semi-small space.

"What brings you out into the cold?" Nicholas asked, motioning for his friend to take a seat at the other side of the desk as he fixed them a steaming cup of tea. His mouth almost watered at the sight, and judging by the eagerness with which Pastor Sam took the cup, he assumed the man felt the same. Both of them clutched the cups tightly, warding off the cold threatening to claim a limb or two.

"I got the feeling to come visit, see how my old friend is doing." Pastor Sam sipped from his cup, a small smile playing on his lips. He knew the man long enough to know there was some hidden agenda behind this visit. "How have things been going over at Noelle's?"

And the hidden agenda reveals itself. Nicholas shook his head, "You would know better than I do, I haven't seen her since last weekend."

"And why is that?"

Nicholas scratched the back of his neck, choosing his words wisely and trying not to sound like the judgmental person he was sometimes, as Pastor Sam had advised him. He was unsure how to say it and how to convince Pastor Sam that he was better off distancing himself from her, when even he didn't believe it.

"I think I am beginning to understand what you meant when you said there is more to the story regarding Noelle's lack of...heartbreak surrounding her husband's death. But I am struggling with a certain role she made me play."

"And what role is that?" Pastor Sam said, contemplative. "One a husband might fill?"

He sat for a moment, even though he wanted to burst out laughing at the irony of his guess. And while in essence, it might be true—considering she'd told those people that he was her husband—it also wasn't. She didn't expect him to stay with her and care for her, didn't expect him to meet the child and be the man in the house. She didn't expect anything of him besides play along as she told that one lie. And if he was being honest, was it truly so bad?

"Without tarnishing the name of Noelle—"

"You are safe to speak with me, Nicholas. Noelle is a friend of mine, I know her character." Pastor Sam smiled, reassuring him. It meant the world to Nicholas, who felt less than excited about discussing the woman with anyone. He was never one for gossip, and he felt horrible, but knowing his friend would not make a snap judgment, he felt much better.

"There was something she demanded of me—or rather, something she dragged me into without my prior knowledge of what was happening." Nicholas almost cringed; he wasn't making any sense.

"And what would that be?"

"Well, when I went to drop off the compensation money, some of the representatives of the orphanage had come for a home visit—Noelle claims she forgot about it, which I understand but..." Nicholas took a sip of tea, wetting his throat and taking the moment to gather his thoughts. "She told them I was Henry—that I am her husband. She lied to them and dragged me right in there with her, without giving me the option to deny or accept her request to aid in her lie."

Pastor Sam stayed silent, but nodded for him to continue.

"I feel uncomfortable with the lying, but it's the whole situation that angers me. The impracticality of it all. How does she expect to care for the child? She can't work and take care of the child while attempting to run the ranch. She hasn't thought any of this through."

Pastor Sam set his cup down, wiping down his mouth as he sat back and regarded Nicholas with open honesty and respect. "Why does this concern you, Nicholas? If you forgive my asking."

He was silent for a moment, wondering why it *did* bother him so. He had no answer besides being a good, concerned citizen, but didn't that make him a meddler as well?

"Let me remind you of a story, if you don't mind." Pastor Sam said, not waiting for Nicholas to answer before he continued. "At your age you might have forgotten." He winked at Nicholas, teasing. "About the story of a wounded man stranded on the side of a road."

Nicholas almost immediately knew where he was going with this, but stayed silent out of respect for his friend and what he was trying to teach him. He had never steered him wrong before, and was one of the few people Nicholas *felt* was deeply connected to God.

"Of all the travelers passing by him, not one stopped, and some didn't even glance his way—either out of fear of getting involved, or were too busy to consider the simple act of a good deed. And so, he suffered for hours on end, until someone finally stopped."

His friend needn't have said more, as Nicholas was already nodding, glancing down at his hands in shame. The tale of The Good Samaritan was one all of them had learned early on in Sunday school, how an act of kindness can change someone's life. He had forgotten the tale, but its lesson remained ingrained in his brain.

"I understand, Pastor. Forgive me if I have been selfish."

"We are all human, and it is in our nature to put our own needs and judgment before others." His friend said, ever gracious and kind. He didn't think the man had a malicious bone in his body. "Do not be fooled by Noelle's desperation for a family—there is more to the woman than you have seen of late."

"Is that so?" Nicholas smiled. "I don't plan on sticking around much longer to see what she makes of herself, I'm afraid. I just wanted to make sure she was settled after the death of her husband. My job is done."

"I see." Pastor Sam nodded, staring into the small fireplace behind Nicholas. "I'm afraid I have to go now, but I do hope to see you this Sunday in church. We're going to do a special Christmas sermon."

Nicholas nodded, standing to usher the man to the door. They exchanged a brief grasp of the hand, the cold fully chased from their fingers thanks to the tea. However, he doubted the warmth in Pastor Sam's hands would last long, judging by the frosty wind blowing through the crack in the window. Before the man departed, he glanced back at Nicholas,

"She's fetching her little girl this afternoon."

He had no idea why his friend decided to tell him, or why it made his heart skip a beat. Nicholas also had no idea why he felt the urge to go to her home now, and why he heard the echoes of Pastor Sam's departing words in his ears. Nor did he have an idea why his mind suddenly changed. But that afternoon, after work, Nicholas raced over to the ranch to meet Noelle's daughter.

Chapter Eleven

Noelle was about two seconds from bursting out of her skin from excitement. Her hands were sweaty on the reins, her face stuck in a smile for the past hour since she'd gotten word from Sister Beatrice that Carol was ready to come home. Not only did she hop with excitement with every bounce of the wagon on the bumpy winter road, but she also almost urged the horses to go faster, despite the ice that lay thick on the path.

Her heart beat in time with the hooves of the horses' footsteps, her breaths leaving white puffs in the air every time she laughed to herself. She was sure she looked a little nutty to passersby, but she couldn't care less. Noelle was bringing her baby girl home, it would take a volcanic eruption to ruin this day for her.

Especially now that everyone had started to hang their Christmas decorations, green and red and white and gold everywhere. The snow added to the festive nature, gold decorative balls shining beautifully in the stark light reflecting from the white sheet of snow on the ground and on the roofs of houses.

Despite the raging winter around her, she felt a warmth wrap around her, her heart full of sunshine. Something she'd last felt when her mother had embraced her when she was little and scared. She had waited years to have a child, months for Henry to finally agree even when she knew it was a long shot; had *lied* to bring Carol home—and here she was, finally on her bumpy way to bring her child home.

She wondered what Carol's thoughts on this were, what she made of this situation, and if she was excited about moving in as she had been since that last visit. Did she want this as much as Noelle did? Would she adjust positively to this change?

Suddenly, Noelle felt her smile fade as the reality of what was about to happen set in. How would she look after this child now that she was officially coming home? She hadn't even prepared dinner or lunch, had just set out the door in a rush once she got the letter that the adoption had been approved. Not to mention the whole problem of Nicholas "Henry" Birch. Would he need to be present? As the husband, and now father? She hadn't even thought of that.

Butterflies quickly turned to knots in her stomach, making her breakfast push up into her throat. There was so much she hadn't considered, so much she still needed to do to make the home livable for a child. She hadn't even gotten the chance to buy Carol new sheets, her very own sheets for her very own home. Not to mention that she completely forgot about clothes for her, and possibly even some brushes and mirrors. Did Carol like such things? She looked like she did, judging by the nature of their conversations. Noelle felt ill-prepared, for the first time in her life.

However, Pastor Sam's words came back to her, telling her to pray and trust. So she did, her nerves flowing away on a current of faith, soothing her troubled mind with its calming water. Beatrice would not have approved the adoption had she thought Noelle unfit for the role, nor would she have approved if the house was less than child-friendly.

Somehow, Beatrice believed in Noelle, so she could too. She would be the best mother she could, odds be damned, and she *would* make a life for Carol—the beautiful life she deserved.

So Noelle went, pulling into the rocky road of the orphanage just as the first bits of snowfall started. If they were lucky, they would make it home semi-cold and not freezing as the snow threatened. She could no longer contain her smile of excitement as she spotted Beatrice and Carol, suitcase in hand, through the tinted windows of the little orphanage foyer. Her boots crunched through the snow as she rushed, hurriedly tying the horses against a nearby tree. The wagon was no use attached to fleeing horses, and she was not going to walk home in a storm with a child.

Her dress dragged through the snow, leaving the whole hem wet and soggy and covered with bits of mud peeking through the carpet of white. Her boots protected her toes from frostbite, but her ankles were not so lucky—but Noelle would be lying if she said she felt anything but anticipation.

The cold was a distant sting over the roar of overwhelming, child-like joy. The white front door neared, her hands shaking as she reached for the biting-cold round doorknob, swinging the door open and stepping into the warm foyer, and into a new future.

Carol was smiling as broadly as she was, dropping her suitcase and rushing forward to encircle Noelle in a crushing hug. She almost knocked the wind out of her, but all was forgotten as she crouched to embrace the girl fully. Tears were streaming down her cheeks, Carol's own tears wetting the space between her neck and shoulder as they sobbed, happiness spilling over and barely able to be contained.

Beatrice stood still as they had their moment, picking the girl's suitcase up from the ground and handing it to her with a soft smile when they finally broke apart. However soft the woman may be with children, she turned as hard with adults—it was evident in the hardened look she gave Noelle, no trace of the tender woman that had glanced at Carol just a moment before. That look seemed to be a warning and a congratulations all in one, as if saying *"Congratulations mama, but we'll take her back if you ruin her. Be warned."*

Once at home, Carol's eyes grew the size of saucers once she took in the sprawling ranch house, and grew even wider (which Noelle didn't think was possible) once she showed her the guest bedroom that would now become her bedroom.

"We'll go to town tomorrow morning and buy some new sheets and clothes for you." Noelle said nervously, but Carol was too busy looking around the room to bother about the sheets on the bed. It had the same wooden floors as the main bedroom did, with cream walls and wooden shutters to cover the window. Along the wall opposite the windows stood her wooden armoire, a coat rack, dresser, and a pretty engraved vanity. Sadly, it had no alcove for a washroom, but the second washroom in the hall opposite the main bedroom would be hers, since Noelle had her own washroom.

As soon as they were done with the house tour, and a tour of the barn, then the ranch itself on horseback, they settled into the second living room, snuggled beneath blankets and hot cocoa in hand.

"What do you think? Is it up to your standards?" Noelle teased, winking at the 6-year-old.

She nodded, curls bouncing. "I like the chickens the most."

Noelle laughed in surprise. "They're...uh...they're definitely something."

The girl nodded, twirling the hair of the doll in her lap. Noelle looked on, leaving the girl to adjust as she saw fit. But then, to her surprise, Carol started talking of her own accord.

"We used to have chickens at the orphanage, but then some of the naughty kids started hurting them so Sister Beatrice had Mr. Banks take them away," she said. "It made me sad, because one of them was my friend."

"I'm sorry, what did he look like?" Noelle asked, scooting closer in interest.

"It was a she," the girl corrected her, not unkindly.

"Oh, my apologies," she said, "what did she look like?"

"She had black and white feathers with a big claw on the back of her legs. It was scary, but she never hurt me."

Noelle nodded as the girl told her stories upon stories. Carol talked and talked for hours, telling Noelle everything she wanted to know and more, sometimes crying as she went through her memories. Noelle was there for it all, laughing with her, and then consoling when needed. When she became quiet, Noelle got a great Christmas idea that would make the girl feel right at home.

"Do you want to make some cookies?" Noelle asked, widening her eyes in excitement. She wanted to give the girl good memories; joy to wipe the stain of sadness from her heart. The girl gaped, nodding eagerly. They were bonding over another cup of warm cocoa when a knock sounded at the door, prompting both of them to spin towards it and frown at each other.

Noelle stood, wrapping the blanket tightly around Carol as she did, and went to see whoever braved the cold to visit them. Suddenly, what she'd said earlier about a volcanic eruption ruining her day took form as Nicholas Birch. Her smile vanished almost immediately, not even returning at the sight of the candy he held out. She cocked an eyebrow, staring him down in distaste.

He was handsome though, cocking a sheepish grin that made those whiskey brown eyes lighten with humor. He was still dressed in his work clothes, which made her wonder if he'd rushed over after work immediately—and why he would do that.

"I deserve that look, and I'm sorry. I'm sorry for being so brash, and for being harsh on you and ruining the day for you." He began sincerely, lifting the bag as he continued. "I brought candy for good fortune."

Noelle opened her mouth to respond, but was bumped to the side by a curious little head. Carol squealed as she beheld what Nicholas held outstretched, grabbing the bag from him. Noelle almost scolded her, but quickly remembered that these things would take time—she would need time to adjust and realize she would have everything in abundance for the rest of her life.

"Why don't you introduce yourself, Carol? This is Mr. Birch." She said gently. But Nicholas shook his head,

"You can call me Nicholas."

The girl waved shyly before dashing off again, Noelle casting him an exasperated and apologetic look. "She's still learning, but thank you for the sweets."

She smiled, wordlessly letting the door open fully, stepping aside to let him in. Nicholas' smile told her everything she needed to know, saw the gratitude, relief, and wonder at Carol in that crooked grin. She whispered, "We're making some cookies, care to join?"

Chapter Twelve

He was almost offended when he saw surprise widen her eyes when he nodded. Was he truly so sour that she thought he'd deny her invitation to make Christmas cookies? He had come in, hadn't he? Did she expect him to just sit around and be served?

Her home was beautifully decorated in red, gold, and green. Ribbons of those three colors decorated the banisters of the staircase from the bottom to the top, matching cushions scattered all over the couches. Mistletoe hung above the foyer entrance, Nicholas took care to avoid the mischievous plant at all costs. He wondered whether she would get a tree; if she'd choose one and cut it down herself or if she'd get one of the ranch hands to help her. He hoped it was the latter, if only to stave off some guilt if he wasn't there to help.

The atmosphere was cheerful, as it was in the rest of the town also artfully decorated in the festive colors. He'd even seen some stores have their own Christmas trees inside, decorated; some quite artfully with on-sale items. Nicholas wasn't one for all the festivities, hadn't been since his father passed.

He could remember his unending love and passion for the holiday when he was younger, but it had passed along with his father—the one he'd spent every Christmas with. Seeing the green, red, and gold brought along with it heaps of memories that made the muscles in his heart pull and a knot take hold in his throat. His eyes burned, and he quickly blinked them away when Noelle returned from hanging his coat.

After quick introductions, Nicholas followed her to the kitchen, making way for the tiny little tornado that was Carol, screeching in excitement. A small snicker escaped him, his eyes meeting the exasperated cerulean eyes of Noelle. She quickly instructed the child, giving her the task of measuring all of the dry contents. She also helped her to look for the cookie cutters—festive shapes like trees, bells, reindeer, and even a little angel.

Nicholas watched them as they laughed, Noelle gazing lovingly at Carol as she made a complete mess of the kitchen. It was like they had known each other for years, not as if she had only fetched Carol this afternoon for the first time. He realized that this was what Noelle had talked about when she said Carol was *hers*. They had a soul-deep connection that he'd only glimpsed a few times in his life, like two souls finally reunited.

Noelle suddenly glanced at him, momentarily distracted from mixing all of the contents together. She smiled slightly, their gazes locked in silent surrender. Something happened in the air, it became warmer, thicker, and more loaded. Before he could say anything, she shoved the wooden bowl into his hands from across the counter.

"Your turn," she said, promptly turning to wash her hands in the bucket in the corner. She then proceeded to hand him a wooden spoon, nodding to the bowl of flour and liquid. "Don't over-mix the dough, otherwise it won't rise properly in the oven."

"Yes, ma'am." Nicholas said, starting to mix the contents together. Afterward, he was instructed to form little balls of dough that would be squashed and formed into cookies. Saluting the woman before plunging his hands into the dough, it was only then that he realized he hadn't washed his hands. His head snapped up, but Noelle was already staring in silent horror. Carol, quick to catch on, just quipped,

"It's okay, his boogers add extra protein."

They all burst out in laughter, the echoes of it ringing out into the many halls of the home, and deep into the caverns of his heart.

Later, after indulging in far too many cookies, Nicholas felt like he was going to burst. He voiced as much, which had Noelle tapping her own distended belly in mutual agreement. Carol, on the other hand, was still eating, shoving her pretty little cheeks full of cookies as she poured over the book Noelle had given her. Apparently, the girl loved to read, and funny enough, Noelle had the perfect children's adventure fantasy books to gift the girl.

They both glanced at the girl, happily munching, and reading till her heart's content. It was in there, beneath the light she read under, that he was able to see the scars on her face and hands for the first time, as a result of the burns she'd suffered in the house fire that claimed her parents' lives. He had known she was scarred, but the dim light in the kitchen had only allowed for a slight discoloration to be seen. Yet it did not take away from her beauty. Noelle nudged him.

"Thank you for being so kind to her," she said, her eyes filled with gratitude. "And thank you for coming. And for the sweets that will keep her up all night."

Nicholas snickered. "It's my pleasure—wouldn't want you to have too early a night."

"Oh, you've made sure of that." Noelle joked, pointing at a still-wide-eyed Carol who was nowhere near sleep.

"I'm happy to see you enjoying yourself, to see you this happy."

A brief moment passes between them, their eyes locked on the other's, before Noelle promptly ended the moment. "What are you doing for Christmas?"

Nicholas snapped out of it, shrugging as he considered her question. "Not much I don't really have anything planned."

"Truly?" Noelle asked, "Well, why don't you join us for lunch then?"

"Oh no, I don't want to intrude on your holiday. Christmas is family time." Nicholas shook off the invite, suddenly feeling very shy. He didn't know when last he'd spent Christmas with someone other than himself and a good book. And while it usually bothered him on the day, it had started to lose some of its sting over the years.

Noelle clucked her tongue. "Nonsense. Christmas is to be spent with those we care about. Or do you have some secret family I don't know about," she teased. He laughed, shaking his head.

"If I do, then they are a secret to me too."

Laughter rang out in the living room, prompting Carol to lift her head in curiosity. When she'd satisfied her curiosity, she returned to her reading, humming contently.

"Then you have no reason not to come." Noelle placed a reassuring hand on his forearm, making him tense involuntarily. If she felt it, she didn't mention it. "We would love to have you join us."

Nicholas looked back at Carol, considering her offer. He sighed, deep and with humor. "Oh, since you so desperately crave my company, I suppose I could find some time in my busy day to join you."

She swatted him lightheartedly and without meaning. "Then it's settled."

The evening stretched on, hours going by as they patiently waited for Carol to wind down. Nicholas glanced outside, the snowfall light enough that he wouldn't have to spend another evening in the barn. He didn't know if he was relieved or thankful—he supposed a proper gentleman would be relieved. But these days, he wasn't so sure if he was as much of a gentleman as he wanted to be. Being with Noelle did things to him, made him irrational and impulsive. Whether it was a good or bad thing, he had yet to decide.

The girl was still reading, but thanks to some Christmas miracle, her eyes were starting to blink slower and slower, sometimes even staying closed for a minute or two as she "rested her eyes" according to her claims of lack of tiredness. Noelle and Nicholas talked for the hours it took the girl to finally fall asleep, about anything and everything.

The conversation went smoothly, and without any real effort. It was a comfortable exchange of words and interests, opinions, and perspectives. They even went as far as debating on some of the topics, laughing at each other and challenging when needed to express their own opinion. It must have been a good hour or two before they finally noticed Carol fast asleep, face down in the book laid flat on the carpet, snoring softly.

Noelle snorted, an awful sound that was closer to a pig than an actual laugh. Nicholas' head snapped to her, mock horror and confusion marking his face before a smile burst forth. Noelle turned blood-red, her cheeks flamed, and her eyes stretched as big as Carol's had been, once she'd seen the bag of sweets.

"My apologies" Noelle said, covering her shy smile with a pale hand. But before Nicholas could say anything witty, he just burst out laughing. The combination of a face-down, snoring Carol paired with a snorting Noelle was all he could take. Tears rolled down his cheeks, making him sniffle and wipe at his eyes to clear his blurry vision.

"I didn't know you were hog farmers." Nicholas gasped out in between fits of laughter. Noelle gasped, swatting him on the arm before she moved to pick Carol up from the floor. However, she stepped on the bag of peppermint sweets, almost cascading to the floor as she did. He tried his best to reach out and catch her, but her face was stuck in one of surprise, her mouth forming an 'o' as she regained her balance. That prompted a fit of laughter from both of them— whether it was a result of the sugar, the embarrassing moments, or simply the late hour; they just could not stop giggling and laughing.

It was the first time in a while he had laughed this hard, had so much fun that wasn't as a result of one of his friends doing something foolish. Soon, however, they sobered up and tried their best to rouse Carol from her sugar-induced sleep-coma. The girl was out like a light, though, and nowhere near light enough for Noelle to carry upstairs.

"Here, let me help," Nicholas said, crouching to pick the girl up from her sprawling position on the carpet. The pages of the book stuck to her drool-wettened cheek, making them giggle once more, before they made their way upstairs, Carol cradled in his arms like a babe.

Noelle opened the covers, white linens with pretty yellow daisies on them, for Nicholas to place Carol in the bed. Her head lolled to the side, falling onto the soft pillow as he leaned, gently placing the rest of her tiny body on the bed. She barely moved a muscle, stirring only to wet her dry mouth and then went back to snoring. If Nicholas was being honest, it was kind of endearing.

Nicholas turned to her in the hall, his hands wringing together. "I should get going now. It's late."

Noelle nodded, descending the stairs before him, trying her best to keep quiet. He supposed it was for Carol's sake, who was not yet accustomed to the natural sounds of the home. Nicholas grasped his coat from the hanger, shrugging it on as Noelle wrapped a blanket around herself to ward off the cold. His breath already puffed in the air in front of them as they moved towards the front door and away from the heat of the fireplace. He wondered how his horses were, and how much of a hassle it would be to hustle them out of the barn and fasten them back to the wagon. His mare wasn't one for the cold, so she would be the worse of the two.

"Thank you for the lovely evening, I really enjoyed myself—especially when you got those cookies out of the oven."

Noelle smiled warmly, "You're always welcome. It was our pleasure; thank you for stopping by."

Silence fell between them, both of them looking as if they wanted to say more, but stayed silent out of fear or doubt. So Nicholas gave an awkward wave "Have a lovely evening."

They both reached out to the doorknob simultaneously, their fingers brushing as they did. Noelle gasped quietly, Nicholas going wholly still as the warmth from her seeped into his skin, his bones... his very *soul*. Their heads snapped up, whiskey and cerulean meeting in a clash of passion, curiosity, longing and perhaps maybe even interest. He swore he could burst into flames at the heat that raged between them. It felt like electricity was racing up his arm, and from the surprised expression on Noelle's beautiful face, he suspected she felt it too.

However, as fleeting as it had begun, the moment ended. Leaving both of them blushing and uncomfortable at the passion that had just passed between them. Nicholas smiled crookedly, rubbing his neck as he pulled the door open. With a small wave, he exited, closing the heavy oak door behind him. His hands were shaking when he fastened the horses to the wagon, and not from the cold.

Chapter Thirteen

Noelle had never answered so many questions in her life, nor had she had to explain so many things in a span of a few minutes every time. Carol was a very curious and inquisitive child, one with such liveliness that Noelle sometimes felt drained at the end of each day—in the best way. Everything she saw or thought of was discussed or asked about, which was especially tiring while doing housework (which she helped with of her own accord) and some of the ranch work.

Noelle enjoyed every conversation, and every bit of information she offered up of herself, as it brought them closer. They spent their time bonding over chores, talking about Carol's favorite colors and prints in anticipation of her appointment with the seamstress that afternoon.

She could barely keep her excitement in check as they rode down the path into town, clapping her gloved hands together when they passed any Christmas decorations, or the stores in town, or basically anything that piqued her interest. Noelle smiled along, but her heart grew heavy at the way Carol got excited about the most mundane things, everything she'd taken for granted. It was like the child had been introduced to a new world. Noelle had known she'd come from poverty, but she didn't think the child had been secluded from the world.

The seamstress' shop was right on the corner, across the street from Noelle's favorite tea shop. The windows were glass, with a pretty pink bow painted on the front, and a big wooden sign advertising her services. She was the best and only seamstress in town, and it helped that she was kinder than half the people Noelle knew. She couldn't recall a time the woman had said or done anything rude in the long while she'd known her, which made her the perfect seamstress for soft-hearted Carol.

A soft chiming came from the bell hung above the door as they entered, announcing their presence to Kara, who was all the way in the back of the store working on pieces she was donating to the orphanage for Christmas. They had spoken about it in church a while back, and Noelle had wondered if she would go through, with it considering the amount of work it took. And money.

Everything cost an insane amount of money these days. She was so thankful for the money Nicholas had brought the other day, as it would keep her and Carol afloat for a few months while she figured out what to do about the work situation.

Kara greeted them with a warm smile, crushing Carol in a bear hug, and placing a quick kiss on Noelle's cheek. The former giggled, staring up at the beautiful blonde in wonder. Noelle had always known the woman to be affectionate, and she much appreciated it and preferred it to the coldness some of the others displayed. Blue eyes twinkled as she beheld their clasped hands, absolute happiness shining through from her towards Noelle. There was not one person in this town and in church that didn't know how much Noelle had wanted a child. It warmed her heart to see her friend's happiness for her.

"What are we doing for y'all today?" Kara drawled, her country accent thick. "Some new dresses for this pretty young lady"

She squeezed Carol's little cheeks, the child giggling as Kara teased. Her heart swelled, knowing how Carol felt about her scars and how they so often bothered her. It meant the world to both Noelle and Carol that Kara had gone out of her way to compliment the girl. She nudged the girl, encouraging her to speak for herself.

"I would like a new dress," Carol said, speaking clearly and confidently. "Please," she added upon a nudge from Noelle.

"And what color material would you like..."

"Carol," Noelle supplied with a smile. "And we would like red, please."

Kara nodded, motioning for them to join her at the back of the shop where measurements would be taken. The room was wonderfully decorated in all shades of purple, white, and beige. Curtains separated the front and back of the shop, a deep purple that looked almost black, with a beige dais in the middle of the room in front of a full-length mirror.

To the side, Kara had all of her customized hats displayed—each and every unclaimed piece she'd ever created that had either been forgotten and never picked up, or made because she was bored and desired to perfect her craft. She was a woman of many talents, and Noelle was thankful she'd chosen this specific town to plant her roots.

Carol took a step up onto the dais after some guidance from Kara, twirling before she finally stood still and glanced at herself in the mirror. She reacted as she usually did, her smile fading as she beheld the burn marks in her face. Noelle tried her best to build her up every chance she could, and scolded her anytime she spoke badly about herself. But there was only so much she could do until Carol saw her own beauty. As if sensing the shift, Kara placed a hand on the girl's shoulder, squeezing,

"Beauty cannot be found in a mirror, my darling," her voice was soft, as if speaking to a frightened animal, "it can only be found within ourselves."

Carol looked up at Kara, and then back to her reflection. Suddenly, the girl's shoulders lifted, the light returning to her eyes and face as Kara's words hit their mark. Noelle supposed her message could be interpreted two ways; one, that true beauty lay in the person you are and will become, and two, that you can find beauty within yourself by believing you are beautiful no matter what. Both meanings were beautiful, and Noelle was eternally thankful Carol got some encouragement from someone other than her mother. Daughters rarely believed their mother's compliments in any case.

Carol told Kara all about her dream dress; the silhouette coming in at the waist, and puffing outwards in a short ball gown-style dress, complete with puffy sleeves and a bow at the back. They took her measurements, Kara even going as far as tickling the obviously uncomfortable girl to make her laugh. They were done within the hour, Noelle having paid for the special dress and three extras just to make sure she had enough.

"Thank you so much for your time, and your kindness," Noelle said, grasping the woman in a tight hug as they made to depart.

"Of course! I'll have those dresses done within the week, then she can wear her special dress on Christmas day." Kara clapped her hands in excitement, as if she was the one that was going to wear the special dress. Carol soon joined the clapping, and even got Noelle to clap with them. Soon, the three of them were jumping up and down like children. It must have been a sight to see for any passersby.

Carol and Noelle were still giggling about their outburst at the seamstress earlier when they went shoe shopping, buying Carol a fresh new pair of black boots she could wear with her special dress. The streets were bustling with wagons and people, teeming with life and laughter. Many people stopped them as they shopped, inquiring about Carol, and Henry, and what she would do when Carol was adopted. She answered all of their questions gracefully, but grew tired of them fairly quickly.

Noelle supposed that she couldn't complain, since they all cared deeply—or rather, *most* of them did—about her journey for a child. It was only natural for them to be curious. However, it did grow a bit irritating once her true friends departed and the town gossips moved in for the kill. So they crossed the street, making a beeline for her favorite tea shop. She glanced back as they went, waving and smiling politely at the women shouting after her, desperate for their own piece of gossip to spread.

She was so desperate to escape their claws that she didn't look where she was going, colliding with a hard chest. The breath *oomph*ed from her, chased from her lungs by the man before her. Strong hands grasped her arms as she tittered over, one foot slipping off the cobblestone sidewalk, and the other twisting as she did. Carol's hand slipped from hers as she fell, almost in slow-motion, before being held upright by none other than Nicholas Birch.

He gave her a crooked grin, "You don't have to fall for me, sugar. I'm already your husband."

He leaned in lower, whispering in her ear. "Or rather, *fake* husband."

Noelle blushed, goosebumps pebbling her arms as she did. Was Nicholas flirting with her? She straightened fully, smoothing her hands down her dress. A small giggle escaped. "Thank you for that."

"No problem," he grinned, making her heart melt. The man's smile was extraordinary, like none she'd ever seen. It almost threatened to knock her off her feet. "Who are you running from?"

She glanced back, tucking her wild hair behind an ear. She'd worn it loose today, which she was severely regretting since the wind had decided to make a rat's nest of her red locks.

"Suzanna and her gaggle of geese."

Nicholas laughed, a burst of sound that had her smiling along. Carol also giggled along, hugging his leg as they finally stepped apart. Nicholas grasped her under the arms, picking her up as he replied. "I see. I'd run too."

Noelle smiled, her heart bursting at the sight of Carol and Nicholas hugging each other.

"Got anymore candy?" Carol inquired, making Noelle gape. Nicholas wasn't fazed though, as he just shook his head, patting his pockets,

"Sorry sweetheart, the candy shop was closed today. Maybe tomorrow." He set her down, patting her blonde hair and turned to leave. Somehow, Noelle didn't want him too. She opened her mouth, grasping at straws to keep him with them. Glancing behind them, she blurted,

"Would you like to join us for some tea?"

Nicholas glanced around, as if looking for the time, and then he nodded, extending the arm for Noelle to lead the way. They entered the small little tea shop, immediately embraced by the smell of eggnog and ginger-bread cookies. Decorations of red, gold, and green littered every surface and hung from every hook in the walls. A large Christmas tree stood to the side of the west wall, tucked against the small fireplace but just far enough to not be a fire hazard. If Christmas was a room, this would be its defining feature.

Carol ran to the first table she saw with four seats, claiming the one at other end of the table, between two of the seats. They shuffled between the surrounding tables, greeting familiar faces and waving at those behind the wood counter on the other side of the room.

Noelle reached over to drape her coat over the chair, pulling it out herself. However, Nicholas gently pushed her hand aside, pulling the chair out for her and pushed it back in once she was seated. Carol watched this in silence, eyes glittering, smile widening, and the smallest giggle escaping from that small little mouth. Noelle was blushing by the time the server came to collect their order, stammering as she spoke. Nicholas, however, was calm as ever.

"One of the kids from the orphanage told me this story about this big tree…"

It was horrible to say, but Noelle barely heard what Carol was saying as her eyes met Nicholas', who was already staring at her. He smiled softly, draping an arm around the back of his chair. Her cheeks heated, turning red all the way down to her neck. Noelle blushed like a little girl with a crush, and she was still blushing when their tea came, and they silently drank it while gazing at one another. All the while, listening to Carol's unending stories about Christmas trees.

Chapter Fourteen

Nicholas' boots thudded off the wooden porch as he ascended the steps to Noelle's front door. Today was one of the colder days again, with Nicholas having left his wagon at home and risked the path on horseback. The snowfall was heavier, and carpeted the ground beneath them in an unyielding trap. Already, he had passed many wagons that were abandoned due to being stuck in the snow, no-one being dumb enough to risk a winter night exposed to save a wagon that might very well still be there in the morning.

After having safely stowed his horse in the barn, Nicholas gathered his little bundle of tools and made his way over to the porch. He hadn't planned on spending his one Saturday off working all day, but working to help Noelle was different. He almost stuttered over his words when she opened the door.

She was wearing a forest green dress that made her red hair stand out even more, the shade of green complementing her cerulean eyes beautifully. Her hair was braided to the side, draped over her shoulder, and falling down to her waist. She was breathtaking, mesmerizing, and all of the words that made him stare until she cleared her throat, effectively snapping him out of his stupor.

"Morning," he blurted out, rubbing his neck nervously. "I was wondering if I could take Carol tree hunting? I don't want to overstep, but I noticed you don't have a tree, and every home needs a Christmas tree. Then I realized it may be because you can't do it by yourself—not that I think you're incapable—"

Nicholas realized he was rambling, like a schoolboy talking to his crush for the first time. He took a steadying breath, Noelle having covered her mouth to hide her obvious laughter as he tried his best to compose himself.

"What I meant was that I just really want to take Carol tree hunting. I thought she might enjoy picking the tree. I got the idea this morning, and I wanted to give it a shot—with your permission and blessing of course." He smiled crookedly, trying to charm her with the 'ole pearly whites.

"I think she would really love that." Noelle said, placing a hand on his arm in thanks, before ushering him inside. Her heeled boots clucked off the wood floors, the door shutting softly with a click behind them. Noelle disappeared upstairs to wake Carol.

Nicholas made his way to the kitchen, smiling when he spotted cookies decorated with slightly strange-looking snowmen and jingle bells. He supposed they were courtesy of Carol, who had begged Noelle for a chance to decorate her very own cookies. Sure, they might look a little funny, but he knew they tasted delicious. Noelle was one mean baker, and he found himself enjoying almost every meal of hers he'd ever consumed.

Grumbling all the way down, Carol finally emerged from the depths of sleep, still rubbing at her eyes in an attempt to wake up fully. She was dressed in a festive green dress that matched Noelle's, the only difference being the red bows dotting the ends of Carol's twin braids. The red was stark against the white-blonde of her hair, but she looked pretty. She also wore the new boots Noelle had bought for her yesterday, completing her very pretty ensemble.

Nicholas smiled, splaying his arms, and pasting on the most excited look he could muster, "You ready to go do some tree hunting, sweetheart?"

Noelle caressed the girl's head, smiling softly as she continued to rub her eyes. Noelle lifted her eyes to him, giving him a *"she doesn't look that excited"* look. Nicholas gave her an exasperated look back, begging her with his eyes to give him a shot.

"Oh come on, you can't be that tired." He said, lowering his arms and making claws with his fingers. "I bet you're not too tired to *run for your life!" He* roared. Carol screeched, running to the first living room as Nicholas the Night Terror chased her about. He ran slowly, making sure to grasp her dress slightly to keep the chase fun, making her screech and giggle maniacally.

Finally, after three loops through the home, he caught her, faking biting her fingers off. It was something his father had always done to wake him up, and he remembered it to this day. So, he supposed it must have worked—and judging by Carol's wide eyes, it definitely did.

"Ready to go find your very own Christmas tree?" Nicholas asked, eyes wide and a smile stretched over his entire face. The girl placed a finger to her chin, faking a moment of thought before she leapt up, and began to clap excitedly.

"I'm ready!" She screeched. Nicholas laughed, scooping her up and draping her over his shoulder, mindful of her dress. He met Noelle in the foyer, shaking her head as she beheld the way he held her daughter. He shrugged. "She's fine."

"Are you coming with us?" Carol asked, her voice slightly muffled by his back. She hadn't yet called Noelle anything related to mama or mother, and he supposed it would take time. From the lack of disappointment in Noelle's face, he supposed it didn't bother her at all. Of course, such things wouldn't bother her; she was too mindful of others and their feelings to consider her own—and she was especially mindful towards Carol's own deceased mother, always careful not to fill that space but create another for herself in Carol's heart.

Noelle looked to Nicholas, a question in her eyes, and he cursed himself. Why hadn't he thought to say both Carol *and* Noelle? Of course she was invited. So he took the liberty of deciding for her.

"Of course she's coming. We'll need her expertise," he said, winking at her. Gratitude and wonder filled Noelle's gaze, a smile as wide as the continent spreading over her glorious face. She quickly grabbed hers and Carol's coats, shrugging her own on before she blew out all the candles and they moved to the porch together.

"We're going to have to go on horseback, the wagon's won't make it through this snow," he said to Noelle, pulling his coat tighter around himself. He would have to get a new one soon, his current coat having worn down over the years and no longer efficient in warding off the cold as it had been. "Can she ride?"

Noelle nodded, caressing the girl's hair. Both of their noses were already red, the latter's crinkling as she sniffled. "But I don't know how comfortable she would be riding in snow."

"She can ride with me, and you can follow us," Nicholas nodded, inclining his head at the girl, "What do you say, darlin'? Wanna ride with me?"

"Yes!" She squealed, jumping towards him and right into his arms. "What does your horse look like?"

Nicholas thought, looking towards the barn, "Well why don't you come see for yourself?"

And boy, was he glad he made her see for herself. Her eyes lit up like a candle when she beheld his appaloosa mare, her mane just as spotted as her body was. She had one blue eye and one brown eye, her temperament perfectly suited for a child. She was beautiful.

"What's her name?" The girl asked, reaching out a gloved hand to the mare who nuzzled it gently. She was ever the softie, and he was so incredibly lucky to have her.

"Her papers say Winnie, but I call her River." He placed a loving hand on the horse's snout.

"Why River?" She asked again, giggling quietly as the horse nuzzled her cheek. She huffed, stomping a hoof on the ground. She was magnificent.

"Have you ever seen the raging waters of a river? How fast the current flows in the rapids?"

Noelle and Carol nodded, both of them glancing at him. They were eerily similar in their mannerisms, making his theory of soul-connections prove even more true by the day.

"Well, that's how fast she runs." He winked, ruffling the girl's hair when she stared at the horse in awe. Like muscle memory, Nicholas draped her blanket over her spotted back, settling the saddle onto it a moment later. He fastened all of the buckles, tightened them, and tested them all before deciding they were good to go. Next, he went to assist Noelle with her saddling but drew up short when he beheld what was playing out right before him.

Noelle was already seated on a pitch-black Friesian horse the size of a small wagon, sporting a white and black spotted pink nose. He stepped aside as they walked past, smiling down at him.

"This is Goliath," she said, patting the horse on its neck. He huffed a laugh, whistling as he went to lift Carol and mount his own horse.

"Goliath," he murmured, snorting. *Go figure.* The woman would be the death of him.

An hour and a short ride later, they were in the thick of the forest, pine trees lined all around them. They were all different sizes, some tall and thick; and some small and skinny. Noelle and Carol looked over them all, shaking their heads in unison, as if they were truly blood-related. It was a wonder to him, how similar they were for having been two complete strangers just a few months earlier.

They were the same level of tree-snobs, and they liked the same type of tree—which, according to them, was just enough green, and just enough bark. As if that cleared it all up for him. However, he left them to it, his eyes focusing on the woods around them instead.

There was total silence around them, the near-quiet whimpering of birds, falling snow, and rustling trees the only sound. The crunch of snow beneath their horses' hooves filled the gap of silence, all of them content with nature-watching instead of speaking. That is, until Carol spotted her perfect tree.

"There!" The girl screeched, disturbing the woods around them. It seemed to have startled the horses too, as they whinnied and paced, tails whipping in agitation and ears pinned back.

"Whoa," Nicholas soothed River, patting her neck gently as he waited for her to calm. "Good job spotting that tree, sweetheart. Now, try to remember to be a bit quieter, though, as the horses don't like loud noises."

Carol covered her mouth. "I'm sorry."

He felt bad, but she wouldn't learn these things if they didn't teach her. So he winked. "It's okay, now, do you want to go check that tree out?"

She nodded, pointing out the way they needed to go. Noelle quickly followed, soothing her mountain of a horse as she did. He looked back, confirming she was indeed okay, and laughed at her exasperated smile. The woman loved the child to death, but Lord help her was she a handful. Nicholas just smiled, inclining his head to her, and returned his gaze to the front.

It was indeed the perfect tree. It stood at about six-foot-two, with healthy green needles and a thick stump that said it was well beyond its "toddler" years. Nicholas nodded, giving Carol a congratulatory and proud pat on the back.

"Well you ladies are right. This is the perfect Christmas tree." He groaned as he dismounted, limbs stiff from the cold.

Making quick work of loosening the little tool pouch and saw, he chucked them into the snow and removed his outer coat.

Nicholas began the hard work of cutting down the tree, starting with a saw to make a stitch for the anvil to cut into, and then swinging the anvil like his life depended on it. Noelle and Carol busied themselves with the horses, the former teaching the girl how to ride in snow, tame a horse—which was not as effective with a tame horse such as River—and what to do when going down a snowy slope. They used a small hill to the left of them for practice, River patiently playing along as the girl learned how to ride a horse properly.

Soon, all of them exhausted and ready for the warmth of a fireplace, they made their way home, the Christmas tree tied down on a sled he'd manufactured from one of the smaller trees in the area. Goliath had huffed when he'd tied the makeshift sled to him with rope, but settled down quick enough when he offered him a carrot. He was an easygoing companion. It only made sense with Goliath having been bred for this exact reason, as opposed to River who would've struggled with the weight of the sled, himself, and Carol on her back. However, it meant he needed to mount Goliath, as he was the one with the 'sled-pulling' experience and not Noelle—as great a rider she may be, this was another challenge in itself. That left Noelle and Carol on River, which didn't worry him a bit. He was more worried for himself on that maneater mountain of a horse.

Nicholas sighed in relief as the silhouette of the barn came into view, the horses walking faster, as they too realized they were almost home and out of the cold. A half-an-hour later, Noelle was digging out her old ornaments, and placing them on the floor for Carol to hang on the tree.

The girl hummed with delight as she did, finally toasty warm, and content with decorating her own special tree. Finally, when the moment came to put the star on the top, Carol gave a yip of pure and utter joy as he lifted her up, helping her place the star perfectly. Of course, with the events of the day, that was all the excitement Carol could take.

She passed out cold only an hour later, her head lolling to the side and flopping against his chest as he ascended the stairs, gently laying her down in the bed and covering her in beautiful lavender-colored-linens. Noelle had bought them specially for Carol, knowing she would love to have her own personally-chosen covers.

Nicholas inched his way down the stairs, careful not to disturb a sleeping Carol—a difficult task with the endlessly creaking floors. He'd have to do some maintenance when he got the chance, if only to make life easier for the girls. On the bottom step, right as he stopped off, Noelle came around the corner from the kitchen.

Noelle shouted and recoiled, spilling the cup of hot cocoa all over her hand. He grabbed at her, steadying her as he took the cup from her hand and covered the other with a rag he'd had in his pocket.

"We have to put this under cold water." He dragged her to the washroom, sticking her hand into the wash basin that was filled with icy cold water. Noelle hissed, the fingers on her burned hand curling. She was shaking slightly, and kept glancing at his face.

"I'm so sorry, Noelle. I didn't mean to startle you."

He glanced up at her as he held her hand under the water, meeting her frightened eyes. Nicholas understood then; it wasn't a fear of him, but a fear of what she'd been enduring behind these wooden walls. "Noelle, I'd never hurt you."

As if a dam had burst, Noelle started to sob.

Chapter Fifteen

Back-bowing, gut-wrenching sobs shattered out of her. The kind of sobs that emerged when a soul was tired, the kind that made one feel broken and then healed when it was over. Noelle hiccupped, clutching at Nicholas when he put his arms around her. He smelled of snow and a musky scent she couldn't place, but she supposed it was just his natural scent. His beard scratched her forehead as he consoled her, and made soothing sounds as he rubbed her back. It was the scent of Nicholas, and his gentle touch, that eased her until she was finally calm enough to step back.

"I'm sorry." She sniffled, wiping her nose with a handkerchief she kept on her at all times. "It wasn't your fault." Her hand was still throbbing, even with the cold water soothing the burn. There was just nothing that burned as much as scorching hot milk.

"I shouldn't have slunk around like that, I just didn't want to wake Carol." Nicholas said, letting go of her. "I'm so sorry."

"You have nothing to be sorry for," Noelle said, perching on the small seat he'd retrieved for her. "I just... he used to... he'd snap out of nowhere. He'd be up in his study, and then he'd come down after having been angered by some of the finances, and he'd..."

"Take it out on you?" Nicholas supplied, taking her sore hand from the water. Somehow, when he'd gone to retrieve the stool for her, he'd also managed to grab some Carron oil— a mixture of linseed oil and lime water that Noelle kept in the cupboard especially for this purpose.

She nodded, wincing slightly as he rubbed the oil over her tender flesh. From what she could see, there were no blisters, but her skin was tender and red. Although it was nothing compared to the blisters Henry had left on her heart.

"He wasn't a bad man when we first met, and I suppose he still wasn't a bad man later in life before he died. I think he was just a bad husband," Noelle admitted, voicing her thoughts on the matter—as she'd dissected it in recent years. Nicholas grunted, shaking his head,

"I'll have to disagree with you there, darlin'. A man who lifts his hands to a woman is a bad man." His tone was hard, his gaze unflinching.

"I suppose so." Noelle fell silent, watching quietly as he wrapped her hand in a bandage to keep the oil from smudging onto the surfaces of the house. It was only when they were back downstairs, Nicholas fixing her a new cup of hot cocoa after cleaning the mess they'd made, that she began to open up fully.

She told him everything there was to know. What Henry had done to her over the years. She told him of the time he'd almost cut her hand off with a butcher knife after she'd disobeyed his command. She showed him the scar she still bore on her wrist; a thin white line from one side to the other.

Noelle told him of all the times he'd come home drunk, demanding a warm plate of food, when he was the one that had missed dinner. Henry would rouse her from sleep every night in the last years they'd been married, and it made her realize how long it had been since she'd had a good night's rest, before he'd died. Nicholas stayed silent through it all, his body growing tense and his jaw clenched. She could see his hands, resting on the arm rests of the couch, squeezing the wood until it groaned, threatening to split.

She forged ahead, and told him everything. Showed him every physical and emotional scar, and he stayed to listen to all of it. Even when the time came for him to return home, and well after it had passed. Sometimes she cried, and sometimes she grew angry at the memories. Noelle found herself frowning at the scars on her body, a permanent reminder of the man she'd endured. Survived. It was the first time she'd spoken of it, the tale coming out in a torrent of words she couldn't stop.

"Them there came a night when he returned from the saloon, drunk again. I... I prayed for an escape out of this life." Noelle trembled, but steeled herself, as she took a sip of the hot cocoa Nicholas had just refilled for her.

"I prayed for him to leave me alone, and for my life to be changed."

Nicholas had stayed silent through it all, not once interrupting or putting words in her mouth. He only spoke when he agreed, or to help her form the words when she struggled. He simply listened, added wood to the fireplace, and refilled her cup when she needed it.

"And now, you see, ever since his death, I have struggled with the possibility that I may have wished it into existence." Noelle spoke the horrible truth of her thoughts, and what had plagued her so since that fateful evening Nicholas had brought her the news of Henry's death.

She glanced at Nicholas, waiting for the judgment, waiting for the gasp of horror and the look of pure undiluted disgust.

She'd deserve it, after all, she had wished for the death of her own husband. But all she saw in Nicholas' face was understanding. As if he knew what she was going to say before she said it, and knew that it was untrue.

It was late into the night when she finally grew silent, tapping her fingers nervously against the mug in her hand, as she contemplated her life. She didn't notice when she dozed off, or even when Nicholas carried her to bed. She only noticed her relocation when he tucked the soft covers under her chin, his hand lingering inches above her face, and then he left.

The next morning, when the sun peaked in through the curtains of her bedroom, Noelle awoke with a smile on her face. Her eyes were still raw from crying the previous night, and her throat was unbelievably dry, but she felt... lighter. As if admitting all of those things to Nicholas last night had taken a weight from her shoulders; one she hadn't been aware she was carrying. She'd never meant to open up to him about Henry, but before she could stop herself, his kind eyes had sent the words tumbling from her mouth.

Throwing back the covers, Noelle shoved her cold feet into her slippers, wrapping herself with one of the throws on her chair and made her way downstairs. She encountered Nicholas on his way out, his coat already on and his hand on the knob of the front door. She supposed he'd slept on the small sofa by the fireplace. There was no way he could have slept in the barn in last night's cold.

"Going so soon?" She asked, smiling softly. Nicholas turned, slightly startled, and smoothed his short hair.

"I need to get home, there are some things I need to do." He said, and disappointment crashed into Noelle. "Thank you for yesterday, it was great." He turned and opened the door.

She nodded, trying her best not to let the smile slip. But something about what she'd said last night haunted her. "Nicholas?"

He turned back, hand resting on the knob of the open door. "Yes?"

She considered her question, contemplating why she needed to hear his answer in the first place. She did not need his opinion to cast judgment upon herself. So why did she desperately need him to give her the correct answer, to lift that burning feeling from her chest?

"Do you think I wished it? Do you think I wished Henry to die, by praying for my life to change?" She tucked hair behind her ear, gnawing on her lip nervously. "Do you think I'm to blame for his death? That it's my fault?"

Nicholas stood still for a moment, staring down at the ground as he thought. Then, he stepped out of the doorway, shutting it behind him as he turned to her fully.

"No, I do *not* think so," he said, instantly making relief crash through her body. "I think you were trapped in a home with no window or doorway out, and I think you needed help. But I do not think you are the cause of his death."

"But why?" She asked, her voice shaking, before she could stop herself.

"Because you don't have the vindictiveness for it." He answered without hesitation, shrugging. "You don't have an unkind or evil bone in your body."

Noelle was taken aback by his answer, the absolute certainty in his eyes when he'd said it. They were both utterly still, the silence stretching for a moment or two while the both of them tried to dissect whatever was growing between them, and exactly what his words had meant. Were they friends? Something more? Or was she just seeing things because she had grown lonely since Henry's death—peaceful, but lonely nonetheless. Did she even want another man? Was she interested in Nicholas that way?

She certainly did have an attraction towards him, but that was to be expected, was it not? The man was one of the most handsome she'd ever met in her life. Possibly *the* most handsome. Judging by his stare, he was going through the same thoughts as Noelle was, trying to place her in a category and trying to figure out if he even had feelings for her at all. Both of them were unmarried and slightly lonely, so was it interest or loneliness that conjured up these feelings between them?

Noelle opened her mouth, wanting to say something, *anything*, but Nicholas beat her to it.

"I have to get going now," he said, promptly turning on his heel and closing the door behind him as he stepped out into the frigid air. She had barely gotten a word out before he'd left, leaving her standing with her mouth open like a fool. Noelle frowned, her mouth pulling in distaste.

However, while making tea, Noelle thought of the previous night—specifically the way he had touched her so tenderly, and cared for her when she'd burned. She couldn't remember the last time someone had worried about her, especially not Henry. He'd even left her to dress her own wound the day he'd cut her with the knife.

It was strange to her, to have someone help her and so tenderly oil and dress her wounds. She knew it felt good because she was smiling as she thought about it. But her blasted mind wouldn't let the subject go, always overthinking and analyzing everything. She wasn't anything to him; not a family member or a love interest.

And yet, he'd helped her, listened to her, consoled her when she sobbed, refilled her mug when it was empty, and sat with her into the early hours of the morning as she spoke of her life with Henry. And now, he'd given her such a lovely departing comment, even though he'd looked startled afterwards, that she wondered if she were overthinking everything or if they were truly entering developing feelings toward each other.

Her heart galloped when she thought about it, about the way he played with Carol and shared experiences with her. Her smile grew when she thought of his laugh and smile, and the way his eyes crinkled at the corners when he did. Noelle wondered if she was the only one that had butterflies filling her stomach at the thought of him, but then wondered if she ever wanted to be with another man anyway. But she couldn't help it—no, those butterflies demanded to be felt, whether her mind and heart agreed or not.

Chapter Sixteen

Traversing the streets of the town, Nicholas drew the fresh, crisp, air into his lungs, his hands tucked deep into his coat pockets to shelter them from the cold. It was about a week from Christmas, and the evidence of it was everywhere; the lampposts, store windows, trees, and every surface that allowed for a red, green, or gold ribbon, were decorated. Even some of the people's wagons sported ribbons at the top of the buckboards, their festive cheer starting to rub off on him as he made his way to church.

He had closed the mine a few hours earlier, granting the men time to spend with their families this Christmas. Just because he didn't have anyone to spend it with, did not mean others had to suffer as well. However, he realized that it wasn't true—he did have someone to spend his Christmas with.

A smile graced his face as he remembered his lunch arrangements with Noelle and Carol, his heart lightening as he finally didn't have to spend Christmas alone. He couldn't believe he had almost forgotten, but he supposed old habits die hard. Along with thoughts of Christmas, came thoughts of Noelle—and their little moment they'd had the other morning before he'd left. He would see her shortly at the church, for the annual Christmas Caroling, but somehow, it felt like it had been ages since he'd last laughed with her, seen her smile, watched little Carol's chaotic ways.

He wondered what she made of it all. Did she mind his visits? Or did she come to adore them as he did? Was he overstepping boundaries? It didn't seem like it, as she hadn't yet said anything. And, unless he was oblivious to it, she did not seem upset in the least when he visited them or did things with them. Nicholas wondered, thinking back to all the times he'd been with them and how they had reacted to him. Why was he overthinking things in the first place? It wasn't like his friend would change her mind about him at a moment's notice; if she was still a friend and not something more.

That was another of his problems. He didn't know where they stood with each other; if they were very good friends, or if she had become something more to him in the last few weeks. They'd been spending so much time together. He didn't even know if he was ready to have her be something more than a friend. He had been so alone for so long, he didn't know if he had it in him to be a good partner to a wonderful woman like Noelle. Then there was the whole issue of the lying—he still didn't know how to feel about that. Would their relationship be made to last if it was built on lies in the first place? Should they proceed with whatever was growing between them? Or would they be set up for failure?

Before Nicholas could answer his own questions, he turned onto the path that would lead straight to the entrance of the church. It seemed his thoughts and dilemmas would have to wait until after the caroling, or when he was alone.

The church was teeming with people, the carolers dressed in pretty, matching robes, all of them standing side by side on the small, raised dais at the front of the church. They would have a small ceremony, and then a performance before the carolers entered the streets to spread the holiday cheer.

The people around him were all dressed in the holiday colors, most of them sporting the deep forest green of

Christmas cheer. Everyone conversed joyfully, standing in groups and laughing, as old friends and family reunited in the season of blessings. Nicholas' eyes scanned the crowd for familiar red hair and its accompanying blonde. He spotted her standing beside Pastor Sam and his wife, smiling and laughing as if nothing in the world bothered her.

It was so at odds with the sobbing woman he'd seen last night. This woman was so different from the one that had suffered so many years of sadness and abuse at the hands of the man that had vowed to protect her, that should have loved her unconditionally. Instead, Noelle looked weightless, and free. As if her admissions to him had aided in bringing on this carefree mood.

Nicholas weaved his way through the crowd, brushing past his own friends while keeping his eyes on her. That laugh pulled him to her, like a tether, a moth to a flame. He heard no greetings, only the sweet pitch of her wondrous laugh. She smiled brightly at him when he finally made it to the small gathering of friends, Pastor Sam greeting him with a quick clasp of hands.

"Nicholas!" Carol squealed, almost shoving him from his feet with the force of her hug. He rubbed her little back, beaming down at her.

"Is that the special dress you've been telling me so much about?" He asked, cocking an eyebrow at the green dress done with golden thread, puffy sleeves, and an even puffier skirt. She looked like a Christmas ornament, in the most glorious way, and he could see why she called it her special dress. However, she shook her head,

"No, that one's red," she answered incredulously, as if he should have known that. Nicholas lifted his hands in surrender.

"You'll have to wait to see that one," Noelle intervened, placing a hand on the girl's head. "She's saving it for a special occasion."

"What could be more special than Christmas caroling?" Nicholas teased, feigning disappointment. Carol just shook her head, and bound off with some of Pastor Sam's gaggle of children.

Just as she did, Pastor Sam called for the start of the sermon. A shuffling of feet ensued as they all made their way over to the benches, conversation dying off almost immediately. The children were all ushered out of the church and to the adjacent building where they would receive their Sunday school lessons.

It was too cold for them to play outside, so they would have to do with some fun bible stories. Nicholas and Noelle took their seats at the back of the church, a few pews from the middle where all of the people had squeezed themselves together to fit as many people as possible. It wasn't too comfortable where they were sitting, but it was better than the overstuffed middle pews.

The sermon was short and powerful, Pastor Sam having them all in tears at some point or the other. He had made a point of reminding all what the true celebration of Christmas was, and to not let the gifts and merriment make them forget why they were truly celebrating Christmas. Afterward, the carolers gave an outstanding performance of all the well-known holiday songs, their voices mixing angelically.

The songs rose in a symphony that seemed to echo off the wooden walls of the church, captured and contained by the walls of their hearts. It made goosebumps pebble on his skin, as his voice rose with the overwhelming feelings now taking root in his body. During that moment, Nicholas glanced at Noelle, who was singing in-tune beside him, catching her smile just as their eyes met. It almost took his breath away.

Were it the music, the moment she chose to smile at him, or the heightened feelings—Nicholas didn't know. All he felt was the ever-growing feeling in his heart. That growing interest he had contemplated earlier. So he smiled back, wondering what it was that was sparking between them.

There was not a dry eye to be seen when everyone filed out of the church.

Afterward, once everyone had dried their eyes and bonded over the shared crying-experience, everyone disbanded, returning to their homes to await the encore of the carolers who would grace their ears with angelic symphonies yet again. Noelle and Nicholas made their way to her wagon, Carol using the few extra minutes they stood talking to play with her friends.

"What are your plans for the evening?" Noelle asked him, coming to a standstill right next to her monstrous mount, Goliath. He huffed, pawing at the snow-carpeted ground, the air escaping from his nostrils appearing as white puffs in the air.

Nicholas shrugged. "For now, getting out of the cold would be nice." He swore he could feel his toes detach from his feet inside his boots. His hands didn't feel much better, the digits having gone numb from the biting frost threatening to claim his limbs. When he looked closely, he could see Noelle shivering as well, her nose bright red.

Noelle laughed, glancing back at Carol. "I should probably get her out of the cold too. That wet dress is only cause for trouble."

The little girl had fancied herself a boy, and went sliding through the ice on the slide as if it were summer. Her dress had become wetter and wetter the more she went down the slide, resulting in a soaking dress and a freezing child. Although, as he watched her hysterically laugh as she was chased by a little girl twice her size, he wondered if she was freezing or if Noelle was freezing *for her.*

"May I accompany you?" He asked, returning his gaze to the woman before him. "I just want to make sure you get home safe."

Noelle's smile stretched across her face, and she nodded. "Of course." She glanced behind him, looking for River.

"I walked here," he supplied, when she frowned in confusion. "I don't live too far from here."

"But how will you get home?"

He shrugged. "A man walking from ranch to town is different from a woman and child walking from town to ranch."

Noelle considered, shaking her head. "I understand; but that's utter nonsense. You can take Goliath and just bring him back when you visit us tomorrow."

Her eyes were twinkling as she said it, filled with mischief and a determination that suggested it was not up for debate. Nicholas let out a laugh.

"Yes, ma'am," he said, helping her onto the buckboard. Then he whistled, waving an arm at a still laughing Carol. He hoisted the little girl up, then took his own seat and lifted the reins. A quick whip and click of a tongue, and Goliath the Giant Friesian was on his way.

Snowflakes dotted their hair as they made their way home, Nicholas keeping his wits about him on the frozen path so as not to get her wagon stuck in the heaps of snow, or slip on the death-trap they currently rode on. He cleared his throat, trying his best to find a good way to say what he needed to.

"The next time the road looks like this, you leave the wagon behind and come on horseback." He almost cringed at the harshness of his tone, so he added, "Wagons are death-traps on ice like this."

Noelle glanced down the side of the wagon, her eyes assessing the direness of the threat he'd just made her aware of. It was a moment before she nodded, for once not having anything to say back or argue against. No wonder they called Christmas the season of giving.

Carol talked the whole way home, telling him all about her day, what they did, how Noelle baked a delicious bread, and how many friends she made during the sermon. His heart almost burst with joy when she told him, relief crashing through him at the thought of her adjusting well to the recent changes and being happy. Not that he'd ever doubted that she would be happy at Noelle's—the woman had the biggest heart he'd ever seen.

The girl talked so much that he barely noticed the time had passed until they took the turn onto the snow=packed dirt road that led straight to the ranch. It was dark and surrounded with woods, the perfect hiding place for any evildoers. He was suddenly glad he'd accompanied them home, musing that it was better safe than sorry. The dark woods were no place for a woman and child to navigate alone. He had no idea how Noelle had done it all these years, considering Henry was as helpful as a fly on the wall.

Nicholas pulled the wagon to a stop, Goliath's muted stomps no more than a soft crunch as he plowed through the snow. Noelle and Carol jumped from the buckboard, making their way over to the porch whilst Nicholas removed Goliath from the wagon. The horse protested the slightest bit, ripping the lead from his hands a few times, until he finally got him hitched to a tree.

Noelle was waiting for him when he finally walked up the porch, his hands officially numb and maybe slightly frost-bitten from the unrelenting cold. She was bundled up in a throw blanket, but from her shivering he could tell it was no use.

"Thank you for bringing us home," she said, smiling gratefully. Glancing at the woods, she grinned sheepishly. "I would have rolled the wagon toward the woods, if only to speed away."

Nicholas snickered. "They are slightly on the terrifying side of things. It was my pleasure."

Noelle nodded, looking like she wanted to say more, but decided against it. Trying not to feel too disappointed, Nicholas waited until she was safely inside with the doors locked, before he made his way to Goliath, keeping one eye on the woods behind the pitch-black horse. Although he was ashamed to admit it, he had hoped she'd invite him to stay over again—no matter what type of man that made him.

He did not want to return to an empty house, where there was nothing and no one to greet him but the dark. The way home was sad for him, the house empty of their laughter and smiles.

Chapter Seventeen

Copper Mountain, Colorado, 1885

One week before Christmas

Belly-down on the plush carpet before her, head resting on her hands, Carol was humming as she read, swinging her little feet in time with her hums. If Noelle ever saw a happy child in her life, it was Carol. She wore one of her black and red flannel winter dresses, her hair braided away from her face and in a crown around her head. A bright red bow graced the side of the crown-braid, painting her as the perfect Christmas *Carol*. Noelle giggled at her pun, drawing an inquisitive look from Carol.

"Sorry, it's nothing," Noelle waved her off, a small smile still playing on her lips. The girl continued reading her book, content with losing herself in the fictional worlds she so preferred to theirs.

She looked down at the red ball of yarn in her hands, the smallest bit of a shape forming in her knitting work, a wonderfully bright hat for Nicholas to protect his ears from the cold. She had not once spotted him with a hat, so she'd decided to gift him one. Though as she never did get his measurements, she decided to go for three and a half of her hand's widths. However, looking at it now, she wondered if it would be too much.

They hadn't discussed if they were giving each other Christmas presents or not, and she wondered if it would be an overstep of boundaries were she to give him one. Did one give their love interest a gift? Although she supposed she couldn't phrase it that way considering she had no idea what they were, and even less where they were headed. Noelle sighed, the red bundle in her hands suddenly no longer a festive gift, but rather a proposition she hadn't thought to present.

"Are you and Nicholas sweethearts?" Carol suddenly asked, startling Noelle from her deep dive into her courting, or not courting, Nicholas. She shook her head, clucking her tongue at the thought.

"No, honeybee. Not at all." She leaned forward, putting the semi-knitted hat down on the coffee table beside her. Her cheeks were blazing, no doubt leaving a red flush from her neck to her forehead as embarrassment took over her body. "Why do you ask?"

Carol shrugged her flannel-clad shoulders, pulling her face as if she were closer to an old man than a 6-year-old girl. "It looks like it sometimes."

Noelle's back straightened, her eyes growing wide as saucers, "What makes you say that?"

She shrugged again, her eyes no longer focused on Noelle but on the book laying open in front of her on the mat. "He looks at you the way Papa looked at Mama."

Cracks like those in a glacier appeared in her heart, sadness leaking from them as her heart bled for the girl. She had known real love then, before her life had been changed forever. Noelle was grateful for it, that she had experienced that deep connection, so that she may one day find the same for herself.

"That is beautiful, honeybee." Noelle said, leaving the denial for another day. "I'm a very lucky woman then."

Carol looked up from her book, smiling happily at Noelle, before she returned to her fictional world again. She returned to her knitting, her mind no longer keen on focusing on Nicholas any longer. So she continued with her hat, hoping that she hadn't overstepped a boundary.

Later in the afternoon, Nicholas arrived and announced his presence with a particularly perky knock. He wore a grin when she opened the door, her own gracing her face when she laid her eyes upon him. He was dressed in tight-fitting warm clothes, a plain black beanie on his head. In his left hand, he held some peppermint candy for Carol, she assumed, and the right was hidden behind his back. He looked particularly handsome today, his whiskey brown eyes alight with childlike excitement. It was only after he had stepped inside that she realized why, as Nicholas pulled a pair of old skates from behind his back. Noelle gasped, Carol squealing in delight.

"What do you say, ladies, up for some skating?" He asked, cheerfully. "These are my old skates from when I was a boy—they should fit." He held one skate up in the air, shutting an eye as he tried to measure the skate against Carol's foot.

Noelle was ecstatic, rushing upstairs to grab a coat for herself and Carol, along with her own pair of skates—she hadn't been able to use them for years. Henry had never been fond of her hobbies, arguing that they took too much time away from her household chores. She'd argued only once.

They were out the door in minutes, Noelle seated on Goliath, and Carol and Nicholas mounted on River. She had a new blanket draped over her back, a nice patterned one with shades of brown, turquoise, and red. It complemented her coat beautifully, making her look exotic, like something out of a fairytale.

"There's a frozen pond just a ways from here," Noelle pointed towards the back of the house at the woods that sprawled there. "I used to skate there. It's as smooth as you'll ever get."

Nicholas nodded. "Lead the way, your Majesty."

Noelle rolled her eyes, sticking her tongue out at a giggling Carol. She shot them a look, glancing at them where they hung back. A mischievous smile played about her lips, her yip of joy echoing off the snow-capped trees as she spurred Goliath into a gallop. Her hair was loose, whipping in the wind and into her face when she glanced back at them, Nicholas' maniacal smile lighting up his chiseled face as he chased after her. Carol hung on for dear life, slightly terrified but yipping along with her.

She let go of the reins, adjusting her seat as she did, and spread her arms. The wind tucked into her side, making her skin pebble with goosebumps, but she didn't care one bit. Noelle breathed the cold Colorado air into her lungs, her eyes stinging, and felt for the first time in years, what it was to be free. Goliath's gallops were hard beneath her, and she was sure she would be sore, but all she cared about at that moment was having the freedom to do whatever she wanted— she could skate, bake, shop, and decorate whatever she wanted in her home. She felt like a new person, like a newborn taking its first breath.

Noelle rode that high until they came upon the pond, having slowed down to weave through the thicket of trees that they needed to go through in order to access the pond. It lay sprawled before them, a thick layer of ice covering the waters beneath. It was utterly smooth aside from some branches littering the glittery surface. The sun's rays peeking through the thicket of trees to play on the ice, creating a wondrous collection of sparkling colors.

Carol gasped when she saw the fairytale-like pond, her eyes growing when the light hit it the right way and made tiny little rainbows reflecting off the snow, onto the trees around. It looked like something out of a true Christmas story—magical and seemingly impossible.

Nicholas dismounted his horse, hitching her to the tree adjacent to them after he'd lifted Carol from her back. River huffed, pawing at the ground before she reached her neck high enough to nubble some of the needles from the tree. He sighed, his hands placed on his hips as he drank in the scene before them.

"This might just be the most beautiful thing I've seen," Nicholas said, swinging his gaze toward her and keeping it there. Noelle nodded, breaking eye contact and looking over the pond again,

"You might be right," she said, swinging a leg over the back of Goliath, boots crunching in the thick snow as she dismounted. She hitched him right next River, the two of them content being so close to each other. Carol had already started to remove her boots, complaining when the cold bit at her toes and threatened to snap them off. Noelle went over, covering the child's toes with her warm hands as Nicholas retrieved her skates from River's saddle.

They made quick work of tying her skates, making sure they fit perfectly to support her ankle and didn't squeeze her feet too tightly. They were the perfect fit, as if they had been specially made for her, and hadn't been worn by a boy once before. Noelle soon put her own skates on, followed by Nicholas, and they hit the ice together, with Carol dangled between them.

She was not as uncertain as Noelle had thought she would be, the girl quickly letting go of their hands to make laps around the pond. It was decent enough in size that she could enjoy herself without bumping into them at all.

"Where'd you learn how to skate, honeybee?" Noelle asked as the girl came past them, a whirlwind blasting by their very calm skating selves. Carol stood still for a moment—or rather, she wiggled her legs in one place as she answered, which she supposed couldn't be classified as *still*.

"Mama used to take me to a pond in the park. She was the best skater ever." Her voice became high pitched as memories resurfaced. "She used to twirl and jump, and she did this thing where she lifted her foot above her head and spun around. It was amazing..."

The girl was in awe, recounting everything her mother had taught her before she'd passed away. Her voice grew more excited as she spoke, Noelle having had to increase her skating speed just to keep up.

"I can't do all of the things she showed me yet, but I think when I'm older, it'll be easier." Carol twirled slightly, careening to the side and back as she struggled to complete the turn.

"Of course you will," Noelle nodded, taking her hand to assist in the turn. "You're going to be the best skater ever."

Before she could say anymore, Carol skated away, in her own little world. Noelle's eyes were glued to her, to the red cheeks flushed with excitement and exhaustion, and the smile that never seemed to really go away. She saw Carol there, the little girl that very rarely let the world get her down, the girl who had lost her parents and still found it within herself to laugh and smile and be kind.

Nicholas caught up to her, also very at ease with being on the ice, as if he had done it his whole life. She skated alongside him, picking up their pace as Carol also seemed to catch a second breath and went blasting over the surface again... their own little tornado. Catching herself, Noelle almost blanched. *Their?* Since when did she classify Carol as hers and Nicholas'? And why did she have that thought in the first place?

She glanced sidelong at him, as if he could hear her thoughts, and quickly averted her gaze when he turned. Carol was hers, and hers alone. He had made that clear the very first night Sister Beatrice and the other orphanage representatives had come for the house visit. He had nothing to do with them, and despite her very obviously growing feelings for him, they were not the happy family they looked to be. Her stomach knotted. It also didn't mean because she had feelings for him that he had the same feelings for her; he could possibly just be a good friend, there to make sure she was adjusting easily with the recent changes, as she herself made sure Carol was adjusting as well.

But when she looked at him again, her heart softened. Noelle's own thoughts had angered her, but when she saw the way he gazed at Carol—with admiration and pride—she started to doubt herself. Although they were not a family, and he was not Carol's father—adoptive or biological—that didn't mean he didn't care for them. It didn't mean that he didn't harbor some type of love, whether it be romantic or platonic towards her. She had no doubt that he loved Carol; it was evident in the gifts he brought her, the experiences he made sure she got, and the effort he put into making her days fun-filled and lasting.

Noelle was so grateful for him, and for everything he had done to make their lives better and more comfortable. And watching Carol twirling and skating in the distance, cheeks flushed and face happy, she placed her hand on his, *willing* him to see her gratefulness.

"Thank you for everything you've done," Noelle said, willing every single drop of gratefulness into her voice. "Thank you for being so kind to us, and for making our lives so incredibly wonderful."

Nicholas watched her, eyes wide as if he was unsure where this was coming from. But he recovered quickly, placing his own hand on hers as they came to a stop facing each other. He nodded. "I could say the same for you and Carol, darlin', you've changed my life in the best way. Especially that little hurricane over there," he teased, squeezing her hand. Noelle giggled, peeking over his shoulder at the culprit. She squeezed his hand back, their fingers staying entangled until they departed the pond to go home for some hot cocoa. *Did he really call her darlin'?*

Mounted on Goliath once again, Noelle glanced back at the frozen pond, skating lines marring the once spotless surface. Light no longer danced on the ice, as if they had taken all of the warmth and brightness of it into themselves to take home and cherish forever. The snow on the trees had not budged and still reflected some of the rainbows the sun tried to paint around them.

She was sad in a way, that the pond's wonderful surface had been ruined by their skating. But when she thought of Carol's joy, she saw a physical account of childlike joy and freedom. A day spent with those she loved, that would still linger long after they had gone home. It was evidence that there had been life there, memories made and cherished for years to come, all because of nature's grace.

One more look at the pond, and Noelle was content, settling her gaze back on the people before her. Those she cherished above all others, and followed them home.

Chapter Eighteen

Nicholas was almost a hundred-percent sure that their toes were icicles by the time they removed their boots and stuck their feet in front of the fireplace. Carol was seated beside him, her small little toes wiggling as the heat thawed their toe-cicles little by little. He hissed, sticking his feet closer to the flames, willing life back into them so that he might also wiggle his, willing heat into them by using movement.

Noelle laughed as she walked past, already covered in more layers than he could count, and her feet stuck deep into her favorite winter slippers. She'd made a beeline for her room once Carol was sorted, warm and cozy by the fireplace with supervision to make sure she didn't set her feet alight.

"I'll make some hot cocoa for you babies," she teased. "Such melodrama!"

"Hey!" Carol and Nicholas shouted in unison, both of them turning to glare at Noelle as she rolled her eyes and backed away, hands lifted in surrender. He glared a little more just for good measure before turning back to the fire, his toes finally starting to gain life again.

"Alright Sweet Pea, it's time to remove these little chestnuts and get some real ones on this fire," he said, lightly nudging her feet aside. He then grabbed the chestnut roaster and the basket of chestnuts Noelle had set down for them. Carol protested, her glare now turning on him when he laid the chestnuts in the roaster and focused his attention on them, no longer caring for her frozen toes.

"Traitor," she whispered, as he stuck his tongue out at her and grinned.

Nicholas toasted the nuts, as she tugged on her socks—special flannel socks that had sheep's wool on the inside, keeping her nice and toasty. *Toasty*, he thought, as he *toasted* chestnuts. Nicholas snorted, laughing at his own joke.

"Why are you laughing?" Carol asked, tilting her head as she regarded him with confusion.

He waved his hand at her. "Nothing. Just a stupid joke I made."

She nodded, picking at a stray piece of wool on her sock. "Noelle does the same."

"Does what the same?" He shook the little pan, making them rotate every once in a while, to make sure they didn't burn.

"She laughs at her own jokes too." Then she looked up at him, her eyes flitting towards the kitchen briefly. "You make her laugh a lot too."

Nicholas smiled then, lowering to his knees once the flames were the right temperature for the nuts not to burn. He had to keep an eye on them though, they didn't need to be on for that long.

"That's a good thing, isn't it?" He asked, now glancing back at her. She was smiling, her picking having turned to her toes, which were freed from the sock. He frowned, amused with her ceaseless picking.

"Well, yes," she said, pulling her foot to her face, her eyes turning cross eyed as she studied whatever bothered her on her foot. "But you're the only one that makes her laugh."

Nicholas huffed, "You make her laugh plenty, too."

"No," she said, her tongue now sticking out the side of her mouth. He almost cringed at the angle of her hip, wondering how she hadn't popped it out of place yet. Her foot was almost against her nose at this point. Not only that, but he wondered if her sweaty skate-feet would knock her out. "That's different. She laughs at you like my Ma laughed at my Pa."

"How's that?" He asked before he could stop himself, needing the girl to know she could open up to him, talk to him if she needed and wanted to. Maybe for a selfish reason too. Carol sat upright again, placing a finger to her chin, tongue still out as she thought.

"Like she has sunshine in her heart," she finally said, and his own heart about burst out of his chest.

"Is that so..." he said, for lack of better words. Of course, Carol just nodded, completely oblivious to the war she'd just started within him. He left the conversation at that, no longer knowing what to do or say, and knowing Carol wouldn't understand half of it anyway. To her, she had just made a connection between them and her parents, and the similar ways they interacted with each other. To her, it was an innocent observation supported by fact as she'd seen it herself. But to him, who was nothing but a friend to Noelle, he had just been compared to her married parents who had obviously been very much in love.

Noelle chose that moment to return from the kitchen, carrying a tray with three hot cocoas and a bowl of her deliciously fresh-baked Christmas cookies—once again decorated by a very talented Carol. Nicholas took the cup she offered, smiling his thanks, and placed it on the coffee table beside him.

"They're almost done," he said, pointing to the still-roasting chestnuts. She nodded, taking her usual seat in the rocking chair closest to the doorway. He noticed how she always looked for a seat closest to a doorway, as if easy escape was still the first priority over comfort. He knew the rocking chair was uncomfortable, the wood in the back digging into her flesh; but she still sat there every time. He'd have to come up with some ideas to fix that.

A moment later, while Carol and Noelle were deep into a conversation about her current book, Nicholas removes the toasted nuts from the fireplace. He placed them into the given bowl, and put them in the kitchen for whatever Noelle wanted to do with them later on. Back in the living room, while his mind ran wild with Carol's comments, he sipped quietly at his cocoa, almost rolling his eyes as the deliciousness of the drink.

"Can we tell ghost stories?" Carol asked suddenly, eyes wide as saucers and her hands curled like makeshift claws. She made her creepiest face, baring her tiny little teeth and hissed like a monster. Nicholas feigned a fright, carefully placing his mug down, and lifted his hands in mock surrender. Noelle giggled, but shook her head,

"Sorry little bee, but there will be no ghost stories at Christmastime," she said, giving the girl a stern look when she pouted. Nicholas could see the meltdown starting to brim, the girl's cheeks taking on a red hue and her arms tightly tucked underneath each other. Noelle's jaw was set in determination, her eyes not budging as she stared the girl down. He would have to come up with a compromise—and soon.

"What about a special Christmas story?" He blurted, sitting upright from where he'd slouched against the couch. Nicholas remembered the story his father had told him one day, about a big man with a white beard and a sled pulled by reindeer that brought all of the nicest children presents.

He could remember the way the story had made him feel, how wondrous he had regarded the world afterwards, always looking towards the night sky in search of the white beard and the sled of reindeers. He just knew Carol would love this story, maybe as much as she loved those fictional stories she always read. However, he did not know if Noelle would be okay with it—Carol was still so young and easily influenced. He did not want her to forget the true reason for Christmas.

Carol gasped, scooting closer as she nodded profusely. Both of her socks were on again, feet probably picked raw, and she clutched at her toes as she scooted. They were about two feet apart when she finally stopped, bending her legs in front of her, hugging her knees in anticipation of whatever story Nicholas was about to tell her.

He tucked his legs under him, taking the hot cocoa mug in his hands as he leaned forward. He lowered his voice, as if it was just their secret, and asked, "What do you know about Santa Claus?"

Nicholas glanced up at Noelle, seeking any confirmation or rejection to his story. But she smiled, widening her eyes, and gasping when Carol glanced to her. He supposed that was her green button for him to continue, which he did—with a lot of dramatics and theatrics.

"Well, it's a big secret, so you can never tell anybody!" He whispered, coming in close. "He only told our family because my great grandpa helped him with his sleigh one day."

Carol's eyes widened and she nodded, her mouth making an 'o' as she waited for him to continue. He almost laughed then, and especially when he heard Noelle's suppressed giggles, but remained serious.

"Okay, well, this might seem a bit crazy, but I need you to listen carefully, okay?" Carol nodded again, but a frown creased her forehead, the first sign of her growing impatience. He huffed out a laugh before beginning the tale.

"Santa Claus is a very old man, with a big, long beard," he cupped his hand by his face, emphasizing a large beard. "A big belly, and a sleigh pulled by reindeer that run all night long."

Her eyes were wider now, Nicholas bouncing his stomach as he tried to emphasize the belly Santa Claus would have. She scooted closer again, as if her proximity would force the story out of him faster. He leaned in, widening his own eyes to express his wonder and the craziness of the story.

"Every year on Christmas Eve, he goes around the whole world," Nicholas circled his hands, encompassing the whole proverbial world, "and delivers presents to all of the nice little children. His sleigh is packed full of toys, almost spilling over the sides, and he leaves them in every home where the little boys and girls have been nice for the whole year."

"What do the naughty kids get?" She asked, her mouth completely open now. Carol stared at him in wonder as he told the story, making him want to squeeze her to death.

"Nothing," he said, making his fingers wiggle. "All the naughty kids are taken off of the list, and they do not get any presents because of it. Only the nice kids get presents, because they earned them. Although, some say the naughty ones get nothing but coal."

"But that would break the naughty kids hearts!" She said, ever concerned about others. "How do you know if you are one of the naughty ones?" Concern laced her tone now, and maybe even a little mixture of doubt and fear.

"They say you can hear him on the roof when he comes to visit you. His reindeer stomp their feet to count how many gifts you get that Christmas."

Nicholas glanced over at Noelle. She was silent, watching their exchange with a content smile on her face. She rocked in the chair, her cup of cocoa forgotten in her hand.

"But how do they know how many to give?" Carol asked, her hand clutching Nicholas' thumb now. He glanced back at her, smiling.

"They count your kind deeds towards others. How much you do for your friends and family and strangers."

Carol smiled, but he interrupted her before she could conjure the thought he knew was looming. "But, they only get counted when you mean them and when the deeds are sincere. If you are kind because you want more Christmas presents, he'll know, and you won't get the gift."

She frowned, her eyebrows slamming down. "He sounds like a sourpuss."

Nicholas burst out laughing then, Noelle even giving her own huff of laughter. Out of all the things he'd expected her to say, that was the last. Sure, there was a lesson in this story, but he would be a fool to think she'd grasp it at her age. All she cared about at this moment was the presents, and her lack of, if she didn't mean what she did all day. He could understand her observation.

"Yeah?" He asked, still huffing a laugh every now and then. She nodded, getting up and grabbing her book from the coffee table. Apparently, she'd lost interest in Mr. Claus and his terms and conditions. She lay stomach down on the rug, her feet swinging as she removed the torn piece of paper that served as a bookmark. Nicholas and Noelle were officially dismissed.

The former shook his head, still cross-legged on the floor. He glanced out of the window, the previously pink sky having turned dark in the matter of half an hour. He glanced at the grandfather clock against the wall to the second living room, eyes bulging at the time. It seemed to have run away from him, fun leeching the time from the day. Nicholas stood, sipping the last bit of his hot cocoa, before he took the cup to the kitchen, along with Carol's and Noelle's.

She rose from her perch on the chair, smoothing her hands down her dress as he emerged from the kitchen, his hands in his pockets.

"On your way?" She asked, her eyes at half-mast and evidence of the exhaustion today's business had caused. He felt his own eyes were dry as well, a yawn lurking not too far behind. Nicholas glanced outside, the snowfall light enough to make it home without having to rush. He nodded, smiling,

"I think River would very much like to get home as well."

Noelle nodded, walking towards the door alongside him. She was quiet as he gathered his coat and shrugged it on, peeking behind the corner to see little Carol engrossed in her book. He smiled and shook his head.

"Just tell her I said goodbye, I think she'd slap me if I bothered her now," he said.

Noelle glanced back at her daughter, nodding her agreement. "Oh yes, that's her 'don't approach me I'm reading' position."

They both chuckled. Nicholas glanced at her one moment longer, remembering exactly what he'd wanted to ask her since that morning,

"Would you like to go to the Christmas fair with me tomorrow?" He was slightly nervous for some reason, as if he hadn't just spent the afternoon with them and every day before that. He also had no doubt she would accept, so there really was no reason for the slight tremor in his hands.

Noelle smiled brightly, nodding her head. "We would love to."

Chapter Nineteen

Dressed in a special white dress with puffy sleeves—which might not be the best color for a 6-year-old-—hair braided back out of her face with curled edges and a big red bow as large as her face; there was nothing that Noelle could do to contain Carol's excitement for the Christmas fair.

Not that she wanted to, but she had never felt such buzzing energy, like a hurricane waiting to be unleashed. Perhaps her honey-bee nickname Noelle had given her should be changed to buzzing-bee. She even had the black shoes to serve as the little bee's feet; now Noelle only had to get her a yellow and black striped dress and her ensemble would be complete.

Noelle wore a red, long-sleeved tight-fitting corset dress that she'd also saved for an occasion. It was done with a slight skirt, not oversized that served as ball-gown but more of an A-line fit. Her own red hair was pulled back from her face, a red bow matching Carol's keeping the strands in place at the back of her head whilst the other half of her hair flowed down her back.

Red tint graced her lips, and she felt pretty for the first time in a good long while. She had forgotten how fun it was to get dolled up, not that she looked down-trodden other days, but today she had put some extra effort in. Henry had never noticed when she made herself pretty, which could explain why she stopped trying to impress him and stuck to her every-day dresses.

Grasping each other's hands, they set about the town, anticipation making both of them extremely jittery, which prompted them to go on horseback instead of with the wagon. The road was slightly less icy this time, which was a relief. It had originally been Carol's idea, wanting to show her friends how well she could ride a horse, so Noelle indulged her little fantasy. Besides, Goliath's black pelt complimented their red and white looks beautifully.

Noelle supposed she would have to get Carol her own horse soon, seeing as she would grow older and start to become more independent, which meant she would be itching to have her own horse in any case. She'd also been teaching the girl and giving her riding lessons, so she was more than confident in the little whirlwind's riding ability. She wondered how much that would cost though, and how long she'd be able to stretch the money Nicholas had given her. If it would even be possible to purchase a pony for the girl. She would be lucky if it lasted her until next spring, although she highly doubted it.

She was lucky enough already that none of the bankers and estate managers had come knocking yet, but she was a fool if she thought they would forget about her completely. Perhaps it was the Lord's blessing they had already left her alone for so long—and that Beatrice had not yet found out about Henry's untimely death. In a small town such as this one, it truly was a Christmas miracle.

The streets were brimming with festively dressed people, all of them sporting smiles as wide as the banner that announced the entrance to the fair. Although, none of them could compete with the smiles on Noelle's and Carol's faces when they spotted Nicholas there, holding two bouquets of flowers for each of his girls. A smile stretched over his beautiful face, making one of her own appear as well at the sight of the small dimple that so rarely made an appearance.

Carol was beside herself with excitement, almost clamoring down the wagon in her haste to get to Nicholas and the pretty flowers he had chosen just for her. She hugged his legs tightly, beaming up at him.

Nicholas tore his eyes from Noelle, smiling down at the little force clutching at his leg. "Is *this* the special dress?"

Once again, Carol shook her head, giggling with glee as he shook his head and rolled his eyes.

"And when will this special dress make an appearance? I am almost crazy with anticipation," he said, handing Noelle her bouquet as she neared, the reins still in hand. He promptly took them from her, waiting for Carol to answer.

"What's…" Carol glanced up at Noelle in uncertainty. She glanced at Nicholas, tucking her hands behind her back as she leaned down to the girl's height.

"Anticipation," Noelle whispered, biting back a smile. The girl twirled her skirts as she asked again, lifting her chin high,

"What's anticipation?"

Nicholas smiled. "I'm the wrong person to ask for the exact definition, but think of it as excitement."

Carol had already moved on from the subject, however, now gazing at the various activities taking place in the demarcated area of the fair a few paces ahead of them. Nicholas inclined his head to her, taking a seat on the wagon as she waited patiently by the entrance while he found a spot for the wagon. Noelle looked around her as they waited, swinging her arm happily with Carol's when she interlaced their hands, eager to enter the fair and indulge in the joyous activities that beckoned to those wide eyes. Noelle lifted her arm higher, using every muscle in her body to keep upright as the child used her like a human swing.

"Where are we going first?" Carol asked as she swung from Noelle's arm. The girl was barely out of breath and Noelle felt like she was about to lose a shoulder.

"Well, we're going to take a look at all the wares people have to sell, and then we'll get something to eat and take you to the playground to play a little," Noelle pondered. "But it really all depends on what there is to do, honeybee."

Once Nicholas returned, looking disgruntled as he had no doubt struggled to hitch Goliath, and they crossed the entrance together, bouquets of flowers in hand and smiles across their faces. They walked past every stall selling goods, stopping to glance at what they offered, and moved on. They bought Carol some sweets, which powered her up for another bout of running around that had Noelle and Nicholas shaking their heads.

Later, after he had gobbled up a particularly large amount of sweets himself, Nicholas joined Carol in her running, placing the little girl in her white dress on his neck as they spread their arms wide—making duck noises as they flapped their make-believe wings. Noelle laughed, clutching their belongings as tightly as she clutched at her stomach, aching with joy. This only prompted them to be sillier, making funny faces at her before they returned to their duck-migration. She took a seat on the blanket they'd laid out, placing the flowers and their coats next to her as she watched them, joyous and utterly without stress or sadness or guilt. They returned briefly for a quick sweets-break and water, which prompted Nicholas to try and convince her to join.

"Our duck-family needs a mama duck, you know," he suggested slyly, wiggling his eyebrows. "Or does mama duck not have what it takes to keep up with papa duck and baby duck?"

Noelle rolled her eyes. "Mama duck is on vacation. She's not required to work today."

Nicholas grunted his answer, playing dead when Carol stood to pull him up by his hand. But soon enough, there he went, flapping his arms again. Noelle shook her head and chuckled.

They ran in circles, drawing the attention of those around them as they cackled like geese, Carol even screeching in excitement as Nicholas jumped to sell the illusion of them taking flight. Then, they switched animals completely, Carol tugging at his hair as he whinnied. He even stomped on the ground as Goliath often did, blowing air from his lips like a horse. Noelle burst out laughing again, watching a six-feet-tall, full-grown man, imitate a horse was something she'd never thought she'd see in her lifetime. She supposed this Christmas was one with many surprises.

Noelle watched them contently, watching them play together causing her heart to almost burst with happiness. She realized how much she had craved this, and how much Nicholas had finally made a final piece fit into her dream-life puzzle. They looked like a real family, *acted* like a real family.

They had met him at the front of the fair, and they'd entered together, scrolled the available goods together, bought food and drinks and sweets as if they were parents spoiling their child. She was Carol's mother, so she supposed it was true in her case, but Nicholas had unwittingly filled the space a father would. Did he realize it? And if he hadn't, *when* he did—what would he do? What would he say?

They had been acting like a couple in love, even risking small touches here and there that left both of the smiling or blushing; whenever the either had the courage to risk a touch.

Their antics came to a halt, Nicholas removing Carol from her perch on his neck as the band started to play a jolly tune. On the other side of them, couples took to the small patch of open space they'd made the dance floor, engaging in a dance that left the women laughing and twirling. She smiled at the glee on the couples' faces as they danced, mesmerized by the beauty of love.

Some of the couples were older, but looked as if they were just as in love as the young couples around them; and that was what had Noelle staring—that never-fading love that had seemed like a fable to her in the last years of her life. However, she wondered if she would now get the opportunity to experience it for herself. Either with Nicholas or whoever she was meant to be with.

Noelle felt a gaze settle on her, meeting familiar brown eyes when she turned to look. Nicholas winked at her, a faint blush creeping over her face as she tucked a stray hair that always seemed to escape behind her ear. He broke eye contact, Carol's small hands in his, twirling her around and around as they started to dance. Her heart felt like it was about two beats away from bursting, and she quickly looked away as they twirled again. Was this truly something she could have for herself? This family that felt like it was appearing right in front of her eyes?

She glanced around at the people openly staring at her family—or rather, make-believe family—and waited for shame to turn the moment sour. But it never came, and she never felt that feeling of guilt that had plagued her after Henry's death. It was as if it had been washed from her conscience completely, leaving only a crystal-clear speck for new memories to occupy.

She felt no guilt for the emotions swirling in her heart and mind, and the dreams that were steadily becoming real. She also felt no nervousness regarding what people would think of her if they spotted her with Nicholas, acting like they were a couple. In fact, Noelle couldn't care less what these people thought of her or of them—as long as Nicholas and Carol thought she was the best. And maybe Beatrice, too, but for different reasons.

Noelle glanced back at them, tapping her fingers in beat with the music the band so artfully composed, widening her eyes and smile when Carol called for her, demanding she watch. Her little feet were clad in black boots that were now faltering as she tried to imitate the dance steps Nicholas was so patiently teaching her.

As if her gaze were something he could feel as clearly as a touch, Nicholas glanced up, meeting her eyes. He held her stare as they danced, his hand still clutching Carol's while she danced without care beside him. Noelle's cheeks turned blood red, her body warming under his molten gaze. Her breath hitched in her throat, and almost like a loaded wagon, the realization hit her. It threatened to knock the wind out of her lungs, stop time around her, and throw her whole world upside-down.

She was falling in love with him. And there was nothing she could do to stop it. Not when he smiled at her, and stared at her with those beautiful whiskey-brown eyes, and especially not when he danced with her daughter as if she were his own. She could not stop the free-fall that was happening, not when he cared for them and did so much to ensure their safety and comfort.

And especially not when he tugged Carol towards where she sat on the blanket, pulled Noelle to her feet, and danced with both of them; dragging a bout of laughter from her that was so genuine she was almost startled by it. Noelle couldn't recall the last time she'd laughed this hard and this much.

It was like her soul had finally come out of its corner in the dark place where she'd hidden it away, safe from the claws of despair and heartbreak. It seemed to have startled Nicholas as well, because his head snapped to her so fast, she thought he would break his neck, his stare feeling like it would pierce the outer layers of her skin and enter her mind. He quickly recovered, clutching her hand tightly in his as they spun.

Noelle couldn't blame her dizziness on the spinning alone, neither could she blame her breathlessness on the dance. All of it was because of the man beside her, still clutching her hand tightly as they spun threatening to sweep her from her feet—and not literally. She was falling for this man, she realized, her eyes glued to that beautifully rugged face. It was done for, *she* was done for.

Chapter Twenty

Nicholas had never heard a sound so melodious as when Noelle had laughed for the first time. He was not talking about the small giggles or snorts she used to give when he or Carol made a joke, no—he was talking about the genuine laugh that had just escaped her lips only moments ago when they'd been dancing, that red dress of hers twirling like a whirlwind of roses.

It had almost stopped his heart dead in his chest, that laugh; and that was not the first time he'd almost perished. This morning, when she'd stepped down from the wagon in that ridiculously beautiful dress, he'd almost called a doctor to check his pulse. Not to mention the way it complemented her hair and eyes, the blue hue of them standing out like amethyst jewels against the stark of the red. She looked...exquisite.

Even now, where they sat on the blanket once again, all of them desperate for a breath, he couldn't keep his eyes from her for more than a few seconds. She was a magnet, like his eyes couldn't resist drinking in the marvel of her beauty and grace. Nicholas had wondered, many times, what it was about this woman that intrigued him so. He rarely got one simple answer when he thought about it, and he supposed it was not that simple.

Perhaps it was her kind soul that always had time to help others, or maybe it was the way she could find the positive in anything. Perhaps it was the way she took care of Carol, or her nurturing nature. Perhaps it was everything about her. He didn't know. And there was something else he was unsure of. Should he avoid that growing, fuzzy feeling in his chest... or embrace it?

Carol ate another handful of sweets, smiling sweetly at Noelle when she gave the girl a stern look, trying to soften the woman's resolve. She'd already had too many sweets, but it seemed there was no stopping her as she shoved another sweet into her mouth, the hard candy making a bump in her cheek.

"You can have two more," Noelle said, handing the peppermint candy to her before she crumpled the paper bag they came in. Carol pouted, jutting her sticky lip out in an attempt to soften that stern look on Noelle's face. She shook her head, the girl folding her arms in disagreement.

"But it's not enough," Carol whined, her green-stained mouth opening to reveal an even more stained tongue. She was sticky all over, from the corners of her mouth and even her cheeks, to her hands that were littered with leaves and wisps of cotton.

"Honeybee it's *more* than enough. You've had sweeties ever since we got here," Noelle answered, attempting to wipe the girl's hands down with a handkerchief. But the girl was not so easily deterred. She whined again, which only made Noelle look at her even more sternly.

Nicholas left them to their battle of wills and stares, looking around them at all of the Christmas cheer that made the air palpable with it. There was a certain joy hanging around with the snow, as if happiness were mixed with the snowflakes and carpeted the ground beneath them, decorating the pine trees around the park they were currently hosting the fair in.

He glanced over the sea of faces, smiles all around and the occasional child wearing the same look of displeasure that Carol had sported just a moment ago. Children were playing all around, throwing snowballs and shrieking with joy as their friends chased them about.

There was a small playground to the left of them, right where the many stalls of goods ended, and right under it, gazing at the hordes of children she'd brought with her from the orphanage, stood Sister Beatrice. She was clad in her usual black-robe-and-white-coif garb, a slightly softer look on her face than the one she usually reserved for adults—that one was far more sour and standoffish. Nicholas's heart dropped like a rock, a hollow feeling settling in his stomach. He sat up straight from where he'd been resting his weight on his extended arms, glancing over at Noelle and Carol. They were still negotiating the amount of sweets the little one was allowed to get, and paid no heed to the ticking time-bomb that had just spotted them.

He gulped, his hands suddenly sweaty. With so many people around them there was no way she could refer to him as henry without some people noticing and possibly correcting her. Not to mention that Carol referred to him as Nicholas, and not the name of her supposed father—or rather according to Beatrice. Why did the thought suddenly fill him with jealousy instead of fear of their discovery?

Beatrice made her way over, the hem of her robes dragging in the snow. The garment usually ended just above the top of her shoes, but with the snow, the dirtying of the garment was inevitable. He placed a hand on Noelle's upper back, rising from his perch to greet the woman with a warm smile, even though he felt like he was about two minutes away from passing out.

Noelle saw what he was looking at, and rose with him, dusting her skirts off as she did. Carol looked up in curiosity, a smile stretching across her face when she realized who it was. The scars on her face should have been stark, and possibly could have marred her beauty, but every time she smiled, it felt like Nicholas' heart would cease its beating completely. She was wonderful; the scars only made her more beautiful, if that was possible.

The little girl rose quickly, grasping the woman at the hips in a tight hug as Nicholas and Noelle stepped closer, his hand still on her back in support—both for himself and her. He knew both of them were panicking slightly, even though Noelle was the picture of perfect calmness. The only sign of her distress was the way she gripped her hands, wringing them together as an outlet for the nerves she shared with him.

"Sister Beatrice, how nice it is to see you," Noelle spoke softly, ever the picture of grace. "How have you been? Are things at the orphanage still progressing as you'd hoped?"

Beatrice nodded, her face falling from a beaming smile directed at Carol, to a barely pleasant expression as she spoke with them. It wasn't that she was rude, she had possibly just had enough of adults for the rest of her lifetime—which was understandable when one considered her line of work. Every child was not an orphan by tragedy, but rather unwillingly by being unwanted or taken due to negligence. The latter was the case far too many times for his liking.

"We have been doing quite well, thank you," she said, gazing down at Carol for a moment before continuing. "The donations from the church helped immensely. Thank you, again, for your help with that, Noelle."

Noelle nodded, smiling kindly. "Of course."

"How have you been adjusting?" Beatrice said, caressing the girl's golden locks. Her fingers toyed with the red bow for a moment, a slight smile appearing on her mouth when she glanced at it. "I know little Carol can be..."

"A whirlwind?" Noelle joked lightheartedly, gazing at the girl with love. "We have been absolutely wonderful."

"Noelle and Nicholas taught me how to ride a horse," Carol informed the woman, beaming up at her from where she still clutched at her robes. "I am the best at it now."

Beatrice gasped, overdramatically to appease the child, "You don't say! I think you're lying," she squinted one eye at the girl, feigning disbelief.

Nicholas went white as a sheet, sweat causing beads of moisture to roll down his back. He swore he stopped breathing too, his lungs unable to function beneath the crushing weight of his nervousness. He felt Noelle stiffen beside him, her hands now ceasing their wringing and settling for a death grip that was wrapped around his forearm. He draped a careless arm around her shoulder,

"That's right," he said, his forehead beaded with tiny dots of sweat and his voice cracking the slightest.

"And who is this Nicholas, so that we might thank him for his service," Beatrice asked, indulging Carol's incessant need for telling stories. She lifted her tiny arm, a finger poised to point right at him, when he gently grabbed her,

"What do you say we go get some more sweets while Noelle and Sister Beatrice catch up?" He asked, lifting the girl, and settling her right on his arm. She clapped her hands together excitedly, squealing as she did. Nicholas-not-Henry and his horse-riding lessons are forgotten, successfully removing their hides from the firepit of Beatrice's rage should she have found out.

He glanced at Noelle quickly, widening his eyes in silent *good luck* as they departed for the sweets stall. She flashed him a grateful smile, moving to steer Beatrice the other way. She placed a hand at the woman's shoulder, guiding her towards where the children still played on the playground. Carol hummed happily from where she sat perched on his arm, oblivious to the absolute stroke she'd almost caused. Nicholas shook his head, and with it, all of his nerves off.

On their way home, Nicholas glanced out at the snow-capped trees around them, his thoughts falling about in his mind as the snow now fell on the ground. It had started snowing moments ago, prompting them to end their excursion. It had been the most blissful and wonderful day he'd had in a while, and he'd been less than happy when they'd needed to end it. Carol shared his sentiments, the girl still glowering at the snow that now decorated her pretty green coat.

Noelle was oddly quiet, caressing her daughter's hair in silent contemplation as he rode next to them, River occasionally stepping into Goliath's path as she navigated the ever-thickening mounds of snow.

"Would you like to stay a while?" Noelle suddenly asked, her eyes meeting his, as she tore them away from the tree line beside her. He glanced into those blue depths, seeing the

169

nerves there. Nicholas considered, glancing at the weather around them before he nodded. She looked like she needed someone, and he'd be damned if he wasn't going to be that someone.

After placing River in the barn, saddle and all, as he wasn't going to stay too long, he entered the warm home to find an already-asleep Carol, tucked under a blanket in front of the fireplace. He didn't blame the girl, the temperature had been plummeting since they left the fair, and he would be the first to admit that a nap in front of the fireplace was one of the best naps one could experience.

Well, until it got too hot, that is. Nicholas shook his head as he gazed down at the girl, crouching as low as he can to gather the bundle in his arms. Noelle was busy in the kitchen, and from the clang of the tea pot, he supposed it was teatime.

He tried to muffle the thump of his boots on the stairs, going slowly and slightly on his toes as he ascended, Carol not so much as stirring in his arms. He laid the girl to sleep, removing the bow from her hair as gently as he could, trying his best not to knot the hair further. He supposed Noelle would know how to get it out, but still.

When he descended the stairs, Noelle was in front of the fireplace, a cup of tea clutched in her hand and another steaming on the coffee table beside the armchair to the right of the fireplace. The flames set her red hair ablaze, a halo of bronze playing over the crown of her hair as she stared deeply into the embers. She looked ethereal with the fire dancing on her face, her hair like a wild flowing river of lava down her back. The red dress helped with that image, painting her as something from a fairytale.

Nicholas stepped down from the last step, purposely hard enough to alert her to his presence. She turned with a smile, lifting her face to his as he came to a stop beside her. He almost gasped at the beauty, her eyes sparkling like the stars he found himself staring at so often. Before he could stop himself, he tucked a piece of that wild hair behind her ear, his fingers brushing over her cheek ever so slightly when he dropped his hand.

Beautiful, he thought to himself, stepping closer to her, as if he could draw her in, and keep that beauty for himself, forever cherished. He tracked her face, eyes moving over the arched brows, sharp cheekbones, upturned nose, and settled on the rosy lips she'd tinted red. He wondered how soft her lips were, and if they would fit into his as he imagined they would.

Ever so slowly, Nicholas leaned in, placing his hand on the arch of her neck, right where the shoulder meets. Her mouth parted, her eyes locking onto his lips as he licked them. Their breaths mingled, their lips so achingly far apart and yet so blissfully close. If he adjusted ever so slightly, they would press together.

A log in the fire beside them fell from its stack, the tip of it red with embers. It rolled onto the carpet at their feet, breaking the moment between them completely as he scrambled to throw it back in the fire where it wouldn't be a danger. Noelle turned abruptly, taking her teacup and setting it down on the coffee table beside his. He stared at her turned back, then glanced back into the fire and tried to calm the identical fire roaring in his blood.

Chapter Twenty-One

1885, Copper Mountain, Colorado

Christmas Eve

Noelle hummed as she made her way downstairs, stopping by Carol's door. She was still fast asleep, her cap of blonde curls spread over the pillow and trapped beneath a pajama-clad arm. She shook her head, rolling her eyes. She'd warned the girl countless times not to sleep with her arm over her face, warning her of tense muscles, but alas, she always ended up that way. In her 28 years of age, she'd never seen a rougher sleeper than Carol Jones.

Her slippers were barely audible on the plush carpet she'd thrown over the stairs, thinking it might help Nicholas when he put Carol to bed. She didn't miss how he walked ever so slowly every time, careful of the amount of noise he made as he ascended the awfully creaky steps. She'd simply hammered the rug to the steps with nails at either side of each step, and the top and bottom of them, every nail perfectly placed in a corner or nook to ensure no-one had a run-in with a punctured foot.

Noelle collected the dirty tea mugs she and Carol had left in the living room the previous night, taking them to the kitchen and dropping them in the bucket full of ice-cold water. She eyed the state of her hands after she'd rinsed them out, the reddened fingertips screaming for a bit of warmth, and decided to boil the kettle before proceeding with washing any more dishes.

Leaving it to boil over the fireplace, Noelle made her rounds through the house, seeking anything out of place or unsuited for her plans to prepare for tomorrow. It was Christmas after all, she wanted to have everything perfect—including the decor in the house. Every red ribbon was in place, every green strand of mistletoe hung perfectly from doorways all around the house, and every little piece of burlap or furniture was perfect. She even added some throw blankets to the chairs, making them seem more suited for a home people lived in rather than a display home.

She did her rounds in the second living room, her gaze snagging and settling on the crackling firewood in the fireplace. It burned hot and fiery, the wood cracking as heat split it open. Noelle stepped closer, feeling the heat scorch her face as she lowered, staring into that blaze as if she could see the scene play out before her. And by scene, she was referring to the night Nicholas had almost kissed her.

A blush crept up her neck and settled in her cheeks, making the heat from the fire unbearable. It was almost unbearable as the heat between her and Nicholas, a thing so real and alive she could almost feel it now, taunting her. She had not forgotten about that almost-kiss, not once; and it always found a way to haunt her. Or rather, she found ways to think about it—for instance, comparing it to the heat of a fire.

She'd seen that kiss in the dishwater, and then in the mirror when she glanced at her lips, and then in her hands when she'd remembered how he'd touched her, and then she'd seen it when her hand had brushed over the spot where her neck and shoulder meet—the exact spot his hand had rested. Noelle was going mad with the memory of it, consumed by thoughts of it and what it would have been like if that log had not fallen out. Would he have gone through with it? Would he have realized what he was doing and pulled away? Would he have gone through with it—and if he had, where would that have left them?

Noelle narrowed her eyes at a log, suddenly very displeased with the inanimate object. She poked at it with the poker, stabbing the point right through its wooden middle. *What a shame*, she thought, pursing her lips. How pathetic was her life that even a log could keep her from romance?

There was a creak from behind her, a still-sleepy Carol rubbing at her eyes as she glanced over at Noelle. Her hair was an absolute mess of knots and tangles, the wispy pale strands reflecting the rays of sun streaming in from the slightly parted curtains. The fabric of her night gown wrinkled, and paired with the disheveled state of her hair and one closed eye, she looked like she had been through war. Noelle snorted, rising from her crouch in front of her nemesis, and ushered the girl back upstairs.

"Let's get those tangles out of your hair, shall we?" She smiled, dragging a hand down her hair. The girl stumbled around, her feet struggling to work together and her mind struggling to wake. Noelle laughed now, "You can't still be sleepy, can you?"

Carol just rubbed her little eyes, yawning as she did, and stumbled her way down the hall and to her bedroom, Noelle on her heels.

After they'd sorted the rat's nest that was Carol's hair, and dressed her in her yellow dress fitted with a matching yellow bow in her hair, they returned downstairs. The little whirlwind was in a much better state now, no longer rubbing her eye until it threatened to pop from the socket, and very much walking straighter.

"Want to help me with the chicken?" Noelle asked, gathering her ingredients from the various baskets littered around the kitchen. She plopped them all down on the counter, the garlic and lemon making their escape as they rolled off the other side. Carol leaned down and snatched them up, nodding her head profusely at the offer. Noelle smiled,

"Well, we'll have to catch and pluck it first!" She shouted, chasing Carol out the door with grabbing hands and bared teeth. "Otherwise we'll have to cook you!"

Noelle feigned an evil laugh, even lifting her head to the sky in mock malice as she did. Carol screeched, clutching at her stomach as she evaded Noelle's clutching hands. Soon, both of them turned their clutching hands on the chicken prancing around in the chicken coop, evading wings and beaks and very sharp talons.

"I don't want to watch," Carol said, covering her eyes with mitten-clad hands as Noelle prepared to decapitate the chicken, laying it on the wooden table at the back of the little shed Henry had built for himself precisely for this reason. Noelle nodded, pinning the chicken to the table as she grabbed the butcher knife next to her.

"You don't have to, honeybee. You can stand outside if you want to, I'll be right there." Noelle said, waiting for her response before she just went about chopping heads off. What a strange thought. Carol exited promptly, leaving the butchering to Noelle.

Later, freshly plucked and cleaned, the chicken lay on the wooden cutting board in front of her. Carol peeked over the lip of the counter, eyes wide as Noelle widened the back end of the chicken and stuffed a lemon, garlic, and various spices along with some herbs in. She watched Carol as she worked, almost able to see the gears in her head turn as she tried desperately to dissect exactly what was happening here.

Noelle winked at her, inclining her head. "Come over here and help me get started on the stuffing."

Eager to help, as always, Carol rolled up the sleeves of her dress, and readied herself for whatever task Noelle had for her. She searched the kitchen around her, looking for any blunt object sharp enough to be able to cut the hard vegetables and almonds. She settled for the lip of a tin, instructing Carol to be careful of the sharp edge and showing her how to cut with the lip.

The girl set to work, cutting the vegetables and almonds with the tin, and leaving them in strange shapes in a pile on the edge of her own cutting board.

"Are we going to make pudding, too?" Carol asked, breaking the comfortable silence they'd been working in. Or rather, as silent as the house could be with Carol's talking and Noelle's humming. Noelle nodded, widening her eyes in excitement,

"Of course! We're going to make a plum pudding using some of the plums we bought at the market the other day," she glanced back at the basket of fruits. "They should be ripe by now."

Carol scrunched her nose. "That doesn't sound very good."

Leave the honesty to children, but be prepared to receive it. Noelle smirked. "That's just because you haven't tried *my* plum-pudding yet."

Her face didn't change, but she finally relented when Noelle gave her some puppy-eyes and promised a bag of sweets if it wasn't good. After they'd cut all the vegetables, and left the chicken in the oven to keep it covered from any insects, they moved on to the pudding.

Noelle covered Carol's nose with baking powder, evading the little flour-covered hands that threatened to exact their revenge. They ran around the kitchen, hiding from each other and peeking around corners as they waged their bake-war. Ultimately, Carol won, planting two handprints right on Noelle's cheeks when she peeked around the kitchen counter, her bowl of flour just out of reach when her enemy had come running.

They laughed, clutching at their stomachs but immediately stopping when they noticed the state of the kitchen and what should have been plum pudding by now. And when their eyes met, they burst out into laughter again.

Noelle sobered up enough to actually start the mix for the pudding, Carol joining her once again, shoving her tiny body between Noelle and the counter. Her chin barely reached the lip of the counter, her eyes straining to see what Noelle was doing. She would have to get a stepstool for the girl, or risk a few toes judging by the feet searching for any foothold– including Noelle's own.

They spent the last leg of the afternoon baking, Noelle ignoring Carol's not-so-inconspicuous attempt at dropping a dime into the pudding. She supposed it was the girl's idea of a prank, or some tradition she'd had with her parent's that she had yet to share with Noelle. And though she might have yet to share that memory or tradition, she still shared a lot of other memories with her.

"One time on Christmas, Mama tried to make a pudding just like this one." Her mouth was full of the jam-covered piece of bread Noelle had given her just moments before. Smears of it covering the sides of her cheeks and the tip of her nose. Noelle smiled softly, gazing lovingly at the girl as she busied herself with the little material doll Noelle had bought for her at the fair.

"I bet it tasted delicious, didn't it?" Noelle asked enthusiastically, sipping from her tea mug. They were in the second living room, seated in front of the fireplace that was steadily driving the cold from their bones and from the halls in the house. There was a broken window shutter in the first living room that she had yet to fix, but just never seemed to find the time or the will to do it. She supposed she would have to sooner or later, considering it was allowing tufts of cold air into the home.

"No," she said, still occupied with her doll and frantically gulping down the slice of jam-bread. "Mama forgot about it, and it burned. But Papa still ate it."

Carol started laughing, fits of giggles that had Noelle laughing along after a while. "He said it wasn't very good," Noelle removed the empty plate from in front of the girl, listening intently while she told her story. "I don't know why he ate it, because it was really bad,"

Carol hopped the doll around, adjusting her posture as she tried to style the hair of yarn. She wiped at her nose every so often, making Noelle slightly insane with the urge to wipe her nose. But she hated it and always fought her off when she did, and she didn't want to stop her talking.

"Papa always did something for Mama, even if he didn't like it,"

"It sounds like your Papa was a good father." Noelle said, tucking a strand of blond hair behind the girl's ear.

"He was the best papa ever." Carol said, her arms suddenly dropping, the doll falling to the carpet face-down. Her shoulders caved in, shaking with sobs as her little face crumpled, tears spilling down her cheeks. Noelle was by her side in an instant, pulling her into an embrace strong enough to help her through this heartbreak, as if Noelle's arms could hold her together. She let the girl cry, rubbing her back and made soothing noises to try and calm her.

Noelle could feel Carol's heartbreak with every back-bowing sob. The girl might have been happy these last few weeks, and while she enjoyed her time here with her, Noelle realized that it would never replace what she'd had—not that she wanted it to. That sadness will always be there, lurking in the shadows of her mind and heart, even if she chose to play in the sunshine of happiness with Noelle and Nicholas. She would support the girl no matter what, and try her best to fill the void while respecting Carol's parents.

Noelle held Carol as she let it all out, only offering her a cup of tea and a handkerchief. When she was calm, Noelle offered to read her a bed-time story, to the joy of the little girl with the broken heart. She supposed they both needed it, and were mending each other's hearts little by little as they built their life.

They both fell asleep with the children's book between them, snuggled up in Noelle's large bed, and significantly more upbeat than they had been.

Chapter Twenty-Two

Christmas morning, Nicholas found himself smiling as he rode down the snow-covered dirt path leading to Noelle's ranch home. River huffed below him, her strides slightly labored due to the increase in weight because of the rucksack he's strapped to her saddle, the bag filled with toys and presents for Carol and Noelle—perhaps too many of each. With River safely stowed in the barn, Nicholas took a minute to rummage through the almost overflowing bag of gifts, suddenly nervous if he'd gone overboard or if he was about to make their day. They hadn't discussed if presents were going to be exchanged, so he'd just gone along and gotten them without any real second thought—it was Christmas after all.

Outside, on his way to the looming font door, Nicholas took a second to stand in the slightly-warmer sun that was shining down on the snow-capped trees around him, bathing them in an orange glow that seemed to warm his soul. The mounds of snow beneath his boots were soft, like a blanket laid out on a green patch of grass, aching for someone to take a nap.

It was like this Christmas morning held a sense of...comfort; different from the other years he'd spent it alone. Perhaps it was the kind woman and little girl waiting inside that brought upon this change, perhaps it was the ambience of the sun and snow that set a warm tone to the world—but something was different, and for the better.

He barely knocked on the door when it swung open, almost taking his breath away as it revealed the most heavenly sight he'd ever laid eyes upon. It had been a while since their almost kiss, and whilst she'd been in his mind relentlessly, it was nothing compared to the absolute joy of being in her company. Noelle wore her red hair down, the ends curling slightly and the pieces around her face swept back in a face-framing style that accentuated her high cheekbones and full mouth. Her eyes were framed with the slightest line of kohl, and her lips tinted with red. However, it was the dress she wore that had his eyes widening. It was forest green with a corset-like cinch at her waist, decorated with gold thread that reflected off the sun's rays that had warmed his face just a moment ago. The skirt flared slightly, hanging off her hips like a green river of steadily flowing material. She looked...exquisite, magnificent, absolutely beautiful.

"Nicholas?" A slight frown creased the skin between her eyebrows, one of them arched in question.

Nicholas glanced up, meeting her cerulean eyes finally, and trying to get his mind to work. He flashed a quick smile, her own spreading across her face, and lifted the presents he still held in his hand.

"I brought presents," he announced, stepping inside when she moved from the threshold. The air was stuffy and warm inside, the home now fully decorated for Christmas day with parlor tables set with drinks and platters of cookies. There was a whole spread of food on the dining room table, a green and gold tablecloth underneath the platters, and red bows scattered about to complete the festive decor. Mistletoe was hanging from the door underneath the threshold as he entered the small hallways before the set of stairs, both of them coming to a halt underneath it; coincidentally. They glanced up, almost simultaneously, and both blushed the color of the bright red bow in the hair of a sprinting Carol.

She was running from the top of the stairs, her locks bouncing as she descended the stairs two at a time. She wore a bright red dress with puffy sleeves, completed with knee-high white socks and the cutest black clogs Nicholas had ever seen. Her face was alight with joy, and her eyes snagged on the bag of gifts he'd brought right before she jumped from the last step right into his waiting arms.

Noelle carefully took the bag from him, gazing on as Carol almost squeezed the life out of him. She moved into the second living room, the bag hanging from her fingertips. He rubbed her small back, placing her back on her feet when they finally broke apart.

"Is *this* the special dress? Has it finally made an appearance?" He asked, feigning anticipation and desperation. He splayed his arms in enthusiasm, adding to the overall scene. Carol giggled, wringing her hands together in shyness, nodding along, until he gasped.

"So I finally get to see the special dress?" He asked. "I feel very special, might I add. It's absolutely beautiful. You look just like a princess!"

Carol frowned, and over her shoulder, he saw Noelle shake her head. She made a cutting motion on her throat, making a pair of wings with her hands that flapped wildly. Nicholas glanced back at Carol, recovering quickly,

"I mean—you look just like an angel!" But the frown only deepened. He glanced at Noelle again, who was waving her arms crazily. She made wings again, but added a hop.

"No!" He said, looking at an irritated Carol again. "I meant a fairy."

Finally, she smiled, and added, "You should thank your lucky stars that Noelle was here to help you," much to their surprise and amusement. Noelle snorted, Nicholas huffing a laugh of his own when she scampered off.

He joined Noelle in the living room, taking the bag she handed to him, and started to place the carefully wrapped presents under the Christmas tree. They didn't look the best, and he'd had to add pieces of ripped material here and there where he hadn't covered the gifts the first time, but it was the thought that counted. Noelle gazed at him as he did, her hands clasped together. She was uncharacteristically quiet, which prompted him to bump her with his hips.

"Why the silence?" He asked, suspecting it was about their almost-kiss, but what if she wasn't as consumed by it as he was?

She shrugged, "You just surprised me."

Nicholas straightened, placing the bag against the side of the sofa behind Noelle. Her scent hit him like a freight-train, almost making him finish what he'd started the other night. He frowned, following her out of the living room and into the kitchen. It smelled deliciously of roasted chicken, with a side of aromas that had Nicholas' mouthwatering just from the smell. He always gobbled up Noelle's delicious food, but judging by the mouth-watering food around him, he could tell tonight would be even more exceptional.

"In a good or a bad way?" He asked absentmindedly, eye traveling over the spread on the table. Noelle just shook her head, filling the kettle with water before she placed it on its designated hook above the fireplace. She shrugged,

"Good."

"Then I don't see the problem, honey." He drawled, still investigating every piece of food and crumb.

"I never said it was a problem," she retorted, making Nicholas' head snap up. Her eyebrow was arched, mouth set in a deviant smile. He smiled, thrilled by the little bit of claws she kept hidden until needed.

They laughed simultaneously, Nicholas leveling a finger at her, about to say something when her face suddenly fell. Her gaze was focused on his finger, sheet-white, prompting him to look as well. There was nothing out of the ordinary, and when he glanced back, she had turned away. Busying herself with the kettle and teacups, Nicholas frowned at Noelle's back.

Carol came bounding in from the living room, probably after having shaken every gift under the tree to try and determine what was hidden behind its wrapping paper. She was flushed, grasping the edges of her dress as she begged,

"Can we *please* open the presents now? You said we have to wait for Nicholas but he's here now!" She complained, her eyes pleading with Noelle, who glanced up at her from the mugs she was pouring full of water, tiny flecks of tea leaves floating to the surface. Noelle smiled, nodding,

"Of course, why don't you start sorting them for us?"

It was as if the shock from before had suddenly drained from her, replaced by the Noelle he was used to; always smiling. Nicholas was taken aback, wondering what it was that he had done for her to react that way, only to return to normal the next moment. But he left it at that, not wanting to ruin Christmas by bringing up whatever it was that had spooked her. It was not the time.

He followed Noelle to the living room, taking the cup of tea from her as they both took seats on the sofa. He didn't know if it was by chance or if she too felt this innate attraction, a pull that dragged him wherever she was, urgent to get closer. He sipped the tea, his eyes focusing on Carol as she read the names written on the various packages.

"Noelle," she read, walking over to her," from Nicholas."

The woman graciously accepted the gift, her eyes betraying the slightest shock before she composed herself and smiled. "You shouldn't have."

Then, the little girl handed him one, artfully and skillfully wrapped in a paper-like bag with a large red bow tied to keep the edges closed. It was soft and squishy to the touch, and on the label were their signed names. He nodded, thanking both of them.

Next, it was Carol—although most of the gifts were for her—and she squealed in delight when the pile kept growing and growing. He'd bought her toys and books, and sweets that would probably make her teeth rot if they weren't careful. The girl kept handing out gifts until it was finally time to open them, both himself and Noelle watching as she showed them each of her new toys, from building blocks to dolls and a wooden horse she could ride on. They watched her giggle in delight, the scars on her face so incredibly dull compared to the brightness of her joy and her soul. They asked her questions and listened to her babble about each and every toy, and what she would do with it, until it was their turn to open gifts.

Nicholas inclined his head at Noelle, prompting her to go first. He was happy for his decision when her eyes lit up like a forest fire, excitement making the blue depths of them sparkle like diamonds. She tore into the wrapping paper, getting stuck on the strings he'd fastened around it to keep it all together.

He swore he could see the eagerness in her fingertips when she undid the knot he'd made, the paper ripping two seconds later and revealing a hair pin he'd seen in a shop just a few days ago. It was forked with two pins, made of gold, and decorated with a beautiful ruby right on the top of it. He'd thought the ruby would complement the red of her hair, the gold a flash in those curls like the golden halo the fire had made on her hair that night they'd almost kissed.

Noelle gasped, lifting a hand to her mouth, her lips forming an 'o'. Her eyes were wide and caught on the pin in her other hand, her thumb rubbing over the ruby as if she couldn't believe it were real, and held in her very own hand. Nicholas started smiling, Carol coming over to see what she held in her hand that had caused such a reaction. The girl's mouth fell open, revealing a row of corncob teeth—some adult teeth, and some missing from the baby teeth she pulled out so easily.

"It's so pretty!" Carol exclaimed, but didn't reach for it. He wondered why, noticing the girl kept her hands on Noelle's forearm, gazing at it just as Noelle did. Perhaps the girl could see the awe in Noelle's face and didn't want to take it away.

"Do you want me to put it in?" Nicholas asked, motioning to her unbound hair that was still falling over her shoulders in waves, framing her face beautifully, and making her look like his very own Christmas dream. He almost cursed himself for suggesting she tie it up, loving the way it looked now, but needing more to feel its silky tendrils glide through his fingers.

Noelle's eyes snapped to his again, finally knocking her from her daze, and she nodded, handing him the pin. It felt like a weight in his hand, his other hand flexing in anticipation as she stood, throwing the red locks over her shoulders, their strands bathed in gold by the fireplace behind her. She turned her back to him, her proximity making the scent of her cling to him as he neared, pin in hand.

Nicholas gathered her hair into both hands, clutching the golden pin in his left two fingers. Her hair was soft, and smelled faintly of lemon and jasmine, the soft scent so at odds with the fiery shade of her hair and the spark in her soul. She was much shorter than him, the top of her head reaching just below his collarbone, even with the heeled boots she wore. The soft skin of her cheek flashed quickly as she adjusted her neck so that he could capture the short tendrils of stray hairs at the nape of her neck.

His fingers brushed slightly over the delicate arch of her neck as he gathered the hair, twisted it, and transferred the roll of hair into his right hand, fastening the pin into the crevice between the twist and her head, successfully panning the hair in place. It was over in a second, but it had felt like an eternity for him.

And judging by the way her chest rose and fell rapidly, he supposed she felt the same. The simple touch of his hands to her skin had left them both with hammering heartbeats, hers beating through her skin and into his fingertips as he held her neck gently, securing the pin even further so that it would not fall out.

"Okay." Nicholas said softly, his words hardly more than a whisper, and placed his hands on her shoulders. Noelle turned to face him, tilting her head back to look him in the eyes. The face-framing pieces had escaped confinement from the pin, still encompassing her face in their wondrous waves. She stared intently into his eyes, the fire behind them nothing compared to the heat now rushing between them. He lifted a hand, reaching for the soft skin of that cheek that always seemed to haunt him with the desire to touch it.

"It looks so pretty!" Carol exclaimed, clamoring from the floor to get a closer look. Nicholas and Noelle startled, stepping away from each other as the girl raced towards her mother. There was a knock at the door, Noelle stepping away for a moment to answer it.

Nicholas gathered the torn paper around them, taking the brief reprieve to open his own gift. It was a red crocheted hat, done with two hanging tassels. He smiled softly, placing it on his head despite its uselessness in the warm house, if only to show Noelle he appreciated and loved it.

Pastor Sam, his wife, and his hordes of children filled the entryway a moment later, ushered out of the cold by a smiling Noelle. She took their coats, hanging them on the hook beside the door. Nicholas rose from where he knelt to gather the torn shreds of paper, offering his free hand in greeting to Pastor Sam, before pulling his wife in for a hug. On his way to the kitchen, Nicholas spied Noelle staring at the hat on his head, giving her a quick wink that made a faint blush appear on her cheeks. Nicholas smiled, wanting to kiss every inch of that blush on her face, but opted for taking out the garbage for her instead. He was so far gone, and he wasn't even sure he wanted to find his way back again.

Chapter Twenty-Three

The dinner table was the fullest it had ever been, with Nicholas aiding her in pulling up some extra chairs for the seemingly hundreds of children Pastor Sam and his wife had. There was laughing and storytelling, food exchanged along with wishes and prayers that had Noelle's heart soaring.

While Noelle and Carol had spent all day the day before preparing this wonderful lunch, and it had almost killed them, she was far from thinking of the amount of work but rather thinking of the faces of delight around her as they bit into every piece of food. Nicholas was seated at the head of the table, with Noelle right next to him on his left, Carol next to her.

Pastor Sam was at the other end of the table, his wife seated as Noelle was on his left, and their children scattered among the table on the odds-and-end chairs they'd brought in.

After lunch, they were seated in the deliciously warm first living room, which had a lot more room than the second even though it was her favorite, and passed around a box of chocolates courtesy of Nicholas. The pin in her hair that he had gifted still kept the usually unruly locks in place, her stomach erupting with butterflies every time she so happened to touch it or remember it was there.

It had been such a thoughtful gift, and she had been so taken aback by the fact that he had even put in the effort to get her something so beautiful, that she'd lost complete control of her emotions and stared like a maniac. Not to mention that it must have cost a fortune—gold and a ruby? It was outrageous, and yet, he'd still gotten it for her.

The best part of it all was that she wasn't even his wife or even close to something like a partner to him—unless they're considered to be partners in lies? And he had still gotten something for her. Henry had only once gotten her a gift on Christmas, and it had been the diamond ring she'd stopped wearing days ago.

That had been her anniversary gift when he'd still cared, right before he'd become a drunk and started hitting her. Sometimes, when she was feeling bitter, she liked to wonder if it had been a *"please forgive me for what I'm about to become"* gift. The sad part of it all was that it had been but a year after their wedding.

Noelle glanced about the room as the people conversed, Nicholas and Pastor Sam locked in a discussion, with Pastor Sam's wife glancing back and forth between them like she was watching a snowball fight. Speaking of snowball fights, she glanced outside through the window, laughing when she spied Carol taking a particularly big snowball to the back of the head, courtesy of Sam's oldest son, Jack. The little boy laughed, clutching his stomach as Carol turned and ran towards him. They chased each other around, Jack lunging to one side before he ran in the opposite direction.

"They're becoming good friends," Sam's wife said, glancing out the window as Noelle did. She turned to the woman, nodding in delight. Their conversation turned just as fascinating as the men's were then, switching from kids to birth to marriage, and back again to kids. Then they discussed church and the town gossips that were likely to burst into flames if they crossed the threshold, making them double over in fits of laughter that had Noelle rubbing at her eyes to wipe the tears.

"We shouldn't joke about these things," Noelle said, before bursting out in laughter again. Pastor Sam's wife was doubled over, clutching her cup as she tried desperately to stop the ache in her stomach. Nicholas glanced over briefly, the corners of his mouth curling as he spied Noelle laughing. A warm feeling spread in her stomach, their eyes meeting briefly before they both returned to their respective conversations. Pastor Sam glanced over at his wife, starting to laugh as he did. Soon, it seemed they could no longer resist their curiosity.

"What is it that you both keep laughing about?" He asked, tugging at the forest green sweater he wore. For once, the man could dress informally, making him look less like a divine figure and more like a normal man out with his family. Noelle glanced at Katherine, sweeping a finger underneath her eyes. She smiled and shook her head,

"Oh, we're just making some harmless jokes, is all," Katherine said, placing a hand on his. Noelle nodded, their eyes meeting and mischief written all over their faces. They looked like naughty children hiding their mischief from a teacher. Nicholas saw it, rolling his eyes.

The children came bounding in from the snow, leaving flurries of white everywhere they went. Noelle waited for the gripping nerves she usually felt when dirt entered the home, but it never came. She wondered if it had been her own cleanliness that had caused that feeling, or the man that had "disciplined" her every time he saw a speck of dirt. Carol reached Noelle, out of breath and cheeks flushed red with cold and running. Jack came with her, both of them setting their hands on her lap as they heaved, trying to catch their breath to say whatever it was that had their eyes wide with excitement and anticipation.

"Can I spend the night at their house?" Carol asked, pointing at Jack with her thumb. Noelle felt her heart stop, the inevitable question she had so dreaded since getting her home finally making its appearance. She glanced up at Katherine, who was gazing at the children with relaxed expectation. She had known this was coming, and did not look nearly as perplexed as Noelle did. She supposed the woman was used to everything, and had forgotten the lessons Noelle had yet to learn with raising a child. She glanced at Nicholas then, her fingers clutching at each other and turning white with the pressure.

His face was relaxed, his eyes focused solely on Noelle as she made her decision. She met those whiskey brown eyes, seeing nothing but patience, understanding, and utter trust. He knew why she was hesitant, knew what Carol meant to her and why she might dread having her out of her immediate vicinity. But he nodded, his mouth curling into a small smile. Noelle took a deep breath, that reassurance he'd just given her meaning the world, maybe even more than the pin currently keeping her hair in place.

"It's fine with me, if you ask Jack's mother first," Noelle glanced at Katherine, who had been watching the entire exchange, as if wanting Noelle to make the decision for herself without jumping in to help. She knew the woman, and she knew Katherine had given her this opportunity to experience what it would be like in the future, having to make decisions regarding her child that might make her uncomfortable.

It wasn't that she was afraid of what would happen at Katherine and Sam's house, she knew they would treat Carol as their own. She supposed it was her own fears, irrational fears that still kept her up at night no matter how many people reassured her that she was doing a great job of raising Carol. The children bound over to Katherine, the woman rolling her eyes and nodding before they ran off in joy.

Yips and cheers followed them, and judging by the yips and cheers from outside, they'd just informed the others. Noelle glanced at Nicholas again, still wearing the ridiculous hat she'd knitted for him, and found him once again staring back. He inclined his head slightly as Pastor Sam spoke to him, turning back before the man could deem him rude. Noelle's heart soared. He was proud of her, proud of her ability to have made the decision all on her own despite the fears clogging her mind.

When it came time for everyone to leave, Noelle packed Carol's overnight bag with her nightgown, extra clothes, Christmas cookies and her favorite stuffed animal she could never sleep without. The small canvas bag felt so heavy as she descended the stairs, little Carol jumping up and down with excitement beside Jack where they waited for her. He took the bag from her hands, ever the little gentleman his parents were teaching him to be, and made it out the door to the wagon where his parents were waiting with Nicholas.

Noelle turned to Carol, her green coat covering every inch of skin that might be exposed to the cold outside. She tucked a stray lock of blonde hair behind her tiny ear and crouched, enveloping the girl in a hug.

"If you need anything, don't be afraid to ask," she said to the girl. "They are wonderful people."

She nodded, curls bouncing, and squeezed Noelle tight. "Thanks, mama."

Noelle's heart stopped, her blood freezing in her veins. Her eyes widened, her mouth falling open in an 'o'. But before she could respond, the girl had already run out the door, leaving a stunned Noelle on the floor. She had just called her *mama*. And she had no idea how to react—she was happy, ecstatic even, without a doubt. But she did not want to taint the memory of Carol's real mother. But she could not deny the smile that spread across her lips, nor could she stop the tears that spilled over her cheeks.

Noelle made her way outside, wiping the tears away before her guests could see, but kept her smile; even though no small amount of guilt ate away at her. They were all standing at the wagon, Carol already seated next to Jack in the covered cargo-storage in the back. They were playing, making turns at telling stories and making animals with their hands.

She reached Nicholas' side who wrapped an arm around her shoulders, still locked in conversation with Pastor Sam, absentmindedly shielding her from the cold that made her frame shiver. Noelle almost combusted, between Carol calling her *mama* and Nicholas now shielding her from the cold, she wasn't sure she could take any more surprises.

Katherine stepped towards her, giving her a quick hug when Nicholas removed his arm from her shoulders to clutch Sam's hand in quick greeting. Noelle squeezed her tightly, rubbing her back in gratefulness and love. She gave Sam a nod of the head, thanking them for coming and celebrating Christmas with them.

As they watched the wagon round the corner of the trees, disappearing down the road and behind the thicket, the tiny arms waved until they were fully out of sight. Nicholas placed a hand at her lower back as they walked toward the home, warmth from his hand seeping through her clothes and flesh right into her soul.

Her mind was reeling, Noelle unable to utter a word as they started cleaning, the silence between them not uncomfortable but rather...peaceful. They didn't need to speak every single moment to enjoy each other's company. The fact that he had even stayed to help clean said enough about the comfortability and the *change* between them.

Once in the living room, Noelle just couldn't keep the words to herself anymore, stopping from where she was placing empty cups on the tray. She turned towards Nicholas, his back to her as he picked up stray pieces of paper and toys that Carol had left lying around. She cleared her throat,

"Carol called me mama before she left," her voice wavered, tears finally spilling unguarded over her cheeks, making the strands of her hair cling to them. Her lip wobbled, eyes closing as the warring feelings within her made her body overwhelmed, not sure how to process them besides crying. She glanced up, only having a second to brace herself before he scooped her up in a bear hug.

Nicholas crushed her to him, her chest flush with his, a sobbing laugh escaping as he spun them around. He set her down, smoothing the hair from her face as he palmed both her cheeks.

"That's wonderful, honey! Why are you crying?" He asked, eyes so incredibly tender it just made the tears fall faster.

Noelle sobbed, clutching his elbows as she did, trying to ground herself through him.

"Because it's not right," she sobbed, her heart breaking for Carol's own mother and the memory she felt like she was tainting, but soaring for herself. Her body was overcome with emotion, Noelle not knowing which one she wanted to honor, the sadness or the joy. "She has a mother, and it's not right for her. To. call. Me that." The last few words were spoken through bouts of hiccupping sobs.

Nicholas' eyes softened even more, his thumb smoothing the tears from her face as he stepped closer. "Oh, honey. Bless your kind heart."

Noelle shook her head, trying to turn away but he held fast, thumbs pinning her chin in place. He tilted her head up, searching her eyes.

"I know what you're thinking, and I understand. But you cannot compare the two," he said gently, "You will never take her mother's place, but you can fill a quarter of that void."

Noelle shook her head, but he continued, "You care for her, you look after her, you feed her, and you provide for her. She has everything she ever needed and wanted—do you not think that is what a mother does? Why don't you deserve to be regarded as such?"

Nicholas bent down, coming eye-level with her as he spoke, "You respect her parents, Noelle. Whoever doesn't see that is a fool. She wouldn't call you that if she felt it was wrong. Age or no, that child is smart enough to know what she's comfortable with and she's not."

Noelle opened her eyes, meeting the swirling depths of his, sniffling as his words doused the raging fires of her guilt like a cold splash of water. He seemed to calm the raging storm in her, turning it to calm seas and clear skies once more. It made sense what he said, even though she knew she would always feel that way. As if she were tainting the memory of the woman who was Carol's real mother. But for now, she'd savor this moment.

"She called me mama," Noelle said softly, a small smile appearing at last. Nicholas huffed a laugh, still cupping her face,

"Yeah, sweetheart. She did."

The air shifted, his words registering as well as how close they were. Their chests were flush, mouths barely inches from each other, and warmth in their eyes. Nicholas cradled her face tenderly, Noelle clutching at his elbows. She shifted closer, tilting her chin. There wouldn't be an *almost* this time.

Nicholas' eyes warmed, flicking to her lips and back again. He moved his thumbs to her chin, tilting it up even further as he lowered his head. Her breath hitched, electricity sparking in her body as his lips inched agonizingly slow. She dug her fingers into his arms ever so slightly, her eyes fluttering closed as his lips met hers in a tender kiss, at long last.

Chapter Twenty-Four

Nicholas felt like he was flying, his lips pressed firmly against the cloud-like softness of Noelle's lips. He held her face tenderly, careful not to startle or hurt her as they shared this moment. His breathing evened out for the first time, his thumb brushing across her face lightly. Just as Nicholas deepened the kiss, a knock sounded at the door, startling them both.

Noelle ripped away from him, but not in rejection. She glanced toward the door, quickly smoothing her hair where his other hand had intertwined with the strands, and went to answer the door. Nicholas took the opportunity to gather himself, and possibly rid himself of the blush no doubt grazing his cheeks.

Sister Beatrice came into view right behind Noelle, her face set in displeasure, though it wasn't outside of her normal look. However, it was the anger in her eye that was new, and uncharted territory for both him and Noelle considering the nervousness in her face. Nicholas' stomach dropped, his eyes meeting Noelle's as they ushered Beatrice to the living room.

The woman took a seat in the chair across from the sofa, perching on the edge rather than make herself comfortable. She cleared her throat, intertwining her fingers,

"I apologize for intruding on your Christmas, but I must discuss something important with you," she glanced about the room and out into the hall, "Where is Carol?"

Noelle shifted, unsure if what she was about to say would be the wrong thing. Nicholas didn't blame her for her nervousness, he felt uneasy himself.

"She's staying at Pastor Sam's house with her friends for the evening," Noelle said, wringing her hands together. "Can I offer you a cup of tea?"

Beatrice shook her head. "I won't be long."

Nicholas and Noelle exchanged a look, turning back to Beatrice as she continued. "It has come to my attention that you have deceived me. A dear friend of mine made me aware of the untimely death of the real Henry Foster, your true husband, while I was at the fair, much to my dismay."

Nicholas' heart stopped dead in his chest, Noelle inhaled sharply, her hands starting to shake from where she extended them pleadingly. She shook her head, but Beatrice continued still,

"Words cannot express my disappointment in you, Mrs. Foster. I truly thought I had given Carol to a wonderful family where she would be cherished and raised right, but it seems I was wrong. I would say I'm disappointed in you as well, Nicholas Birch, but I have not yet had the displeasure of getting to know you."

Nicholas recoiled at the verbal slap, growing angry at the judgment she spoke over him, as if she had the right. She didn't know anything about it, much less what type of man he was or if it was pleasure to know him or not. But before he could say anything, Noelle interrupted,

"I am sorry, Beatrice. If you give me a moment to explain myself..." Her eyes were wide and pleading, her lips wobbling and her heart beating in her throat.

Nicholas cleared his throat, shifting towards the woman again, "Please, Sister Beatrice. Please just allow her the opportunity to explain."

Beatrice sat back, mouth set in a tight line and looking less than happy to listen. But she stayed silent, Noelle scooting forward as if proximity would lessen the blow of her admittance.

"I know what it seems like, and it is horrible, I agree. I will not make excuses for myself, so I will only tell you what happened and my reasoning for it," Noelle gulped, her hands squeezing each other until the knuckles were white. Nicholas had to fight the urge to place his hands over hers, to ease the knots he knew were now making knots in her stomach. "I have wanted to adopt Carol for the better part of this year, and I have wanted children ever since I was a child. Henry indulged my dreams and we tried for children, but I couldn't carry one to term. We lost a lot of children, and I grew desperate enough to ask Henry to adopt. He agreed, but only on the condition that it be a boy. Henry did not take kindly to being disobeyed, and while I tried desperately to connect to some of the boys at the orphanage; there was none of them that felt quite like mine as Carol did. But he wouldn't relent, and he wouldn't even meet Carol before he said no."

Tears started slipping from her eyes now, and Nicholas swore he could hear his own heart crack. Beatrice shifted uncomfortably, and he could've sworn he saw the hardness in her eyes recede a bit, a glimpse of the compassionate woman shining underneath. Nicholas supposed there had to be some part of her that was not hard, considering that she worked with children day in and day out. And by the way she'd looked at Carol at the fair, with so much love...there has to be more than what she showed others on the surface.

"I thought my dreams were to be just that; dreams, and that I would never have a family of my own. I thought I would have to go back to the orphanage and tell Carol that I would not be able to take her home, and that she would have to find a new family that she could connect with as she did with me." Noelle sniffled, wiping at her eyes. Nicholas rummaged in his coat pocket, pulling from them a handkerchief which he handed to her. She shot him a grateful look, dabbing at her eyes.

"But then he died in the avalanche that covered the mine Nicholas works at, and suddenly I had this vision of a life I could have, one that Henry had denied me at every twist and turn. I was finally within reach of the family I wanted so badly, despite not having a husband or being able to give Carol a father. I took the opportunity to get Carol to come home—but I didn't know how you would react if you learned that I had no husband to provide for us. In my moment of weakness, I was naive enough to go through with the house visit, thinking that I might convince Henry, and when he died, that I might be able to care for her regardless of his presence. However, when you actually came for the house visit, I was afraid that you would deny the adoption if you learned that Henry had died, thinking that I would not be able to care for her. It scared me, and when Nicholas came to check on my well-being, I saw the opportunity to introduce him as my husband, so that I might have a fighting chance in adopting Carol before it was too late. I hoped that with him present, you might look at the woman and mother I am, and not the woman who was without a husband and unable to care for the child you are about to release into her care."

Beatrice was silent as Noelle recounted exactly what happened, and what her thought process was during this whole situation. The woman didn't move, and she didn't interrupt. She simply let Noelle attempt to save herself from the heartbreak that was now impending. Nicholas just hoped that she didn't dangle the hope in front of Noelle like a carrot just to rip it away. Noelle cleared her throat,

"You have to believe me when I say that I wanted to come clean many times, and that I wanted to tell you what the situation was. But I was afraid, Sister Beatrice. Carol is happy here, I am happy with her here—*we* are happy." Noelle's arm encompassed Nicholas as well, making his heart swell with joy and pride. She considered him a part of their family, even though they had not had time to discuss what they would do from here, yet. "We have become a family, the three of us. Nicholas cares for us, he helps us, he takes us on adventures, and he teaches Carol things of life just as a father would. *I* teach her things just like a mother would."

Beatrice shifted then, glancing between the two of them. Her hands were folded in her lap, relaxed, but twitching every now and then as Noelle said something she did not agree with—that was his guess anyway. Her mouth was still set in a hard line, unforgiving and unyielding. But Noelle went on, undeterred by that stubborn look.

"We are happy, she is happy with us. She will be happy with us for the rest of her life if you allow me to keep her," Noelle's voice wobbled again. "What I did was wrong, but I am not a dishonest woman. I am a good, Christian woman who will look after Carol the way that she deserves and more, and—"

"I am sorry, Noelle but I must stop you there." Beatrice's hard voice sounded, cutting her off. Nicholas turned in his seat, the knot in his stomach growing and tightening. He knew that look on her face, and he braced himself for what was coming. He had to be strong now, both for himself and for Noelle, because Beatrice had come here with determination, and not even Noelle's carefully chosen words would deter her. Beatrice continued,

"You cannot sit here and proclaim that you are not dishonest when you have gone out of your way to deceive both myself and Mr. Banks and every person at the orphanage that has had the displeasure of sharing your company. I thought that I had finally found a good and honest home for Carol where she would be brought up with the morals that become a young woman. But now I have come to the conclusion that that is not the case."

Noelle shook her head. "Sister Beatrice, we cared for Carol like—"

"Like she was your own?" The woman asked, eyes settling on Nicholas. "You and Mr. Birch are not even married, Noelle. And yet, that night we spent here due to the snow, it was he who slept next to you in your bed. You have sold that child an illusion of a family, made up by two *friends* who are attempting to raise a child as if they were husband and wife, as if they were parents."

Both Noelle and Nicholas recoiled from the verbal slap, but it was Nicholas who grew angry. He frowned, looking the woman straight in the eye. He opened his mouth to say something, to say *anything* to discourage this false narrative that she had made. But he couldn't, because it wasn't false— whether they had done it on purpose or not, and no matter with what intention they did it, they had unknowingly misled Carol. He was not Noelle's husband, and he was not her father. And he had grown so used to them, that he lost sight of the truth himself. What would have happened after Christmas? What would have happened if Noelle had decided to move? Would he have gone with? Would he have stayed? What was between them, and was it serious enough for him to consider moving with her in the first place? Additionally, what would have happened if real estate and debt collectors came knocking and found him here in the stead of Henry?

"I understand your thoughts and your reasoning, Noelle. But I remain steadfast in my conclusion that this is not a good home for Carol to grow up in, if you resort to lies to get what you want out of life."

Crack. Crack. Crack. Nicholas wasn't sure if it was the sound of the wood cracking under heat or the sound of Noelle's heart, breaking inch by inch, as Beatrice spewed her words like poison. He felt his own heart shatter with hers, tearing itself apart to capture the pieces of hers. He finally relented, moving closer to her and placed a hand on her back.

"Please," Noelle whispered, seeing what was about to happen from a mile away, *"Please."*

"I left this subject for after Christmas because I did not want to ruin it for the girl, but I am afraid that I will have to take Carol back to the orphanage where she will be given to a family that will be able to care for her and teach her valuable life-lessons and morals. Your home is not the correct fit for that child, not after all she's been through—and for how much she deserves. I cannot trust you with her after you have so masterfully deceived myself and Mr. Banks."

"Please," a small whisper from the woman beside him, whose eyes were now filled with fear and silver tears. She clutched at her heart, her hands gripping the cloth of her dress. "Please, I am sorry."

Beatrice was unforgiving, lifting her chin at Noelle's apology and pleading, steeling her resolve. "I will be here to pick her up tomorrow morning. Please ensure she is packed and ready by then."

Noelle stood, moving towards the woman when she made her way to the door. It looked like she was ready to clutch at the woman's sleeve and beg at her feet. Desperation made her face slack and her eyes wide, her mouth moving but no words escaping those lips. The same lips he'd kissed only a few minutes ago, when all had been perfect. How did it go so wrong, so fast?

Chapter Twenty-Five

When the slamming of the door echoed through the halls, Noelle sprang to action, taking two steps at a time as she bounded upstairs to gather their things. She had to get them away, because she knew that once they took Carol, they would never give her back. So they would run, where no one could ever find them, and they would live happily on their own, undisturbed.

Noelle threw open cupboard doors, a canvas bag laid out on the bed and awaiting the clothes she threw into it. She shoved things away, making a mess where she went as she desperately tried to fill her bag with both her own things and Carol's. Nicholas' footsteps thundered as he climbed the steps behind her, entering the room with wide eyes and a disheveled look on his face. He combed his fingers through his hair, his other hand extended towards Noelle, palm exposed, as if she were a wild animal that needed to be tamed.

"Noelle." He said calmly, stepping towards her. But she would not listen, would not wait for two seconds. Her eyes were wide with panic, mouth set in a tight line, and face ghostly white. Her hands trembled where she shoved clothes into the bag, her fingers refusing to work against the pins and needles making it hard for her to do anything at this point. It felt like she was about two seconds from throwing up, but she persisted. Nicholas stepped forward again,

"Noelle." He said a bit harder, placing his hand on her elbow. She ignored him, and he grabbed onto her arm, wrapping his fingers around her bicep. Her lip wobbled, tears slipped down her cheeks once again. His face softened,

"I know you're panicked right now, but I need you to take a moment and breathe. Okay?" He asked, cupping her cheek, the calluses on his palms scratching lightly at her skin. "Breathe with me."

His chest rose and fell as he inhaled and exhaled, Noelle looking deep into his eyes as she followed his lead. Slowly, the panic receded from her, her heart slowing for a moment so that she could just take a moment and *think*. When she moved to step away, calm enough, he held on. Still, Nicholas smoothed his thumb over her cheek, and helped her breathe through it, as if he knew she was far from okay and would benefit from just another moment of his strength seeping into her. Finally, when her rapid pulse slowed to a steady beat beneath his pinky-finger, he stepped away.

"They're going to take her away, Nicholas," Noelle said, her voice wobbling slightly. A frown creased the skin between his eyebrows, anguish making his eyes lighten and fill with sadness. He clutched her elbow, smoothing his thumb along her skin in an attempt to soothe her, and it was working. Little by little, the panic receded and left sadness behind.

Sadness and hopelessness, the very emotions she'd thought she'd never have to feel in her lifetime again. Anger sparked through the fears, making its way to her heart. Why did she not deserve this? Why did she deserve this unending sadness and anguish? Why had she been allowed to experience this brief moment of content and happiness, only to have it be ripped away?

Nicholas noticed the shift in her demeanor, and he pulled her into his arms, her face flush with his chest as she sobbed. Anger and sadness raged a war inside her, one not making enough space for the other to be felt as it should. She felt like a failure, but worse, she felt like a horrible person who had deceived those around her—even though she knew what her intentions were. Perhaps Beatrice was right, perhaps she was not the right parent for Carol. But the little girl had been so happy here, *they* had been so happy here. There was no denying the fact that they had been so unconditionally happy, and had been as close to a family as Noelle had experienced in a very long time. Why did that have to be taken away?

Nicholas smoothed his hands down her back, making soothing noises as she poured her heartbreak out on him, his proverbial hands cupped to catch any shattered pieces of her so that they might not get lost. They stood there, utterly wracked by hopelessness and hands tied like they were at the mercy of external forces. She supposed they were. Suddenly, Nicholas tensed, his back shooting ramrod straight, and she pulled away. He was gazing down at her, eyes wide and sparkling. Noelle frowned,

"What?" She asked, stepping out of his embrace. Nicholas scratched the back of his neck, looking contemplative.

"There is another way to keep Carol with us. But I don't know if it will work—we could at least try though." His voice was gruff, unsurety making him scratch the tip of his chin where the slightest bit of scruffy beard lingered.

Noelle frowned, "What?" She asked again.

Nicholas looked away for a moment, and then stepped to her again, placing his hand at the nape of her neck. "We could get married."

Noelle inhaled sharply, clutching at his sides. Her heart thundered, threatening to beat out of her chest. Her head spun, struggling to catch up to the words spewing from his mouth.

"Think about it—Beatrice had a problem with us not being married and setting a bad example for Carol, as well as you not being able to care for her." Nicholas swallowed, wetting his lips. "That solves both of our problems."

Noelle shook her head, "You're still so young, Nicholas. You haven't married before, it's not right. You deserve a chance at true love."

An emotion flashed briefly before it was gone again. He frowned. "Those things don't matter to me right now," He said it as if she were daft, as if he couldn't grasp why she would think it. He opened his mouth to say more, but shut it again.

Still Noelle persisted. "There's no guarantee it's even going to work. She'll just think it's another ploy. Not to mention how it might look to our friends and the rest of society."

"Who cares what society thinks? I won't let anything keep Carol from us." Nicholas said, "We could at least try."

Noelle's mind snagged on the *us*, the word playing on a loop in her head. Was that how he truly felt? They hadn't really had the time to talk about these things just yet, and they'd only had their true first kiss only moments ago. Did he regard them as his family as she regarded him?

Well, she supposed that answered her question. However, was it only in regard to Carol, or did he share her feelings? And what timeline did this statement encompass? Was this strictly because they needed to get Carol back? So many different questions that she had no time to think about or even answer.

Nicholas let go of her face, reaching towards her dresser, and snatched up one of the gold rings that lay there. It had one ruby, and it had been a gift from a dear friend when she and Henry had married. He clasped the ring in his hand, sinking to one knee in front of her. Noelle gasped, her eyes wide and her throat dry. Her stomach fluttered despite it not being a true proposal, and her heart thundered.

"Noelle, will you marry me so that we can get our dear Carol back?" He swallowed, his eyes holding a lot of emotions, and Noelle tried her best to keep her mind from reeling. It was too much, it was irrational, and it was unkind towards him for her to marry him when he had not yet experienced the authenticity of the act. She would be taking so much from him if they married.

It was unusual and unseemly for Christian couples to get divorced, and was only excusable if one of the parties was unfaithful. That meant that he would be married to her, regardless of whether it was what he wanted long-term or not. He'd be saddled with her, unable to marry ever again, even if he somehow met the love of his life later down the road. If she accepted his proposal, what kind of woman did that make her? Definitely not a good one, that was evident. Could she really be selfish enough to do this? And why did he insist? He was a smart man, smart enough to know the magnitude of his decision. But did he truly grasp what it might encompass, and that it might not be as simple as he made it sound? Was she possibly overthinking this?

Noelle felt like her brain was two seconds away from combusting, especially as the time stretched on in silence, Nicholas ever patiently waiting for her to think it through for herself and give him an answer. Did she even deserve a man as wonderful as Nicholas? She had lied, made *him* lie for her, had made him corrupt his own morals by pretending to be her husband, sleeping in her room, lie to the people of the orphanage. If she were being honest, brutally honest, she didn't think she even deserved to keep Carol. Not to mention the fact that she hadn't even properly mourned her true husband, Henry. In fact, she hadn't mourned him at all.

Nicholas shifted, reaching his hand up to take hers. His thumb caressed the back of her hand softly, understanding and compassion evident in his eyes. Noelle's heart felt it was being pulled into separate directions, one part of her desperately wanting to say yes, and the other begging her to say no.

Sure, it could work in helping her get Carol back, but then it would sacrifice so much more for Nicholas. It hurt her heart, to think of all these things, to act like she did not want to jump into his arms at that very moment and scream yes. She had fallen in love with Nicholas long since that day, but was it not love that one had to be selfless for? Was it not for love that one had to sacrifice one's own happiness to ensure the happiness of the other?

"I can see the wheels turning in your mind, honey. And while I'd wait a century for you to figure it out for yourself, I no longer have the knees of a young man; and we're running out of time to do something about our dilemma." Nicholas said, switching knees for a moment, before switching them back again. He groaned like an old man, bracing an arm on the floor as he shifted. Noelle sneaked a smile, a small giggle escaping.

"If you're going to say yes you need to do it now, honey. We have to get married before tomorrow if we're going to get Carol back," he said seriously. Noelle took a deep breath, nodding once before she smiled widely,

"Yes, Nicholas Birch, I will marry you."

Nicholas grinned, the same old grin that made her heart skip a beat, and slid the ring oh so carefully onto her ring finger. He rose from his kneeling, pulling Noelle into his arms and planted a kiss on her lips. It was over before it started, and then Noelle was left feeling breathless.

"You're acting like you actually want to do this, as if I didn't just force you into another situation again." Noelle said, a knot forming in her throat. While it might feel real, and his reaction might suggest he was happy, she still felt its fraudulent nature like a phantom limb.

Nicholas stopped from where he was on his way to the door, her hand in his, and turned, "Who says I don't?"

Noelle drew back, his words rocking her very world. Nicholas squeezed her hand once, as if he understood her conclusion, but that there wasn't time to talk about everything at that moment. So she silently followed him downstairs, Nicholas grabbing their coats, and out the door. She didn't think to ask where they were going, and only got onto River behind him, clutching at his middle as he rode off into the snowy night. She blindly trusted him, as she always had and possibly always would.

Chapter Twenty-Six

It was achingly cold outside, Nicholas having an arm slung around Noelle's shoulders to protect her from the icy wind as they rapped their knuckles on the white-painted door. Everyone in the house was already fast asleep, if the pitch-black darkness inside was any indication; and he felt bad for waking them, but it was an emergency. One that could certainly not wait until the next morning. Nicholas rubbed her arm, keeping her tucked closely in his side as they tried to rouse Pastor Sam—the only man they could trust with this, and the only man that would not judge them horribly for it, nor deny it.

Noelle was uncharacteristically quiet, but not unhappy. Her eyes were wide, and Nicholas swore if he looked closely enough, he could see her thoughts running wild in her mind. He understood why she might be overwhelmed, and he could only guess what she was thinking, what worries she must have now. But so did he. He also thought they shared the same thoughts—thoughts about them, their time together, and what it might mean if they went through with this.

Noelle kept going on about what it might cost him, but he was honest if he said that it did not once cross his mind; the fact that he might not be able to marry again lest something happen or either of them were unfaithful—which he highly doubted for both parties involved. Neither of them possessed the vindictiveness it took to cheat.

He wondered what exactly would happen after this, where this would place them. Sure they had kissed and shared many moments these past few weeks, and sure they had become somewhat of a family. But that didn't mean Noelle thought of him in that sense—though the way she'd kissed him back and looked at him begged to differ. Even now, as he gazed down at her, she was staring at him in that way of hers; the one that made him feel like he was the luckiest man in the world. Did that not say something?

He had felt like his heart shattered when she'd looked at him with so much uncertainty, and so much shame. It was as if she felt undeserving of this, as if she were robbing him of something that he had no interest in in the first place. But how did he tell her that? How did he tell her what he felt on a night like this, when her whole world was crumbling right before her eyes?

The door opened, leaving Nicholas' hand raised in the air, knocking on absolutely nothing. Pastor Sam looked disheveled and...angry? It was the first time Nicholas had seen the man anything but happy. It wasn't terrifying but it also wasn't pleasant either.

"Nicholas? Noelle?" One of his eyes were squeezed shut, his face pulled strangely. "What are you doing here? Is something the matter? Do you want Carol to come home?"

Nicholas and Noelle shook their heads simultaneously, but he said, "We need to ask you a favor."

Pastor Sam looked behind them at the falling snow, stepping aside to let them in from the cold. They were ushered inside, Nicholas grasping Noelle's freezing hand in his as they did. Once inside, he drew her back to his side again, trying to chase away the cold from her shaking limbs. Pastor Sam lit a lamp that was settled on top of the small counter across from the fireplace. It sparked to life, bathing them all in an orange glow.

"Something's happened," Noelle finally spoke, possibly sick of the waiting. "Beatrice found out that we lied—that *I* lied."

Nicholas squeezed her hand, "*We* lied," he corrected her, glancing down at her as Pastor Sam leaned against the counter. He was covered in a plaid robe, his one eye now fully open and wide awake as he listened intently.

"She came to our house this evening," Noelle started, moving closer to Sam as if that might convince him even further. There was a sad, desperate edge to her voice. "She found out who Nicholas was at the Christmas fair, and she wants to take Carol away."

Pastor Sam's eyes widened, his hand now gripping the lip of the counter. He looked as bewildered and heartbroken as they did, which goes to show just how invested he'd been in this whole situation. Nicholas supposed a lot of Noelle's friends had been invested, hoping for the best for her, for a relief from the horrible life she'd been living before Henry had passed. But now, it threatened to all come to an end.

"Forgive me, Noelle," Sam said softly. "But I don't understand what you want me to do? Do you want me to wake Carol?"

She shook her head, looking to Nicholas for help. He stepped forward, grasping her left hand in his once more, "We want to get married."

Pastor Sam shot straight up, his eyes wide. But before he could say anything, Nicholas spoke. "Beatrice raised some concerns regarding the way we were raising Carol—that we were not teaching her good morals, due to us not being married but acting like married people would. It was one of the reasons, actually the main reason why she took Carol. So we decided to change that, to get her back."

Pastor Sam dragged his hands down his face. "I am thoroughly confused, Nicholas. Nobody has taken Carol, she's upstairs."

"Yes," Nicholas said, growing agitated. "But the decision has been made. She intends to pick Carol up tomorrow morning first thing."

Sam was quiet for a moment, utterly shocked and possibly reeling from all the information just as they had been. He stared blankly at them, no sounds around them besides his hammering heartbeat and the shuffling of Noelle's boots as she shifted her weight from one leg to the other. Neither of the children, nor his wife came downstairs to inspect what was going on, which Nicholas was grateful for because he had no idea what he would say to Carol should she stumble upon them now in their panicked states. Nicholas cleared his throat,

"I'm sorry to ask this of you friend, because I know what you might feel about it," He pleaded Sam with his eyes, hoping the man loved both of them and Carol enough to help them keep their family intact. "Will you marry us? Tonight."

The pastor did not give them a straightforward answer, he only sighed and moved closer to them, his hands spread as he tried to plead with them to reconsider. "There must be another way, Nicholas. It is not right for you to marry simply on the principle of it being the best solution—marriage is the unification of souls, a sacred act between a man and a woman deeply in love."

Noelle suddenly stiffened, moving slightly away from him as Pastor Sam spoke.

"You know Sister Beatrice, she will not take kindly to you rushing to marry in an attempt to sway her decision and let you keep Carol with you," he finished, glancing at both of them. His eyes flicked over each of them, pleading and slightly tinged with annoyance. Nicholas supposed the man had every right to feel this way, but it still angered him.

"You do not understand, Sam," he said, discarding all formalities. This was his friend before him, not the pastor. He spoke to his lifelong friend. "This was not something I decided on at the spur of the moment. It is simply the way things are, with our unification in marriage possibly being the one thing that could keep our family together."

He saw Sam's eyes widen, saw him look between them, and right back into the admittance that Nicholas was certain now shone in his eyes. He let Sam see every emotion, every memory, and every feeling he had for Noelle. He let him witness just how certain Nicholas was about this, and how devoid of fear he was.

He just now realized himself that he indeed wanted to spend the rest of his life with Noelle, had possibly known it since that very first night she'd asked him to stay, and he'd had to hold her the entire night, fighting off her nightmares. Even though she'd made him lie for her, and had almost sent him in the opposite direction, tail tucked and thoroughly freaked out. However he saw it, and understood it from the way his eyes softened, Pastor Sam was still not convinced.

Nicholas lowered his head, his voice barely audible in the silent kitchen, "You were the one who advised me to give it a chance, that all was not as it seemed. Well, all is not as it seems. This is not a hurried decision, I love that woman. And I want to marry her, now."

That seemed to do it for his friend, because he sighed deeply, raked his fingers through his hair and said, "Very well. Give me a moment to get my affairs in order."

The man made his way up the white and brown wood steps, one of them creaking loudly just as he made it to the top landing, disappearing around the corner of the rail. There was the sound of an opening and closing door, then muffled voices—one of which quickly turned fierce. Nicholas raised his eyebrows at Noelle, Mrs. Pastor Sam was not happy at all.

He searched her face for any indication that she'd heard what he'd said to Sam, but there was no spark of interest, no surge of requited love, and no sign that she'd heard anything at all. Nicholas didn't know if he was disappointed or relieved. Noelle was chewing at her lip, tearing small pieces of dry skin from them in nervousness. Her hands were also tearing each other apart, fingers picking at every bump, scratch, or hangnail. He suddenly felt unsure, and guilty, as he beheld her nerves.

Nicholas placed a hand on her cheek once more. "Are you okay? We don't have to do this if you don't want to."

Her head snapped up from where she'd been studying the floor beneath them, her eyes searching his. She frowned. "No, it's not that. Not at all."

"Then what is it? Because your brain is about two thoughts away from bursting to flames," Nicholas said lightheartedly, feigning sniffing in her direction. "I think it already has."

Noelle pinched his arm lightly, a small smile gracing her lips. But she turned somber, her eyes flicking away from his, lashes lowering. "I feel like I'm robbing you, Nicholas."

He almost sighed and rolled his eyes, but remembered that she was utterly oblivious to the inexplicable love he had for her. So he plucked up the last bit of his patience, and pulled her into his arms. He opened his mouth to tell her exactly what he'd told Pastor Sam, in fact, the words were almost out when suddenly Sam came clamoring down the stairs dressed in his usual working garb and wearing a look that was between annoyance and pleasantry.

"Do you want to take Carol with you?" Sam asked, and Nicholas looked at Noelle. It was her choice, as it was her daughter, and she had every right to be the one to call the shots. She shook her head,

"Not like this. This will only confuse her." Noelle said. Nicholas nodded, and took her hand.

They followed the pastor out the front door, Nicholas lifting Noelle into the seat beside him on the buckboard. He made his way to River, following on horseback as closely as he could next to them, keeping an eye on Noelle's face as often as he could. There wasn't enough space for all of them on the wagon, but he didn't mind. He loved riding on horseback, preferring the steady bump to the excessive rattling and rocking of a wagon any day.

The church came up a few feet from them, slightly obscured from view by the wondrous pine trees that surrounded the small white building. Nicholas' heart galloped in his chest, excitement that he had not expected making him almost spur River into a quicker pace. He glanced at Noelle once again, spying the same excitement on her face that he was sure reflected on his own. His face stretched into a smile, his huffed laugh making a white puff of hot air appear. He'd known she felt the same, even though he might have had his slightest bit of doubt. But that small smile on her face, that told him everything he needed to know.

They rushed into the church, the interior utterly silent and dark, undisturbed by the life-changing events of this eve. Noelle was almost glued to his side, his hand resting lightly on her lower back as they waited for Pastor Sam to light the candelabra on the dais behind him. The man smiled,

"It's usually decorated much nicer than this, but we also have more time in those instances." He joked, opening the Bible, and setting everything up as it should be in preparation for their unification. After a few moments of shuffling and moving some things around, Sam nodded at them, "When you are ready."

Nicholas and Noelle took their places on the dais, the ring on her finger already removed and held in his palm. They faced each other, and here in this church, with what they intended to do, it was like Nicholas was seeing her for the first time again. He reached over, removing the pin that still her hair in place, leaving the beautiful waves to cascade down her back and shoulder. Noelle's eyes filled with emotion, and Pastor Sam started their vows.

Clutching each other's hands tightly, they repeated each and every word with passion, perhaps more than they were supposed to, since everyone regarded them as something less than a couple. However others may think that way, Nicholas's ever-growing emotion disagreed.

There in the candlelight that bathed her hair in orange hues, he felt what he'd been denying for so long. Love like he'd never experienced in his life threatened to buckle his knees, threatened to tilt his world right at his feet.

Noelle gazed at him, emotion and passion drilling a hole into his chest, nestling deep into the fold of his soul. He loved this woman, had loved her from the very first moment of their meeting. And he would do anything to protect her and their daughter. No, this was not some idea just to keep their daughter with them. He *wanted* this. Desperately, enough that it felt like he couldn't breathe when he thought of spending his life with her.

When it came for them to kiss, Nicholas channeled every single thought and emotion he felt into it, crushing her lips under his as he kissed her passionately. He grasped her to him, gently but enough to convey just how deeply intertwined in his soul she truly was. Nicholas tilted her chin back, grasping the nape of her neck, and showed her just how much this unification was not just for the sake of Carol, but for them as well. And when they broke apart, chests heaving and tears mixed on their cheeks, Nicholas was the happiest he'd ever been.

He'd just married the love of his life.

Chapter Twenty-Seven

Noelle was riding a high that she had never thought possible. Her lips were still tingling from where Nicholas had kissed her so passionately. It hadn't been like any of the kisses they'd exchanged thus far. It had been a claiming and a declaration all in one. He had sealed their unification with a kiss that was a promise in itself, one that had left her breathless still at that very moment. Noelle glanced at the man riding beside her, astride River and looking more than a little happy with himself. She gingerly touched her lips, a small smile appearing as she replayed the scene in her head.

She couldn't explain the thoughts that had gone through her head as they'd exchanged vows, and he'd stared so deeply into her eyes, she'd almost fainted with emotion. Before they'd gotten to the church, her mind had been full of regrets and what-ifs that had consumed and ruined every moment for her up until Pastor Sam had announced he would marry them.

But when she'd spied the church, and she'd realized what was happening, an overwhelming amount of joy and anticipation had flooded her. Suddenly, there was no more doubt, no more worry, no more pain and sadness and utter hopelessness. When she'd spotted the church, and looked at the man riding beside her, Noelle had felt true happiness, outside of her memories with Carol, for the first time in a long time.

It was when he'd grasped her hands and slid the ring on her finger, that she'd truly realized that she'd wanted this. Although she felt like she robbed him, she also felt like she was right where she was meant to be. Love had made her heart skip a beat as he'd leaned in for the kiss, stealing her breath and made her dizzy with absolute and unconditional love.

Perhaps Noelle had known for a while now that she'd fallen in love with him, and perhaps she'd been scared to face the reality of it all. But she knew for a fact now, that Nicholas Birch was possibly the love of her life.

Maybe he'd been sent to her in the darkest hour of her life, as a message and a blessing from the Lord that her struggling days were over. And he had come exactly when she needed him, when she was so far down the road of despair, that she had seen no end in sight, no white knight that would rescue her from the dragon that was her very own life.

But here he was, in the flesh, healing her shattered heart with every laugh, every kind word or gesture, every teaching moment he shared with Carol, every wink or grin he sent her way, and every single soft kiss he placed upon her lips. She was not naive enough to think Nicholas saved her—she saved herself. But he was there helping her every step of the way, and for that she'd be eternally grateful.

Noelle thought of that night she'd broken down in front of him after she'd burned her hand, spilling all of the secrets she'd kept tucked so closely to her heart, they'd started poisoning it. She supposed it was that night when she'd first started realizing the future she might have wanted with Nicholas. He'd listened so carefully, and he'd sat there for hours with her until she'd calmed down, until she'd gotten every horrible memory out of her system. Not once did he interrupt or silence her, and not once did judge her for the horrible thoughts she'd shared with him. He hadn't even batted an eye when she'd told him she'd brought upon Henry's death, and hadn't even mourned him.

As if he felt her stare like a physical touch, Nicholas' head turned, his eyes meeting hers. Both of them inhaled sharply, his eyes flicking to the ruby ring on her finger briefly before returning to hers again. There was devotion in those whiskey brown depths, and what she hoped was the same as what she felt—love. Of course, she might have felt the emotion in his kiss, but it could also have been the intensity of the moment and the act that they were performing that could have messed with her mind. Whichever way, however, Noelle was happy. And from the way his eyes sparkled, she could see Nicholas was as well.

Pastor Sam brought the wagon to a stop right at the side of his sprawling home, the draft horse at the front huffing and stomping his ginormous paw on the snow-carpeted ground. Snowflakes fell as much as they did earlier, blanketing the trees around them, and coming to rest at the top of their heads. Sam jumped off the side, keeping hold of the reins lest his horses decide to take her on a little road trip.

Noelle gripped the lip of the wagon, her foot searching for grip when Nicholas' hands suddenly gripped her at the waist, effortlessly lifting her off the wagon and setting her gently on the ground. She glanced up at him, his hands still at her waist, and fought the urge to kiss him again. In fact, it was all she'd been thinking about since that passionate kiss that had sealed their marriage. *Marriage*, Noelle thought, realizing not for the first time what they'd done. Her lips parted in a smile, mirrored by one of Nicholas' own, and they took just a moment to stare into each other's eyes.

Nicholas shifted on his feet, pulling Noelle closer as his gaze dipped to her lips. He lowered his head slowly, his lips so achingly close to hers, when Pastor Sam suddenly cleared his throat. Noelle pulled away, blushing furiously. She'd forgotten he was here, so caught up in Nicholas and his distracting kisses that she'd lost track of what was going on around her.

I think we should go rouse Carol," Noelle said quickly, tucking now-loose strands of hair behind her ears. Snowflakes fell from the locks as she did, decorating her coat. Nicholas extended an arm for her to go first, placing a hand on her lower back as they went. He was always there, not too far behind, just in case she needed it. Noelle didn't know how she hadn't seen it before, but she was thankful for his presence. She knew he would always be at her back, for protection and support, forever.

They entered the house as quietly as they could, the front door only creaking slightly as they slipped inside, away from the relentless cold that was slowly eating away at the warmth her coat provided. She was also sure one of her fingers was about two seconds away from frostbite, which was not a welcome thought. The house was deathly silent, no sign of anyone having been roused from sleep by their loudness, and especially no curious Carol bounding down the stairs to ask what all the commotion was about—Noelle was especially relieved at the last one.

She pointed a finger up at the stairs, tilting her head to let Sam and Nicholas know she was going to get Carol. They nodded in unison, Pastor Sam already unbuttoning his heavy cloak and draped it over one of the chairs at the small round breakfast table. She wondered how many times they used it since there were only four chairs, and about what seemed to be a hundred of their kids.

Noelle inched her way upstairs, hand gliding over the smooth, white-painted wooden banister. Her boots thudded quietly on the plush carpet Katherine had laid over them, and she wondered if she could get away with sneaking Carol out without waking the others up. She just knew Katherine would have her hide if she woke one of the kids up, because there was no way they'd go back to sleep—meaning Katherine had an all-nighter waiting for her.

Noelle strode to the end of the hall and stopped at the door on the left, right across from the main bedroom where Katherine was blissfully asleep judging by the lack of noise. Well, except for some light snoring that made Noelle have to muffle her laughter. She turned the round golden knob quietly, pushing the door open to reveal Carol soundly asleep next to one of Katherine's daughters. Apparently, they'd made them a huge Christmas bed down with two beds pushed together, what seemed to be a million pillows, and a heap of blankets that made the whole thing look like a cloud. Carol laid at the end of the bed on the right side, right by the door where it was easy for Noelle to reach her.

She glanced around the room in search of the cream rucksack she'd packed for her, the bag stuffed in the corner of the room right by the armchair stacked with toys and dolls and clothes. Noelle reached for it, slinging it over her shoulder before she crouched beside the bed, laying her hand softly on Carol's arm so as not to startle her. She shook the girl gently, stifling a giggle as Carol's little arms shot up in a stretch almost immediately.

Her eyes shot open, confusion twisting her face as she looked around the room. Noelle smiled at her, whispering softly. "Come on, honeybee, we have to go home."

The words struck a chord in her heart, a spear of fear and emotion threatening to level her to the ground right where she sat. The girl's eyes fell closed again, her mouth going slack as she went right back to sleep. Noelle took the moment to center herself, swiping at the tears that had escaped.

Fear gripped her heart like a vise, and uncertainty made her nauseous. If Beatrice took Carol tomorrow, Noelle wasn't sure what she would do. It would absolutely shatter her, break the last bit of her that she had spent so long nurturing and keeping safe. It would undo all of the healing Carol and Nicholas had unwittingly helped her with. It would destroy the last of her hope, and Carol would take the pieces of it with her.

She swallowed, rousing the girl again. She finally awoke, smiling softly when she saw Noelle. She motioned for the girl to follow, slinging the bag over her shoulder, and inching out of the room softly. They closed the door with a nick, disturbing nothing but the small dusting of snow on the floor.

At home, Noelle was seated, Nicholas was fixing them a cup of tea, and Carol was once again fast asleep in her bedroom upstairs. They were tired, but Noelle couldn't find sleep, not when her mind was running rampant with memories made, and the possibility of memories unable to be made starting tomorrow if their plan didn't work. Knots in her stomach, Noelle accepted the cup of herbal tea that Nicholas handed to her, smiling gratefully before she returned her stare to the crackling fire.

He sat across from her, close enough for support, but far enough to grant her the space she needed to sort the thoughts in her mind. Her mind wandered to the first day she'd met Carol, the memory seeking an outlet, pressing against her teeth. So she let it out.

"The first day I met Carol, she wouldn't come out of the house, because she thought I wouldn't like her because of her scars." Noelle said, Nicholas shifting his body to hers, intently listening. "But after some convincing, she finally came out. We bonded instantly, talking about all sorts of things for the hour and a half that I was allowed to visit. I tried with some of the other kids, but it just didn't feel as special as my bond with her."

Nicholas took a sip, eyes set on her, his gaze burning on her cheek as she stared into the fire, letting the memory wash over her.

"But when I got home, and I told Henry about it. He didn't want to adopt a girl, and he told me it was a boy or nothing." Noelle swallowed. "It absolutely shattered my heart when he said that, and I felt like my dreams had been crushed all over again, like they had been every time I'd had to grieve and bury my unborn children."

A warm hand covered hers as salty tears spilled over her cheeks, Nicholas' strength seeping into her chilled skin like his warmth did.

"It felt like he'd robbed me from a family I never got to have, one I'd thought possible when I saw Carol step out that front door. And then Henry had died, and I'd been able to adopt Carol, and I'd experienced real unadulterated joy for the first time in a long time." Noelle smiled, a sad sort of nostalgia creeping in. "My time with Carol had made up for years of unhappiness, replacing every bad memory in this house with one of her playing, singing, laughing, running, and breaking something."

Noelle laughed, Nicholas following suit, as she continued. "I am so incredibly happy, Nicholas. With you and Carol in my life, I feel like God has finally blessed me, and that it was finally my turn to experience the type of happiness I'd only heard of in stories."

She was crying fully now, tears of sadness or happiness, she didn't know. "But now, that happiness is threatened again. I am once again about to lose the greatest love I have ever known, and I cannot help but feel like I am being punished for something."

Nicholas took a seat beside her now, pulling her into his embrace. He was warm and solid, a wall of flesh that she could lean against when she got weary. His breathing was even, like a lullaby to her ragged heartbeat that was trying to force blood through her icy limbs. She leaned deeper into him, as if she could absorb his strength.

"Nicholas?"

"Mhm," he murmured, and Noelle looked up at him. His eyes were shuttered, so she could not gauge his emotions thoroughly. But she asked anyway,

"Do you think us getting married is going to work? That Beatrice will let Carol stay?"

He was silent for a moment, contemplative. He scratched his chin where her hair tickled him, his eyes settled on the fire in front of them before meeting hers. "I hope so, honey. I pray it'll be enough."

They fell silent, staring at the flames and the crackling wood. Nicholas held her when she started crying, silent tears rolling down her cheeks and into the hem of her dress. She snuggled deeper when it got colder, both of them too comfortable to throw more wood on the fire. They held each other on the sofa until dawn peeked through the windows at them, bringing with it a morning of what-ifs and maybes.

Chapter Twenty-Eight

Nicholas' eyes opened to a strand of sunlight assaulting his pupils. He glanced at the window, the one sliver of light that slipped through of course settling for antagonizing him. His mouth was horribly dry, his side unusually warm and pressed against a lightly snoring Noelle. Nicholas smiled softly, rubbing his eyes until he saw stars, before he carefully laid her down on the sofa, and stalked to the kitchen. He stands still, hands on his hips as his gaze traveled over the different ingredients Noelle had.

Nicholas got to work, grabbing a skillet from her stack in the cupboard, along with some eggs and bread. He squeezed the loaf, considering the freshness before he shrugged and placed it on the cutting board next to the 6 eggs he'd taken. He placed the skillet on the small stone ledge, bringing forth the metal stand and taking some of the wood to place under it. Small embers floated in the air before him as he placed the skillet on the stand, a dollop of animal fat immediately melting under the heat.

He left the fat to melt, moving to the cutting board to chop some tomatoes Noelle had harvested from her garden just two days before. Nicholas let the knife glide over the board, chopping the red fruit into small cubes he'd add into the eggs along with some salt and pepper. His mind wandered to what awaited them later today, the possibility of losing Carol almost too much to bear. Tears flooded his eyes, but he blinked them away, not yet willing to give in to the sadness and hopelessness he'd been fighting since Beatrice had confronted them.

How would he even begin to console Noelle when their idea didn't work, and Beatrice took Carol from them. She would be a wreck, utterly heartbroken at having lost her daughter she'd grown to love so deeply. And he had no idea to stop the inevitable breaking, no way to put those pieces back together.

The stairs creaked, a still-sleepy Carol inching her way down them as she started to wake. She rubbed at her eyes, her white nightgown crinkled, her hair stuck up in all directions. Carol stopped at the bottom step, looking over at him in confusion. Or rather, they looked at each other in confusion—Carol was never up this early.

"Why are you awake this early, honeybee?" He used Noelle's nickname for the girl. She shrugged,

"You were making a lot of noise." Her voice was whiny, and he huffed a laugh.

"Apologies, m'lady," he bowed, holding a broken eggshell in his hand. "Why don't you go lay down and I'll bring you breakfast in bed."

She nodded, turning, and spotted Noelle. Instead of going back upstairs to her own bed, she crawled in next to Noelle on the sofa, squeezing tightly to her so as not to fall from it. He shook his head, continuing with scrambling the eggs. Nicholas added the tomatoes, generously seasoning the breakfast with salt and pepper, before he toasted the bread in the same pan after removing the eggs.

He went about setting the dining table, placing three plates, one at the head, and two at either side of the head. He placed glasses, cutlery, and some flowers he picked from the garden in the middle. It was then that the princesses decided to rise, both of them looking like they'd been through a war rather than dreamland.

Noelle's eyes widened when she spotted the food on the table, gratefulness shining in her eyes. Carol took her seat on the left side of the table, rubbing her tiny hands together in glee. Noelle dragged her hand along his back as she took a seat on the right, leaving the head of the table to him. They both looked up, expectantly, and he realized that this moment, and what he decided in this moment, would have a monumental outcome. He had unknowingly set the table, and posed a question to himself that he was only semi-sure to answer. The expectancy in Noelle and Carol's eyes posed that same question, and he had to decide, fast.

If he took the seat, he took all the responsibilities that came with it, and the family that was willingly offering themselves to him, for him to protect and cherish. Nicholas swallowed, the egg spatula still in his hand, and wondered if he would be able to fill the shoes that now waited for him to step into.

Would he be able to protect them? He couldn't even protect them from Carol being taken away, what about other things? How would this even work? He has never been a father, nor a husband, and he had no idea if this thing was made to last. But as he gazed into their eyes, that seat looming over him, waiting, he felt his heart settle. The knots in his stomach dissipated like dust blown by the wind, and he slid into the wood chair.

They dug in, Nicholas scooping serving Carol a little bit less than he did for himself and Noelle, seeing as she barely ate more than a mouse. They dug in, but Nicholas didn't miss when Noelle stayed still, her eyes trained on Carol, sadness seemingly oozing from her, tainting the air with its potency. She might have been grateful about him making breakfast, but it didn't diminish her sadness.

Afterward, Noelle helped Nicholas clean as Carol played in her room, talking cheerily to herself. Nicholas was busy cleaning one of the plates when she asked,

"Do you really think this will work?"

Nicholas' head swung to her, taken aback by the bluntness of her question. He had that same worry, had laid awake until the early morning hours with its echoing in his mind. He was worried, sometimes doubtful, that it would be enough, but he also remembered that it wasn't always in their hands whether something worked out or not. It was in no one's hands besides their Lord's. Nicholas set the plate down, took her hands in his,

"I don't know, sweetheart. But what I do know is that faith can move mountains. So have faith, and all of this will work itself out as it should."

Carol chose that moment to return, looking beautiful as ever, face bright. Noelle's eyes lingered on him though, heartbreak lingering there. They were lighter today, the blue changing based on her moods and emotions. Carol stood next to Noelle, her mother's hand toying with the short ponytail of blonde hair. Her eyes were glued to the girl, her face crestfallen and her skin pale. Sadness seemed to ooze from her, like an illness with no cure.

"I was thinking we could do something today," Nicholas said carefully, her eyes meeting his over Carol's blonde head. "What if we went caroling in the woods?"

Like one mind, both Noelle's and Carol's eyebrows scrunched in a frown.

"In the woods?" Carol asked, thoroughly confused. He nodded, a warm memory making him smile.

"Me and my father used to do it when I was little—we can all come up with our own little performances and perform for each other."

"Can we be on the same side?" Carol pointed her finger at herself and Noelle, clutching at Noelle's dress. Nicholas nodded,

"Of course, honeybee. You can do whatever you want today," he said, but quickly added, "within reason."

He knew better than to tell a child they were without reins, it would lead to straight disaster with this little hurricane. Though he was tempted to see what would happen.

Nicholas gathered their coats, Carol and Noelle having gone upstairs to layer themselves against the biting cold—he could feel it from the breeze that flowed in from the bottom of the door. He laid their coats out on the little foyer table, stepping out into the cold to gather their horses.

He saddled Goliath with no trouble, the steed giving him no lip as he tightened the buckles at the underside of his belly. River, however, was far from excited to be out in the cold, reaching around to bite him every chance she got. If he didn't know her so well, he'd have worried about an injury, but there was nothing wrong with his mare besides her stinking attitude.

Noelle and Carol joined him in the barn moments later, the former taking Goliath's reins from him, mounting the gargantuan horse in one smooth motion. He was awe-struck by the regal way she sat on him, like a queen on her royal steed, off on some adventure.

Nicholas lifted Carol onto River, the girl frowning at the mare in distaste when she tried to nip at her. He almost scolded her too, but relaxed when he saw the little girl pat her neck, soothing her. River's pinned down ears relaxed slightly, pushing back again when he mounted and nudged her into a calm walk.

"Why is she so grumpy today?" Carol asked, her hair tickling the bottom of his chin. He shrugged,

"She only gets this grumpy when it's cold. She'll feel better once we warm her up a bit."

"And how do we do that?"

Nicholas smiled, mischief making him giddy. He nudged her into a slow trot, leaving the mare to set her own pace as her muscles warmed up. Unsuspecting Carol glanced at the woods around her, thoroughly searching for any wandering fairies, elves, or any mythical creature she read about in her books. Nicholas grinned broadly when River started to pick up the pace, Goliath not too far behind and kicking up a storm of snow as he trotted.

"We make her run like the river." Nicholas said, lightly kicking River's sides, the horse sprinting full speed. Carol squealed, throwing her arms out in joy,

"We're flying!"

Nicholas glanced down at her, his heart pinching when he realized that this might be the last time he could share a moment with her. That it might be the last time Noelle had the opportunity to hear her laugh, make a memory with her, keep her close. It could be the last time they ever saw her, and Nicholas couldn't bear the thought.

They arrived at a small clearing, bringing the horses to a halt as they spotted one lone stump in the middle of a circle of trees, the perfect seat for a judge to watch the carolers. Nicholas hitched River to a tree, and then Goliath, helping Noelle and Carol from their seats. They made their way through knee-high snow, Carol on his neck, to the stump where he laid his coat over its icy top.

"Shall I go first?" He said, feigning straightening his lapels. Noelle and Carol giggled, the former smiling for the first time since the morning. Nicholas moved a few feet away from the stump, taking center "snow" as he did. He felt like a true performer, straightening his back, and puffed out his chest. Nicholas sang, awfully and dramatically, a melody so complex and hard that his voice cracked sometimes. He continued on however, prompting Carol and Noelle to cringe and the little one to cover her ears, shaking her head back and forth.

Nicholas sang and sang, melody after melody, until his daughter finally stood, having had enough of his less than stellar performance. She took his hand, shaking her head profusely,

"I think it's our turn now!" She yelled over his last ending note. Nicholas bowed deeply, only grinning when Carol shoved at his back. Noelle shook her head, grinning as she passed him. They took their places, standing where he had been just a moment before.

"This song is for my mama and papa in heaven, and my mama and papa here," Carol said, making Noelle's head snap towards her. Nicholas stared at the little girl, robbed of all words, just as Noelle was. His wife stood there, staring down at the girl with a type of sorrow he'd only ever seen in people who were grieving.

The little girl sang, her tiny voice shaking, but angelic. Carol hit every note of Silent Night, never wavering, or stumbling over the words, just flawlessly executing a tribute to her parents, and her adoptive parents. Noelle grasped the girl's hand tightly, frequently swallowing as tears streamed down her face. Nicholas felt himself having to swallow back tears himself, blinking profusely to clear his blurry vision.

That was when he realized just how much her departure would scar him, how he would miss her tiny little self, and how he would miss their days together as a family. He'd only accepted his role in this situation last night, but he felt like this had been his family for far longer than he realized. His hands trembled as he placed them in his pockets, emotions strangling him.

What would they do without her? She was *theirs*. And she had no idea what was going on, had no idea what waited when they returned home. He'd done this to keep their minds off of it, to grant them all one last memory just in case it didn't work out as they'd hoped when they'd hatched their plan last night. But now, he wondered if it would work, and what that would do if it didn't.

Nicholas' thoughts died off just as Carol's last note did, the little girl smiling brightly at them. Her joy faltered, her eyes dimming as she saw their crestfallen faces.

"What? Was I terrible?" Her voice shook, lip wobbling. Noelle and Nicholas snapped out of it simultaneously, both of them rushing to the girl's side.

"Not at all, sweetie," Noelle said. "It was absolutely beautiful."

"Then why are you crying?" Carol asked, clutching at Noelle's dress in uncertainty. Nicholas grasped her tiny hand, almost abnormally dwarfed by his large one.

"Because it was so pretty, that's why," he reassured the girl. Noelle's eyes met his, absolute heartbreak in their blue depths. It threatened to knock the breath from his lungs. He had no idea how he would fix the broken pieces of his wife's heart if they should lose Carol. And for the first time in his 29 years of age, Nicholas Birch was absolutely terrified of what would happen.

His fear gripped his heart in a vise-like grip when they returned home, Beatrice waiting for them on the front porch. He heard Noelle's gasping sob from behind him. He quickly pointed at something in the trees to keep Carol distracted while Noelle composed herself, not wanting the girl to see her mother crying and breaking apart. He shifted his body, keeping Noelle from Beatrice's sight as she quickly pulled herself together.

When he glanced back, he saw her wiping tears from her cheeks with the sleeves of her dress, nodding at him in confirmation that she was okay, and that he could relax. Or rather, be relaxed as he could be with the potential threat of having his adoptive daughter taken away. Nicholas straightened, turning to the front just as Beatrice pulled her face in disappointment. He didn't know much about women, but he knew enough to know that this convincing wouldn't be easy.

Chapter Twenty-Nine

Noelle felt like she was about two seconds from throwing up. The bodice of her dress suddenly felt too tight, the skirts too heavy, and her legs too leaden to comfortably trudge through the snow on their way to the porch. Carol was in Nicholas' arms, her husband—*husband*—seemingly taking this stroll easier than she was, even though she could see his nerves in the way he protectively clutched at Carol. His body was angled in a way that shielded Carol from Beatrice, as if he was subconsciously keeping the girl from her reach. Noelle's breathing was ragged as she tried desperately to calm herself.

Her heart was breaking with every step they came closer to the porch, her stomach twisting and turning, her throat becoming dry as a desert, her tongue thick and tingling. Her hands shook as she clutched at her dress skirts, pins and needles making their way through her body. Noelle had no idea how she would handle this situation, and how she would even be able to talk around her heart that was now beating in her throat.

"Good day, Sister Beatrice," Nicholas greeted cheerily. Noelle supposed it was for Carol's sake, the little girl still not aware of what had transpired last night, or what was potentially about to happen. She had thought about telling her, but how did you tell a little girl you were about to lose her because of lies?

How would she be able to make her understand that it wasn't that she didn't want her, that it wasn't because she was giving her back to the orphanage. But that it was because of other reasons, beyond her current mental capacity, and beyond her understanding. Not to mention how she would tell Carol that she and Nicholas had married, and that they hadn't been married all the times he'd done things with them, made memories with them, spent the night.

It was when Noelle had had that thought that she'd realized that Sister Beatrice had been right, that they'd only confused the girl and that she'd be given the impression that the way Noelle and Nicholas were doing things was right. And it wasn't, no matter how she tried to justify it. Their faith had taught them enough for them to know that they were wrong.

Of course, Noelle had mused that they were only human, that they were prone to sin no matter what. But almost immediately she felt shame and guilt about those thoughts. While it had never been her intention to teach Carol the wrong things or to set a poor example, and while her heart had been in the right place and she was still a good person, that didn't make things right. Not by a long shot. Noelle had always been a woman of faith, sometimes so much so that it had annoyed Henry in some cases. But now, she felt like she was a fraud, like she had no business asking for help from God when she'd disgraced Him.

"Good day Mr. Birch, Mrs. Foster." Beatrice said, her nose scrunched in displeasure, but her tone civil. Nicholas cleared his throat, set Carol down on the porch, and opened the door for her to go in. The little girl hugged the Sister first, beaming up at her.

"Why don't you go inside for a moment, honeybee." Nicholas said, "We'll be right there."

When their daughter had entered the warm cocoon of their home, Nicholas turned to Beatrice and said unceremoniously,

"It's actually Mrs. Birch now."

Beatrice frowned, her gaze returning to his from where it had lingered on Carol's exiting frame.

"Pardon?"

Noelle cleared her throat, steeling her spine and her resolve. "I'm no longer Noelle Foster. I'm Noelle Birch, now."

The Sister's gaze passed between the two of them, lingering for a moment on their intertwined hands and the golden band winking in the light on Noelle's left hand.

"Why am I only being made aware of this now?" Sister Beatrice asked, a softer tone to her voice than before. But while it might seem like they had a chance, Noelle knew she was about to blow her casket when they revealed why.

"Because we got married last night." Nicholas said, his voice not wavering, and his chest puffed out in pride. Noelle marveled at him, her eyes glued to his face, the jaw set in stubbornness. He was proud to be her husband, proud to announce it to the world, and those that stood posed to break theirs.

Beatrice's eyes narrowed, her face pulling into a look of such pure disgust, Noelle felt lower than the horse dung that stained the bottom of their soles. The woman was angry, her face flushed with red, and her hands balled at her sides. She took a step forward, the softness in her voice honed into nothing but hard steel,

"Please explain yourselves so that I might not jump to conclusions."

Noelle took the Sister's hand before she could react, squeezing it gently. The woman looked down at their hands, her features softening somewhat at whatever was projected in Noelle's face at that moment. Perhaps desperation, sadness, hopelessness. Whatever she felt was displayed there, as she could never hide her feelings.

"Sister Beatrice, may we speak as friends?" Noelle asked, voice bordering on begging. "Not as an orphanage overseer and an adoptee, but two women who want the best for Carol—no matter what that may be."

The Sister was quiet, so was Nicholas, so Noelle continued, "We were married last night in front of a Pastor, in a church, as tradition requires. We are a good Christian family, one that will look after Carol and love her, and see to it that she has everything she'll ever need and more. We love Carol, Sister Beatrice, more than we even love ourselves, and we cherish her above all else—and will continue to do so until our last dying breaths."

Something turned Beatrice's face back into a scowl. "Mrs. Foster, you cannot claim to be a good Christian family when you have only married in order to convince me to let Carol stay. That is not love, and it is not honest—it is a blatant disregard to the sanctity of marriage."

Nicholas stepped forward then, a wall of muscle and strength behind her. He looked down at Beatrice, visibly angry at the Sister.

"Forgive my rudeness, Sister Beatrice. But you are wrong—about all of it." The woman opened her mouth, but Nicholas continued, much to Noelle's dismay. If he angered her now, they could lose Carol just out of her spite. "I love Carol, and I love Noelle—deeply. I did not marry this woman as a ploy to get you to leave Carol with us. I have loved Noelle since the first time I laid eyes on her, even though I didn't know it back then. And every moment spent with her and Carol, with *my family* has only strengthened that love. You cannot take our daughter away from us, not when we're happy and Carol loved."

Beatrice only scowled, his words falling on deaf ears, but not Noelle's. She looked up at him, wonder and awe and devotion making a knot appear in her throat. Her eyes burned, vision becoming blurry as she realized what he said, what he proclaimed as if it was the easiest thing he'd said in years. The words had rolled off his tongue like honey, the warmth of his proclaimed love wrapping around her shattered heart and keeping the pieces together. The moment was short-lived.

Sister Beatrice ripped her cold hand from Noelle's, taking a step away from them, as if their sins could rub off on her. As if they were disease-ridden and not two parents desperately trying to keep their daughter at home with them. Noelle felt rejection wrap around her like a snowstorm, pushing the air from her lungs, jabbing its rotten, icy finger into her heart. She knew, without Beatrice having to utter the words, she knew what she'd decided.

"Please," Noelle whispered, dropping Nicholas' hand—that she'd not even realized she'd held—and stepped forward. She reached for Beatrice. "Can I please say goodbye first."

Nicholas started, but shut his mouth when Noelle stepped forward. "Please let me say goodbye to her. I can't bear the thought of her thinking I don't want her anymore."

Sister Beatrice's eyes widened, but her face shuttered again only a moment later. She nodded, a snap of her head that had Noelle dashing off.

She found Carol in her room, playing with her dolls as if there was nothing wrong or out of place on this day. And Noelle supposed there wasn't, not in her world. She crouched beside her daughter, her beautiful, wonderful daughter, and smoothed blonde wisps of hair from her little face. Carol giggled at the little tickles it caused, trapping Noelle's hand between her cheek and shoulder.

"Honeybee," Noelle started softly, as if Carol was a startled animal two seconds away from bolting, never to be seen again. "I have to talk to you about something. Do you think you can stop playing for just a moment?"

Her daughter looked up from her dolls, immediately attentive, and then concerned when she spotted the stream of tears wetting Noelle's cheeks.

"What's wrong, mama?"

Noelle swallowed the surge of emotion, the burning in her throat twin to the ache in her heart. Splinters of sorrow pierced her ribcage, almost making her back bow with the force of the sob that threatened to escape. But she kept it in, steeled herself, for her daughter.

"Sister Beatrice is here," she started softly, her hand resting on Caro's knee. This was the last time she'd get to touch her, the last time she'd ever get to hold her.

"I know," Carol said cheerfully. "I saw her."

"Well, she's here to pick you up, honeybee. Only for a little while until mama can sort some things out," Noelle said. The girl's smile faltered, a frown creasing the skin between her eyebrows.

"But why can't I stay with you?" She smiled brightly again as she added, "I can help you!"

Noelle closed her eyes against another surge, another back-breaking sob, another splintering piece of her heart.

"You can't right now, honeybee. Mama needs to sort this out herself, you can't help me with this one."

"But I can still stay. I won't be in the way, I promise," Carol's lip was starting to wobble. Her eyes were filled with tears, and she scooted closer. Noelle shook her head quickly,

"You're never in the way, honeybee! You have to know that," Noelle said. She pulled the girl closer, urging her to listen closely, "You are never in the way. And you are not leaving because I don't want you here, baby. There are just some things Mama can't control."

The girl started crying now, making Noelle's tears spill over once again. There were footsteps on the stairs, light ones, and heavier ones right after them. Noelle pulled the girl into a hug, one so tight she was scared she'd crush her to death. Carol squeezed her back even tighter, the girl clutching at her back.

"Please, mama," Carol hiccupped. "I don't want to go. I love you!"

Her daughter screamed the last part, and Noelle had to squeeze her eyes shut against the pain. Her body started shaking, wracked with sobs.

"I love you, baby," Noelle sobbed, soothing the girl's hair. "I love you so much. It's only for a little while. And I need you to know it's not because I don't want you—I love you so much."

The door creaked as it opened, revealing somber faced Nicholas, and Beatrice right beside him. Noelle started shaking her head, pleading with the woman with her eyes. But she persisted, grabbing a rucksack from the chair beside Carol's bed, and started packing some of her clothes.

Carol started sobbing harder, her nails scratching Noelle's back as she did. Nicholas sat beside them on the ground, pulling them into the V of his legs, and held them as all of them sobbed. His strength seeped into Noelle, but it was not enough to keep her heart from shattering completely. Carol would take its pieces with her, wherever she went in the world, and it was the thought of their reconnection later in life that held a small piece of Noelle alive.

Beatrice cleared her throat, "We have to go," she added softly, having enough of a heart to not bombard this moment with her crassness. Carol screamed then, wailed like a baby, and Noelle felt herself slipping into herself, no longer aware of what was happening. Nicholas' arms tightened around them, as if he could keep them together with strength alone. As if their despair had not taken the form of Sister Beatrice. Noelle shut her eyes again, gasping for air. She felt panic, and then numbness.

Chapter Thirty

Nicholas stood, using every ounce of his will to leave Noelle sitting on the floor. He helped her stand, Carol still clutched in her arms, her eyes so incredibly numb that it was a miracle she was still moving. He felt his breakfast surge in his throat, his stomach in knots, his heart beating irregularly.

Nicholas kept a hand on Noelle's back as she descended the stairs after Beatrice, the woman's back ramrod straight and her shoulders squared. Noelle looked much more defeated, her shoulder curving in toward the girl, as if to shield her from Beatrice's sight, as if she could hide her until the Sister forgot about her. Her usually fiery red hair was suddenly dull, the color of her skin paler than the snow outside. Nicholas willed some of his strength into her, begging God that it would be enough to save his wife from absolute devastation.

Beatrice stopped on the porch, turning to them, and reached her arms out in expectation. He clenched his jaw, almost snapping at the woman. He knew she wasn't as cruel to children, and that she did not necessarily mean to be this cruel to Noelle, that anger blurred her empathy in the slightest, but it still angered him. The woman's jaw was also set in determination, or rather, maybe she was trying to keep her emotion separate from this. Nicholas almost thought there was hope, but then she opened and closed her fists in impatience, and the hope dissipated like snow in the sharp morning sun.

Noelle's hands started to quiver, her shoulders started to shake, and Nicholas knew he'd have to help. His wife wasn't weak; not in the slightest. Because it took a certain strength to offer your child up to someone to take them away—against your will or not. She needed him now, needed him to take this final step and help her where she could just not let Carol go completely.

Nicholas supposed it also had to do with the symbolism of it—that Noelle giving Carol to Beatrice would signify she was giving her away, that she no longer wanted her. And while his wife was obeying Beatrice's command to surrender Carol to her care, this was the last bit of defiance she could show her. The last bit she could prove to Carol that this was not her choice, that she was not unwanted. So he stepped forward, shoving his own heartbreak aside, and grasped Carol from her.

Nicholas took Carol from Noelle, so that she might know that her mother had not *given* her away. But that she'd been taken, and that Noelle would never willingly give her away to anyone, no matter what. Nicholas swallowed his tears, the burning in his throat. He clutched the girl tightly, whispering to her. "I love you baby girl."

He handed Carol to Beatrice, willing his eyes to convey his every emotion as they met Beatrice's. He could have sworn he saw regret flicker there, but he must have been mistaken. Nicholas released Carol, stopping to plant a kiss on her forehead before he stepped away completely, leaving his daughter in the arms of the woman that just broke apart his family. His heart stayed there, on that red spot on her forehead, forever to be carried with her where she went, just as she carried Noelle's heart with her.

Carol reached for Noelle, the Sister placing a hand under her arms to keep her from falling. Sister Beatrice shrugged the rucksack higher on her other shoulder, suddenly avoiding all eye contact as she started her trek back towards the buggy. Noelle fell to her knees, sobbing fully now. Hoarse gasps escaped her, "*Please.* Please Sister Beatrice—I am sorry!"

Carol was crying profusely, her face scrunched in his sadness. The scars on her cheeks were wet with tears, her small hands clutching at the air in desperation. Her mouth open and closed, silent sobs, words unable to break through the thick barrier of heartbreak and betrayal. And Nicholas knew that was what she felt—she was too young to understand that Noelle had no choice, all she knew now was that she was returning to the orphanage, she was betrayed. And while Nicholas knew it was not the truth, she did not. And she would not until she was old enough to understand. This day would stick with them forever, the trust and hearts that were broken.

Nicholas felt his own knees threaten to give in, the sound of her begging a horrid sound to his ears. It was so broken, so filled with despair, that even Beatrice hesitated, stopping dead in her tracks. She did not turn, but Nicholas knew she was witnessing the heartbreak Noelle felt. It was strong enough that Nicholas thought even the fall of snow stopped, that one word loaded with so much desperation and devastation that even nature stopped to bear witness to this moment.

It harbored so much love, that Nicholas swore the angels in heaven stopped to bear witness to its existence. Carol wailed again, Noelle sobbing, "*Please!* I'm sorry!"

But Beatrice walked again, placing Carol in the closed back of the buggy. Noelle begged and begged, but Sister Beatrice left her there. Nicholas crouched next to Noelle, pulling his wife into his arms as she begged the woman to bring back their daughter.

Nicholas' own heart strained, finally shattering when the buggy disappeared from view, Carol reaching towards them from the back, before she disappeared from view, and from their lives. Noelle bowed, her forehead laid on her hands on the porch, her body shaking with sorrow. He closed his eyes, cast his face skyward, and granted himself the moment to feel.

Despair made his stomach hurt, his throat and eyes burn, made him feel like he was helpless in this world. They'd lost their daughter, despite trying everything they could to keep her. He saw Carol's face flash before his closed eyes, her smile, and heard her laugh echo in his ears. He saw the puffy red dress he'd worn, and hoped Beatrice had packed it as well. She loved that dress, and she deserved to keep it.

Nicholas opened his eyes, pulling Noelle back into his chest as he sat back against a pillar of the wood porch. He drew its strength into him, its unyielding nature, and siphoned it into Noelle. Her hands were wrapped around his arms, her face buried in the crook of his elbow as she struggled to process this loss.

"*Please,*" Noelle begged, her voice hoarse. But it was no use, her begging fell on the snow like phantom snowflakes. Her please went unheard, and unfelt. Beatrice was gone, and so was Carol, and all they had to do now was ride the storm until it passed. Nicholas squeezed her tighter, Noelle turning to sob into his chest.

This was the hardest thing Nicholas had ever had to witness, the most soul-shattering experience he'd ever gained. Seeing his wife in pieces, seeing his daughter reach for them, it was *torture*. There was no other word for it.

Nicholas was angry at this whole situation. Angry at himself for allowing it, angry at Noelle and himself for putting them in this position, and angry at Beatrice for not having a heart. He was angry at the world for ripping this away from him, for ripping Carol away from Noelle, and leaving his wife broken once again, after she'd just healed herself.

His father had always asked him what kind of man he wanted to be. And, being just a boy, he'd never understood the question. To him at that age, there were only two kinds of men—good men and bad men.

Very obviously he'd answered that he wanted to be a good man, incredulous that his father would even consider something else. But now, he understood that the question encompassed much more. Would he be the man that sat back and allowed this, or would he be the Godly man his church and faith taught him to be—a provider, a protector, a *good* man.

He had made mistakes, had sinned, and had forgotten to stay true to who he was. And while he hadn't done this intentionally, or with bad intention, he still did it. But would that define him as a man from now on? Or would he pray for forgiveness and return to the path of righteousness?

Nicholas was at a forked road. One path leading him to hopelessness and a lifetime without Carol, always left with a vast emptiness that she'd once filled. And the other led him down a road of solutions, Carol coming home, himself returning to his faith, their family reunited and happy.

He stared down the road, particularly at the bend around which his daughter had disappeared what felt like hours ago. He allowed himself to feel her absence, the sting that came with the disappearance of her smile, and her light from his life. And then Nicholas steeled his resolve.

He kissed Noelle on the top of her head, his wife still sobbing relentlessly.

"We'll get her back," he vowed to her, to Carol who was not here to hear it, and to himself. "We'll get her back no matter what. I promise you."

He spoke the promise to Carol, praying that the cold winter wind would carry the words to her, prayed that God would plant the word in her heart, and allow her to know just how determined he was. Just how loved and cherished she was, is, and still will be.

"You hear me?" Nicholas asked, lifting Noelle to look him in the eye, her face red and swollen. Her eyes were filled with tears, the blue light with sorrow. "We're going to get her back home, Noelle. I don't care how long it takes. We'll bring her back home."

She fell back against his chest, her cheek laid against him as she stared at the same bend he did. They stayed there for hours, the cold seeping into their bones, soothing the raging emotions inside them, a welcome balm to the scalding fire of heartbreak.

They sat there, Noelle in the V of his legs and pressed tightly against him, Nicholas seated against the pillar as if it might keep them grounded. They watched until the snow became more, the sun became dimmer, and the night enveloped the road. It was as if they expected her to return, as if Beatrice had played a cruel joke on them and wanted to test how much they truly wanted Carol. But they never came back, and Nicholas and Noelle were forced to pick their broken hearts up and return to the warmth of the home.

However, even though it was heat that enveloped them when they entered, the house still felt colder than the porch they'd been seated on for the past however many hours. Noelle's hand was clutched in his own, both of them paused on the threshold of the home and scanned the spaces before them.

Traces of Carol were everywhere—dolls, books, torn newspaper strips as a result of one of her crafts. *She* was everywhere, but she also wasn't. Her laughter didn't fill the hallway, her dolls didn't litter the steps, her little feet didn't echo off her upstairs bedroom floor. She was gone, and Nicholas wasn't sure if she'd be back soon enough for them to still experience these things with her in her childhood.

It would take *years* to reestablish that trust with the orphanage, and they didn't have years to spare with her.

Noelle came to the same conclusion, her face crumbling again. Nicholas swept her up into his arms, cradling her like a baby against his chest. He took her upstairs, placing her in the bed before climbing in beside her. Nicholas held his wife all night, soothing her tears when she was awake, and calming her when she awoke through the night, her very own nightmares replaying her separation from Carol. He held her until the morning hours, never leaving her side, even when his own sadness pressed on his chest, and he struggled to breathe.

Chapter Thirty-One

Noelle stared at the mug of tea in her hand, the small shavings of tea leaves floating on the surface like tiny boats on a still sea. They didn't do much, in fact, they didn't do anything but bob in the same place when she shook the cup slightly. She felt like the tea leaves, bobbing in the same place as life shook the sea beneath her, never moving forward or backward, just staying in the same place.

The house was eerily quiet with Carol gone, the absence of her screeching and laughing louder than any scream she could've uttered in these halls. It yelled at her, the silence; demanded her attention when the static in her ears and mind didn't have center stage. And when even the silence didn't yell, she was left with a numbness as vast as the tea-ocean in her lap, no ending in sight.

The only sounds in the home were of Nicholas, scurrying around its halls trying to hide any traces of Carol that had sent Noelle into a sibbing fit when she'd seen them this morning after waking, making meals she didn't eat, bringing cups of tea filled to the brim that stayed full.

She had felt bad, still did, because she saw the black circles underneath his eyes. She saw his own tears that he tried to hide from her. He tried to feed her, tried to get her to eat something, but she just wasn't hungry. There wasn't a desire to eat at this moment, so she didn't. Her thoughts didn't leave enough room for an empty stomach anyway, filling the hunger with endless *what-ifs* instead of food.

Sometimes, when her mind granted her the blissfulness of forgetting Carol had been taken, Noelle almost got hungry enough to eat. But when she rose and saw the emptiness of her home that had been filled with love and laughter just an evening ago, she wasn't hungry anymore.

Sometimes she grew angry with Beatrice, but then she realized it wasn't the woman's fault, and then she grew angry at herself. She wondered why she hadn't just told Beatrice the truth from the start, wondered why she had been so overcome with panic and desperation that she'd resorted to dishonesty to get what she wanted.

Noelle wondered what Carol was doing at the orphanage, what she was thinking and if she truly believed that Noelle had simply not wanted her anymore and had given her back to the orphanage. And that was the thought that made it so much worse for Noelle.

She didn't want her daughter to think she'd been given away without second thought, that Noelle had deemed her unworthy of the love she'd been given while living with her. She didn't want Carol to think that she was unimportant to her. It broke her heart to think that her daughter was possibly feeling abandoned and betrayed, and worst of all, forgotten.

Nicholas' heavy footsteps echoed from the foyer, his boots muffled by the carpet as he came to take a seat across from her, his own steaming mug of tea in his hand. He looked disgruntled, his hair stuck up in all directions, his eyes sad and ringed with dark circles.

His clothes were rumpled, and his boots unlaced where they sat on his feet. Nicholas Birch looked like a tired man who was carrying the weight of the world on his shoulders, and Noelle felt ashamed. He was just as devastated about Carol, and yet, he'd taken care of her. He *was* taking care of her, since yesterday when Carol had been taken from them.

"Are you okay if I leave just to grab a quick change of clothes?" He asked, voice gentle and understanding, nothing but pure concern and care. He met her eyes, the first time she'd looked at anything besides the tea leaves and the crackling fire in a good while. She could have sworn her heart fluttered, but it was gone so quickly, she was unsure if it was just her mind playing tricks on her. He looked handsome, even though he looked a bit worse for wear.

Noelle nodded, returning her gaze to the fire, before she placed her teacup on the coffee table and stood, the blanket from her lap left discarded on the floor. She smoothed her hands down her nightgown, she hadn't even bothered to dress this morning.

"I think I'll go lay down while you're gone," she said, her voice barely more than a whisper. "I'm...tired."

Noelle was tired. She was tired of having her dreams ripped away, tired of feeling this vast emptiness that she had fought so long, that Carol had filled so effectively, only to have it be ripped open again when she'd been taken. Noelle Foster Birch was tired of being heartbroken, and she was tired of working so hard to get what she wanted only to have it be ripped away by those around her.

Granted, it was her one fault, but even she couldn't blame herself for doing anything it took to get Carol home, when she'd already wanted it for so long. First Henry had ruined it for her, then even in his death he'd stood poised to ruin it again, so she'd adapted and overcome. And yet...

"Okay, sweetheart. I'll be quick, I promise. Do you need me to help you with something before I go?" He asked, immediately rising to his feet and came to her side. Noelle's heart almost broke again. Nicholas was so considerate, so loving and caring and kind. He was all she'd ever dreamed of in a husband, and she had no idea if she even deserved him.

She shook her head, making her way up the stairs. The wood floors were biting cold against her feet, but she barely felt it. Nonetheless, Nicholas followed her up, opened the covers for her to slip in, and sat on the edge of the bed right next to her. His broad hand covered a large part of her back as he caressed her, soothed her. Just as he had since yesterday, all night last night, and this morning when she awoke with a new wave of sadness.

He was good to her, and Noelle had no idea what would happen to them now that Carol was gone. Sure, he had proclaimed his love for her yesterday to Beatrice, but had that been part of his idea to keep Carol? What if she had read too much into this arrangement, what if he really had just married her to help and he didn't feel that way for her. It would have been fine if Carol was still there because she knew he loved Carol, and that was the reason they had done it in the first place. But what would happen now?

Nicholas rubbed her back until he was sure she'd fallen asleep, only leaving when her breathing turned even enough to sell the illusion. She almost reached back to grab at him, almost asked him to bring all of his belongings with him when he came back, that he never had to leave for anything ever again.

But if he did not feel the same, she could not handle the rejection at this moment. So she stayed quiet, kept her breathing even, even when he bowed low to press a kiss to her temple. Noelle waited until the door closed behind him, and she heard River's whinnying; then she let herself cry again. Only when she was certain he'd left, when she felt truly alone, did she let herself cry.

The bed shook with her sobs, her back and ribs straining against the breathless cries she made. A sound of utter despair escaped her, broken and horrid to even her own ears. Noelle cried herself to sleep, eyes swollen and pillow soaked in the pieces of her broken heart, and didn't rise until four hours later.

***

Noelle was roused from sleep by a slightly cold hand on her back. The room around her was bathed in darker afternoon light, indicating that she'd slept to late noon. She turned, smiling smally at Nicholas when she saw him, dressed in fresh clothes and looking a lot better than he had earlier. Her eyes burned and her face felt swollen and hot, Noelle blushing when she saw the concern and sympathy in his eyes. She didn't want his sympathy, not at all.

"Sorry for waking you," he said softly, as if she were a startled animal, "Pastor Sam is here. He came to see how you were,"

Noelle almost cried again right then, the knowledge of everyone in town knowing what had transpired almost too much to bear. She never cared what anyone thought, but if they knew, then there would be rumors spread about— rumors that could get back to Carol and give her the wrong information about what had truly happened. She nodded, throwing back the covers when he stood to give her space. Her body felt stiff, her stomach and ribs tight with all of the crying. Her mouth felt dry, and her head was pounding.

"I'm just going to freshen up." She said, her voice hoarse and awful. She was sure she smelled awful too, but she couldn't really care. "I'll be right down."

Nicholas nodded, his mouth opening as if he wanted to say more, but he didn't. Turning on his heel, he left, shutting the door with barely more than a nick. The room was silent once again, the only sounds were the beating of her own heart and the static in her ears that had been there since Beatrice had made her decision.

She made her way to the washroom and quickly washed her face, then she brushed her hair, looking duller than she'd ever seen it. Noelle stared at herself in the mirror for a moment, drinking in the full glory of her sadness that was displayed there. Dark circles rimmed her blue eyes, her face was gaunt and pale, her hair closer to rust than the rich red it usually was. She looked like a living corpse, a shell of the woman she once was. And yet, she couldn't bring herself to care.

Her bare feet padded off the wooden floor, the cold slightly unbearable but much preferred to the uncomfortable fit of her boots. Nicholas and Pastor Sam's deep voices filtered out from the dining area of the kitchen. She'd only shrugged a robe over her nightgown and combed her hair. She hoped Pastor Sam didn't focus too much on her appearance, had come as a friend and not a pastor.

Both of them turned to her when she came around the bend of the wall, Pastor Sam standing to greet her. He was not dressed in his formal attire, and Noelle was glad to see her friend. She took a seat next to Nicholas at the dining table, her husband—*husband,* it was still so strange—rising from his seat and going to the kettle. He fixed her a cup of tea as she and Sam started talking.

"How are you feeling?" Sam asked, placing his hand on hers in support. "I heard from Katherine, who heard what happened from some of the women at church."

Noelle nodded, tears falling silently from her eyes. His face softened.

"Am I being punished, Sam? Is that why I can't seem to keep my grasp on happiness?"

Her friend's eyes softened even more, his own sheen of tears appearing. He knew her, had been by her side so many times when Henry had broken her spirit. He had been there when she'd first met Carol, when she'd adopted her—he'd been there for everything. Sam was one of her dearest friends, had shared in her victories and now shared in her failures. His tears rolled down his face as she sobbed,

"Is this my punishment for not mourning Henry as I should have? As his wife? Is this because I lied to Sister Beatrice?" Noelle truly did not understand, and she truly felt like she was being punished. She felt like her happiness was the price to pay for her sins.

Sam shook his head, Nicholas placing his hand on her upper back as he set the cup in front of her, taking his seat beside her. He had his own track of tears falling down cheeks.

"No, Noelle. I do not believe you are being punished." Sam said. "God doesn't punish, he redirects us to the right path."

"Why was she taken from me, Sam?"

Sam's head bowed. "I don't know, Noelle. I do not know the way of the Lord. But I do know that he would never intentionally hurt you or Carol."

Noelle sobbed harder. "I just don't understand, I don't understand why any of this turned out like this."

"I know, my dear friend. I know, and I'm sorry for your sorrow." Sam was crying with her now, no trace of that smile he seemed to wear like jewelry. He clutched her hand tighter. "The only advice I can give you is to pray, Noelle. Pray, talk to the Lord. Do not ask for anything, just allow Him to understand what is in your heart, allow Him to help you. To take your sorrow."

His words settled over her like a heavy blanket. She realized that she had prayed these weeks, but only to ask and not to give. She realized that she had expected, and not given the Lord the opportunity to work inside her heart, as He always had.

She had only prayed to say thanks and to ask for more, not to give Him her heart, to allow Him to understand what she was feeling as Sam had said. And while God did not punish, she felt that she would have deserved it if He did. She'd unwittingly pulled her Lord into a one-sided relationship.

Sam squeezed her hand again. "Have faith, Noelle. God is not done with you yet."

Chapter Thirty-Two

Nicholas and Sam stood in the foyer of the home, hands clasped in farewell. His friend looked back towards the direction of the kitchen, to his wife that was still seated there, hollow. His face was solemn, and his eyes were sad,

"Neither of them deserves this," Sam said. "They deserve a bit of happiness in their lives. The Lord knows they've both had tough starts."

Nicholas nodded, thinking of Carol's scars and about her parents perishing in a fire. Then he thought about Noelle, and all the things she'd endured while Henry had been alive.

"I'm going to get her back," Nicholas said. "If it takes years, I don't care. I'll bring Carol back home."

Sam nodded, stepping back. "Noelle deserves someone who will fight for her, and so does Carol. I have no doubt you'll do what it takes. Just make sure Noelle stays whole through it all."

Nicholas nodded, opening the door for his friend. The air was frigid outside, almost knocking the air from their lungs with its brutality. Sam whistled, rubbing his hands together before he made his way to the barn. Nicholas waited for the man to disappear around the bend before he went inside.

Noelle was still seated in the kitchen, staring into the cup of tea that he'd made for her. He was sure it was ice cold already, but she still took a sip, not even a grimace appearing. Her head was hung low, her shoulders drooped, and her hair hung limply down her back. It was paler red than usual, not as vibrant.

Her very essence felt dull, like the shine had been stolen from her and carted off with Carol. Nicholas took a seat across from her, weariness finally slowing him down for the first time in a while. He felt bone tired, like a man that had been awake all his life and never had the chance for restful sleep.

Noelle tapped her nails on the side of the cup, contemplatively gazing into the contents. At first, when she'd done it for the first time, he'd thought that he'd made her tea wrong. Granted, there had been more tea leaves left over floating in the cup than when she made it, but he was trying his best.

He even went as far as following her exact tea-making routine, down to tapping the spoon on the side of the rim two times. But now he didn't know, she probably just felt a bit more at ease, finding some sort of solace in the dark red-and-amber liquid.

"Can I ask you something?" Noelle suddenly said, her voice strong and clear, unlike the soft and hoarse sound it had been earlier in the day. This was serious to her, if the clarity with which she spoke the question was any indication. "Something I'm unsure about. Actually—quite unsure about if I'm being honest."

Nicholas nodded. "Ask away, sweetheart."

He sat back in the chair, leaving his arms relaxed on the arm rests, not wanting to shut her off with his body language.

She suddenly looked up, her eyes clearer than they had been, mouth set in a determined line, and her body rigid. "When Beatrice...yesterday when you said those things—that you love me?"

Nicholas had to compose himself, keep the smile from painting his face, when he realized just where she was going with this. He should have known she would have second thoughts about it all, would question his devotion to her—and he didn't blame her, considering the way they were unified and the reason why. And even though he now knew that he had loved her long before these three days, she didn't, and he'd barely had the time to tell her properly. He'd hardly call blurting the words out to Sister Beatrice while she was taking their child away the proper moment, or even the moment where it would have sunk in.

"Did you mean it? Were you...were you serious?" She finished.

Nicholas almost flipped over the back of the chair with the urge to reassure her. How could she even ask? How could she not know? But he did not think she'd appreciate any sarcasm or incredulity today. So he stayed silently amused, nothing but seriousness on his face as he answered.

"As serious as a hangman's knot, honey."

Almost immediately, a frown creased the skin between her eyebrows. "I'm serious, Nicholas."

Oh, she's *very* serious, and definitely not in the mood for his antics. Nicholas sobered up, pushing the amusement far away, replacing it with nothing but sincerity. He shrugged. "I am too. I didn't say those things yesterday because I felt they would help our cause—I said them because I meant them, and I couldn't bear Beatrice minimizing our marriage and our vows."

Noelle stared at him for a moment, so intently, that he almost felt prone to start straightening his clothes. It felt like she saw *through* him, as if she was peeling back layer upon layer to see what lay at his center. And usually, he didn't squirm so easily, but this woman...this woman had the power to undo everything about him. She could be his downfall, and he'd go down smiling. But when she still said nothing, when she just looked at him as if she was expecting the other shoe to drop... his heart broke again.

Nicholas stood from his seat, walked around the table, and pulled out the seat right beside her. He turned it towards her, and then he grasped the upper and lower part of her chair, turning it towards his. Taking his seat, he scooted closer and closer, until their knees touched, and he placed his hands on the armrests on either side of her. Nicholas leaned in close, making sure she would internalize every single word he said.

"I am in love with you, Noelle. I have been from the very first moment I saw you, even if I didn't know it yet. Everything I feel for you is genuine, and it is deeply ingrained into my soul. *You* are deeply ingrained into my soul." He swallowed, Noelle's eyes wide as they stared into his own. "I have felt happiness like no other in my short time with you, and while I would have preferred a more prepared and romantic wedding..."

They both laughed quietly, puffs of air mixing and mingling.

"I am still so extraordinarily happy and blessed to have married you. I want to spend the rest of my life with you, with

Carol and maybe a few more children someday," Nicholas grasped her hands, placing them against his lips. She was crying fully now, tears streaming down her beautiful face. "You will want for nothing, you will never experience pain or heartache again. Not if I can help it."

Noelle started nodding, clutching his hands tightly. His own tears stained her hands where they were pressed to his face. "I love you, Noelle Birch. And I will love you until the end of my days, to my very last breath—if you'll have me."

She gave a gasping sob, crashing her face into his shoulders as she clutched him closer. Nicholas released her hands, gathered her up, and settled her down on his lap. He held her tightly, as if the wind blowing against the door might find a way to blow her away from him. Her breath left hot puffs of air on his neck, her tears wetting his shirt and staining his heart. They held each other for a long while, both of them unable to move and not really wanting to.

Noelle suddenly lifted her head, face red and puffy but looking beautiful as ever, and Nicholas palmed her cheek. He let her see what he felt, put every scrap of emotion and love into his gaze so that she might finally see his sincerity... that he truly did love her. That she was *worthy* of love, despite having been shown the opposite her entire life. Nicholas showed her every raw emotion he could, and prayed to the Lord that it was enough, that he was enough for her.

Silence stretched as they gazed into each other's eyes, a silence that did not need to be filled. One loaded with such emotion, it could have had a mind of its own. Noelle's gaze flitted between his eyes, searching for the answer to a question she no doubt had posed in her head. So he sat quietly, patiently waiting for that wondrous mind of hers to decide.

Noelle spoke then, and he'd be damned if they weren't the most beautiful words he'd ever heard. "I take you, Nicholas Birch, to be my lawfully wedded husband from now until my last days, up to my very last breath."

Nicholas' heart beat out of his chest, threatening to burst through his ribcage.

"I love you, Nicholas. Unequivocally, and unconditionally." Her lips trembled as she spoke the words, her hands poised on his shoulders. "I *love* you."

Nicholas kissed her tenderly, almost grunting at the unearthly softness of her lips. He kissed her deeply, for every kiss they didn't have before this, and for every kiss they didn't have to go without from now on. They loved each other, and while they were both far from being whole, they had each other. And when he woke the next day, he'd march down to that orphanage, and they'd have Carol. They would be a family again, no matter what.

The next morning, when Nicholas awoke, he was almost humming with determination and purpose. The morning air was crisp and cold to his lungs, almost burning with every breath he inhaled. The pine trees swayed in the soft winter breeze, the snow like a cozy blanket on the earth as he made his way to the front door of the orphanage. He'd left early that morning, careful not to rouse Noelle in his haste to get there.

The wooden porch groaned beneath his feet, the white paint chipped and peeling in some places. He knocked twice, his gloved hands making a dull sound. He hoped Noelle slept until she was rested, seeing as she hadn't gotten much sleep in those last few days. She looked worse for the wear, and he was starting to get worried.

There was a dull thud of boots as someone came to open the door, Sister Beatrice's smile fading when she laid on eyes on him. "It is no use, Mr. Birch. Carol is better off here, go home."

He stepped closer, a palm on the door she tried to close in his face. Annoyance flashed in her eyes, her skirts seemingly vibrating with her irritation. He did not mean to be rude, but he would not leave there without having Sister Beatrice listen to what he had to say.

"Good day to you too, Sister," he gritted out, barely containing his own annoyance. "I don't mean to be rude, but I'm not leaving here until you've heard what I have to say."

Nicholas only noticed the other patrons sitting in the living area once the words had left his mouth. He nodded sheepishly. "Respectfully."

Sister Beatrice considered it briefly, still holding the door partially closed, before she sighed and opened it fully. Nicholas stepped inside, inclining his head in greeting to the patrons who had just witnessed his demand. Beatrice motioned for him to follow and led him to a back living area that wasn't as occupied as the one they'd passed at the front.

It was a large house, the interior as big as a mansion with multiple bedrooms, seating areas that served as playrooms, and bathrooms to accommodate the horde of children currently under the orphanage overseers' care. Nicholas took a seat on one of the plush chairs, Sister Beatrice excused herself briefly.

She returned a moment later with Mr. Banks, who also looked less than happy to see Nicholas but was civil enough to grasp his hand in greeting. They took their seats opposite him, making it very apparent that they would listen, but it was very obviously Nicholas vs. them.

He rolled his shoulders back, unsure how to start. Nerves made a bundle of knots in his stomach, his throat feeling like it was closed up for some reason. He scratched the back of his head, and then he began. "I completely understand your reasoning with this whole situation, Sister Beatrice, Mr. Banks." He glanced at both of them in turn. "But there is more to the story than either of you realize."

Sister Beatrice's shoulders tensed immediately, and Mr. Banks shifted his weight. They were already aching to leave, already uninterested; and he'd only just begun. Nicholas swallowed, willing every ounce of confidence he had into his voice and body as he continued. "Noelle only told you the gist of what happened, what made her decide to go ahead with the adoption despite not having a husband."

"With all due respect, Mr. Birch, we have places to be and an orphanage to run..." Mr. Banks said, sitting forward. But Nicholas just went on, unfettered.

"When Henry was still alive, Noelle experienced something a woman should never have to. He was an unkind man, an alcoholic with the habit of picking on his wife whenever he returned home from the saloon, reeking of whiskey," Nicholas said, hoping he wasn't betraying her trust. "Noelle tried for years to give him a child, despite the horrible husband he was to her. But she couldn't carry the babies to term." He wondered if it was the fault of Noelle's body or the countless beatings she underwent whilst trying to grow a baby. He supposed the answer was obvious.

"And when she proposed the idea of adoption, Henry was adamant for a boy. He did not want Carol, the little girl Noelle had an instant connection with; he wanted a boy that could inherit the ranch after him upon his death—as he was the last living descendant of his family." Nicholas spoke with confidence, hoping this would be enough to convince them that Noelle was not a horrible person; that they were not bad people. "And when she pushed him, asked him again if she could bring Carol home, he hit her and—"

Nicholas trailed off. Details were not necessary, and he did not need to tell Beatrice every single thing Noelle had disclosed to him to get his point across.

"And you know what she did? She asked again, and again, took every beating he gave; trying to get Carol home. To adopt the little girl she was *sure* was sent to her to be her daughter." Nicholas looked straight at Sister Beatrice when he spoke again. "Noelle Foster Birch, the same woman you scolded and treated like dirt, took countless beatings trying to adopt the very girl you took away from her."

Mr. Banks cleared his throat, trying to speak, but Nicholas persisted. "She might have lied, and she might have deceived you. But she apologized, and after the things you said to her, well, she is devastated—and make no mistake, Sister, she did it all for Carol, just as she always would. She'd lie, steal, and deceive to keep Carol safe and happy; something I personally don't think is that bad of a quality in a mother."

Sister Beatrice looked away first, her throat bobbing as she swallowed. Nicholas looked at his clasped hands. "What she did, I agree, it was wrong. But is she not allowed to make a mistake?"

With that last parting question, Nicholas rose from his chair. He did not bid them goodbye, and he did not glance back as he left the orphanage. He only paused to get one look at a little blonde head, but left disappointed. He hoped his words were enough. Nicholas prayed that it would be enough to bring their daughter home.

Chapter Thirty-Three

Nicholas was gone when she awoke, the bed beside her cold and empty. She rubbed the sleep from her eyes, placing her palm on the pillow where he'd laid his head. His scent still lingered, a balm to the raging fire in her heart.

Noelle was still heartbroken, and she still cried whenever she was reminded of what could have been, and what she'd lost. Her eyes were sore and dry, her tongue thick in her mouth and devoid of any moisture. She was also sure she smelled like stale bread and dust bunnies.

Noelle rose onto her elbows, looking around the naturally lit room, in search of any trace that Nicholas was just down at the kitchen, but his boots were gone, and there was no tell-tale clattering of skillets to keep her company. She frowned, trying not to be too disappointed. She had grown so accustomed to him being here, it was almost a sad sight to see the vacant spot where his things always were. Noelle supposed it was also time for her to ask him to leave and get his stuff, and never leave again. If she were to throw out Henry's things—

The thought made her cheeks blush immediately, the red stain of shame, guilt and embarrassment leaving a stain down her neck and chest. Noelle almost drew the covers over her head, trying to hide from her own thoughts and lack of empathy. It was one thing to not feel guilty about his death, but quite another to think about throwing away his things to make room for another man. Another *husband*. Granted, Nicholas was much more to her than just another man in her life; but the principle still stood.

Noelle threw the covers back and padded over to the washroom, almost gasping at the sight of herself in the small mirror that hung above the basin. Her cheeks and eyes were gaunt and shadowed by the darkness of despair. Her hair hung limply from her shoulders, and her nightgown was crumpled from having been in it night and day for days now.

Noelle left the washroom, hoping to find some purpose by cleaning her home, or trying to do something she'd enjoyed before she had shared her hobbies with Carol. But when she got downstairs, the home was empty and clean. No trace of dirt or messiness lingered anywhere, and no trace of Carol or Nicholas to keep her company.

She wandered through the halls of her home, trying at first to find something amiss that she could fix, and then knitting. But when she thought of the day she'd knitted the hat for Nicholas, how she and Carol had shared so many laughs, she almost dropped the needles like they were on fire. Aimlessly, Noelle wandered her home, searching for something—anything—to do. Eventually she found herself back in the washroom, staring at herself again, trying to find some semblance of determination left. She supposed she could straighten up a bit, seeing as there was nothing else she could, or wanted, to do.

She splashed the cold water in her face, the icy temperature like a balm to her swollen and sore face. Next, she brushed her hair, gritting her teeth against the matted bits that pulled relentlessly against her scalp. However, with every stroke of the brush, and every rinse of her teeth, Noelle felt closer and closer to being human.

The ache was still there, and she still felt her eyes sting every time she thought of Carol; but she felt better physically.

Moments later, she was dressed and layered against the cold, her hair in loose waves around her shoulders to keep her ears warm from the cold. Not bothering with jewelry or the beautiful pin Nicholas had gotten her for Christmas, Noelle stepped out onto the porch.

The winter air bit at her nose and cheeks, the skin of her hands tightened immediately, and a shiver cascaded through her body. But despite the intruding cold, the day was beautiful. Snow fell softly to the ground, glinting off the bit of sunlight that shone through the clouds.

The pine trees that surrounded their home were capped with snow, birds nestled in their depths, singing cheerily in the morning despite the winter threatening their lives. It truly was a beautiful morning, even though Noelle didn't want it to be.

Grief was a strange thing. And she was grieving Carol, like she hadn't grieved Henry when he'd passed. Noelle wanted the earth to stand still while she mourned, the very wind to stop blowing while she just caught her breath for a moment. She wanted the serenity in the air around her to cease existing, and to bathe the day in gloom. Noelle wanted the earth to mourn with her, wanted it to acknowledge what she had lost and just grant her a moment to feel whatever it was she needed to. And this cheery winter morning would not grant her that.

She'd taken this walk with the purpose of finding some peace and quiet from the thoughts in her head, pressing and pressing. The same thoughts that left her crying herself to sleep, and her head pounding in the mornings when she woke. But with every step, her mind wandered farther away from the clarity she so desperately sought. Thoughts fell from her subconscious like snowflakes from the sky, littering her consciousness like the snow-covered branches littered the forest floor her boots walked on.

Noelle didn't know if she walked for minutes or hours, but soon, she didn't see the forest around her, didn't hear the birds chirping cheerily from their warm nests in the crooks of the trees around her. All she heard and saw were memories of her life before and after Carol's arrival in her life. She thought of Henry, and the charming young man he'd been when her father had sold her to him. Then she thought of the fateful night it had all changed, and he'd returned home drunk from the saloon for the first time, and hit her so hard she'd awoken the next morning with a split temple and a headache that lasted for a day.

Since that night, it had become a habit; a sort of game, between them. She was always the loser, and he was always the victor that got out unscathed. Noelle wondered if she had told her father then, when she was still young and Henry had not yet stolen the most precious years of her life, if he would have done something to help her. She doubted it, but perhaps it was the little girl deep inside her that still held some semblance of hope that things could have been different for her.

What would have happened if she had met Nicholas instead of Henry? She would have been happier, without a doubt. But would she have met Carol then? Who knew pain and heartbreak as she did?

Or would she have her own horde of children and not worry about someone else's? It did not take Noelle long to realize that it was not her body that rejected her children, but their father that beat it so relentlessly that it was unable to keep them alive. Noelle wondered if she had the choice between a life with Nicholas from the start, or a life with Henry that would lead her to such despair and eventually to Carol, which she would choose for herself.

A sprawling building came into view as Noelle ducked beneath a low-hanging branch, her heart ceasing its beating when she realized just where she was. The mine Henry had worked at sprawled before her, a looming presence that represented much more than just the hard-working men of their town. Noelle sank to her knees in the snow, barely feeling the increasing wetness of her dress as the snow melted beneath her.

This mine represented the looming shadow of him over her, just as the building hid the sun from her now, casting her in coldness and darkness. Henry had stolen her *life* from her. Not only the years, but also the girl she had been—so full of love and laughter and joy, she had been compared to sunlight many a time before her marriage to him.

Soon, people had started to notice her rapid "maturity" and increasing silence; chalked it up to married life and the same path that all unhappily married women walked. Instead of looking deeper, people had turned their cheeks, selling themselves the illusion that she herself had also indulged in.

Noelle had been convinced that it was only her childish nature taking its leave, making space for the woman she was on her way to becoming. Never suspecting that it could have been that exact childlike naivete that would make her accept behavior that had no place in the loving and warm home she was desperately trying to build for herself, and for her future children.

Tears, scalding hot on her frozen cheeks, dripped into the snow below her. A wail escaped her, swept away by the wind that seemed to blow right through her. It served as her friend now, carrying her sorrow away from Henry's phantom that stood posed to gobble it up once more.

Noelle was sure she didn't hate the man, but she also did not love him as a wife should love her husband. She did not feel one ounce of heartache for him, did not contribute one tear to his loss. No. She felt the heartache for herself, cried these tears for the girl she had been, so incredibly in love with the idea of love, she'd let a man ruin her.

Noelle cried for herself, let every wail voice the despair she had felt for years, let every broken piece of her manifest, and be felt in this cold snow. She let it all out, every single broken piece of her heart, every single shattering he had caused and reveled in, and felt it all.

Every bottled scream, every stitch she'd sewed into her mouth, every broken bone she'd had to mend on her own, every single cut and scar he'd left on her body. Noelle let herself feel every bruise, and every ounce of fear she'd had to push down in these years.

And when she was done, when her tears left dry streaks of pain on her face, and her heart cleaned every festered wound; she stood from the snow. Her dress was soaked, the hem of it icy cold with the evidence of her emotional release, but she stood taller than she ever had before.

Noelle looked up at the mine before her, stared it down like a giant posed to crush her beneath its meaty foot, and turned her back on it. She left Henry there, his spirit and his memory, left him with her pain so that he might not bother

her again. And when she ducked beneath that branch again, she let it stand in the way of his lingering memory, adamant on following her for the rest of her life; let it serve as a barricade between her and the trauma she'd suffered. Noelle left that little clearing before the mine, decorated with her despair, and didn't look back.

***

Noelle was cold and shivering by the time her beautiful ranch home came into view, a very worried and equally as beautiful man waiting for her on the porch. She smiled smally and gave him a small wave as she crossed the last of the distance between her and the porch. Her toes were close to falling off, her knees felt like they had aged at least seven years thanks to the cold and the wet dress, and she was also fairly certain that her nose was nothing but a dripping, snotty mess by now.

Nicholas rose from the porch swing, setting the blanket draped over his lap on her shoulders as she ascended the last step onto the semi-warmth of her home and her husband. He enveloped her in a bear hug almost immediately, rubbing her arms and back as he escorted her into their home. The fireplace was already going, bathing her in its warmth as she entered the foyer, immediately sighing at the relief from the biting cold of the outside.

Noelle took a seat on the sofa, sinking deep into the cushions as Nicholas draped another blanket over her lap. His face was set in a frown, his eyes traveling over her body as he set one last blanket on her lap for good measure. She smiled her thanks, not saying anything until he posed the question,

"I was worried about you. Where did you go?" Nicholas asked. His tone was anything but accusatory, and his concern for her warmed her heart. He sat across from her, intent on hearing her answer.

Noelle stared into the fire before she answered. "I just went for a walk. I needed to clear my head. It... it felt like I was drowning in my own thoughts."

"Do you want to talk about it?" He asked, always concerned, always supportive. Always her dream husband. Noelle considered it, but decided that she did not want to give it another thought. She'd tell him in time, when she felt better and more up to talking about it.

Noelle shook her head, smiling softly to let him know that it was not because she did not trust him, but because she wasn't ready to tell him that part of her history yet. She had only made her own peace with it an hour ago, and she was not ready to confront it again just yet.

Nicholas looked at her for a moment, contemplating what to say. He finally nodded. "Okay sweetheart. I'm just glad you're safe. You want a cup of tea?"

She nodded again, unable to express her gratitude. He winked at her, and made his way to the kitchen. She listened to his clamoring, her mind finally silent enough for her to just... be. The vast emptiness in her still remained, as it always would without Carol here; but she could finally sit with herself, without feeling like bursting out of her skin with sadness or anger or despair.

Nicholas returned with her tea, placing the warm cup in her hand before he took a seat next to her. Noelle leaned into his embrace instinctively, making herself comfortable, as she could always be with him. Only him.

"Where were you?" She asked, more curious than upset. "You were gone when I woke up."

Nicholas tensed suddenly, his body rigid against her back. He cleared his throat, the sound of his fingers scratching at his beard reached her ears. Noelle frowned, he only did that when he was nervous or unsure. But before she could jump to conclusions, he spoke.

"I hope you won't be too angry with me," he started, which already had Noelle tensing. "But I went back to the orphanage to talk to Sister Beatrice."

Noelle sat upright, causing the tea in her cup to splash over the side. She turned to face him, her mouth fell open in shock and the utter disbelief made tears pierce her eyes.

"What?" She asked, breathlessly. Nicholas surged forward, cupping her cheek.

"Are you angry?" He asked uncertainly, but Noelle just cried.

"You did that for me?"

Nicholas' face fell, softening as he realized it was not anger that made her sob uncontrollably again. He took the cup from her hands, set it on the coffee table, and drew her into his chest. Nicholas, her wonderfully selfless husband, held her as she sobbed. He rubbed her back, soothing her cries, and once again supported her when she needed him most.

Noelle had never felt loved like this, had never experienced the crushing embrace of a partner that cared as deeply for her as she did for them. She almost said as much, but a knock at the door spurred them both. They exchanged a look of confusion before Nicholas rose, taking a long-legged stride to open the door. Noelle almost sobbed again at the sight of Sister Beatrice, shivering and cold on her porch, and a softness on her face she'd never seen from the woman.

Chapter Thirty-Four

Nicholas almost fell on his back at the sight of Sister Beatrice, hardly believing his own eyes. And judging by the surprised sound she made, neither could Noelle. The Sister was smiling softly, clutching at the coat she wore as she tried to ward off the ever-increasing cold. The snowfall behind her cast a strange picture of an angel, the little flurries serving as strange depictions of her make-believe wings.

He stepped aside quickly, ushering the woman inside before their angel froze to death on their very own porch. As hopeful as he wanted to be, Nicholas had seen the way she'd looked at him before he'd left. He had known it would be a long shot to go see her and try to convince her, when she had been so adamant in her decision from the first moment she'd found out about their deception. So he kept his expectations low, prepared himself for another verbal scolding, and angled himself to protect Noelle from the same. He would not tolerate this woman tearing his wife down again.

"I apologize for just barging in this late in the afternoon," Beatrice said, glancing around the home. All traces of Carol had been tidied up but not removed from where they had originally been kept. Nicholas had only wanted to help Noelle with the transition, not remove Carol from their lives and thoughts completely. Something flickered in the Sister's eyes.

"It's no worry at all, Sister," Noelle assured her. "Would you like something to drink? A cup of tea to warm your hands perhaps?"

Sister Beatrice nodded, smiling with gratitude as she took the seat Nicholas offered to her, sinking right into the cushions of the sofa opposite to the one they'd been seated on. She extended her hands to the fire, seeking its warmth. Noelle was back in only a moment, the kettle still hot from where he'd made tea for her just moments before.

"How can we help you, Sister?" Nicholas asked, scooting over to make space for Noelle. Sister Beatrice didn't miss how he tucked Noelle into his side, or how she placed her hand on his knee. His wife's eyes were wide, her focus solely on the Sister. If Beatrice saw how run-down she was, she didn't show it.

"Firstly, I would like to apologize to the both of you," Beatrice started, taking a deep breath before she continued. "The way I acted, and the way I spoke to you—it was horribly unprofessional, and it was unkind."

Noelle drew back, sitting against the back of the sofa and his arm now, clearly surprised by the Sister's willingness to apologize. Nicholas had to admit that he was, too. Sister Beatrice did not look like a woman who admitted to doing wrong very easily.

"After you left, Nicholas, our dear friend Pastor Hastings came for a visit." She took a sip from her tea, closing her eyes against the warmth that spread through her belly. Pastor Sam had visited the orphanage? "He spoke to Mr. Banks and me about what had transpired between us all, and why Carol had been taken when she'd been cared for so diligently."

Nicholas' eyes widened of their own accord. Noelle glanced up at him, confusion marking her features, possibly twin to his own. Pastor Sam had spoken to them about Carol? He knew what had happened, why she'd been taken away. They turned back to Beatrice as she continued,

"He raised some particularly interesting points that he felt we should be made aware of, as did Nicholas. And I fear that I might have judged you two too quickly." Nicholas could hardly believe his ears, could hardly hold his breath at the possibility of what was about to happen. Beatrice set her cup down on the coffee table in front of her, and smoothed her hands down her dress before she admitted, "I feel like I have made the wrong decision regarding Carol's adoption, and her residence here."

Noelle clutched at his hand, her nails digging into his palm. Nicholas barely felt it, could barely think around the rapid pounding of his heart in his ears. It couldn't be, could it? Had God truly granted them this Christmas Miracle? Had they truly been blessed by His fortune?

"I would like to return Carol to your home and to your care, if that would please you. I think she would like it very much to be reunited with people who evidently love her very much. I understand my behavior has not been seemly, but I do not think the child should be denied a home becau—"

"Yes!" Noelle exclaimed, moving to grasp Beatrice's hand across the coffee table between them. "Yes, Sister. We would love to have her back."

Nicholas nodded when the Sister's eyes settled on him, her face surprised but delighted as Noelle still clutched at her hand. Tears welled in her eyes, her face pulled in a mixture of joy and tears as she nodded again. Sister Beatrice squeezed his wife's hand again, smiling down at her. It was the first time he'd seen the woman smile at anyone but the children she cared for, and he was the first to admit that she truly was beautiful.

That was when Nicholas realized that Beatrice had not been the villain all this time; that she had not broken his wife's heart and separated their family because she wanted to or because she had set out to from the beginning.

Sister Beatrice was simply a woman who cared deeply for the children she looked after, who loved them just as their adoptive parents did, and who wanted the best for them after they'd had a horrible start at life. She was not a woman out for blood and wrecking families where she went. She was a woman who sought only the best for her charges, and would fight tooth and nail, would ruin her own likeability, to make sure they got just that.

Nicholas gazed at Beatrice with newfound respect, the woman returning the sentiment when their gazes met. Noelle sat back against him, her face alight with a smile for the first time in days. He gazed down at his wife, overcome with joy and love and gratitude. She looked up at him, her eyes once again alight with the possibilities their future now held.

"I will return Carol to you tomorrow morning at the earliest convenience," Sister Beatrice said, standing, and smoothed her hands down her robes. "We all know how she likes to sleep in."

They all laughed, Noelle's a bit more breathless as the rest of them. His wife stepped forward, her hands clasped together. "Thank you for your kindness, Sister Beatrice. You were not unkind with your words before. You were simply a mother who sought to protect one of her children."

Sister Beatrice's eyes shone with a sheen suspiciously close to tears; but she blinked them away quickly. She nodded, squeezing Noelle's hands before she walked towards the front door. They escorted her out, and Nicholas remained on the porch to see her safely down the path before he returned inside.

Noelle was in the living room, gazing at the door as he entered. He stopped right in his tracks, smiling broadly at her and bellowed his laughter when she sprinted and jumped right into his arms. They laughed joyously, Nicholas spinning her in the air, her hair creating a curtain of red as they spun.

"She's coming home, baby," he hollered. "Our baby is coming home!"

Noelle laughed and lowered her head, kissing him deeply when he stopped spinning. They kissed each other passionately, Nicholas clutching his wife tightly against him as they shared in their joy. For the first time in his life, Nicholas Birch didn't want for anything to be different.

***

He didn't know which of the two of them woke first, or woke up more excited. Nicholas and Noelle were both up and dressed before they knew it, making pancakes and eggs and a breakfast spread that would have Carol jumping for joy when she saw it. Granted, it would be cold depending on when Beatrice brought her home, but she'd be happy, nonetheless. Minutes felt like hours, and hours felt like days.

Both Nicholas and Noelle were fighting the urge not to pace by late morning, their limbs jittery with anticipation, and their eyes glancing at the pathway leading to the ranch house every other minute.

"This is torture," Nicholas said, slightly annoyed. "Absolute and unadulterated torture."

Noelle snorted. "Tell me about it."

Nicholas' eyebrows shot up his forehead at the sound, not because she laughed, but because she *snorted*. Catching his look, Noelle rolled her eyes.

"Oh please," she said, "You're the last one to judge me about my laugh."

His mouth fell open. "Is that so?"

Noelle nodded and leveled her pointer finger at him, "You sound like a donkey seeing a mare for the first time."

Nicholas burst out laughing, absolute shock and denial making his mouth fall open once again. Noelle shrugged, giving him a less than remorseful look. "The truth hurts, pal."

Nicholas shook his head, rolling his eyes. "Okay, honey. Whatever you say. Guess we'll be a family of donkeys and pigs then,"

Her head snapped towards him, eyes narrowed and a reluctant smile on her face. He shrugged as she had, allowing his insinuation of her laughing like a snorting pig to hang in the air. Nicholas sat forward and smiled conspiratorially.

"Have you noticed Carol laughs a lot like one of the chickens you have in the coop?" He said, whispering as if the little girl might hear him. Noelle's eyes widened, and she pointed at him again.

"That's what it is! I've been trying to figure out what it sounds like with no such luck!"

They laughed again, Noelle gasping. "A family of donkeys, pigs, *and* chickens then!"

A fit of laughter overtook them, both Nicholas and Noelle clutching at their stomachs in an attempt to stave off the cramps that plagued them. The house around them seemed to echo with it, the reverberations of their joy sinking into the walls like a memory into their minds.

Just as they caught their breaths, silence descended once again, and they heard the clumsy clamoring of a buggy over the less snowy pathway leading up to the house. Noelle and Nicholas both went rigid, quiet as the mice that sometimes plagued the barn and bit the chickens in their coops. When they were certain of what they heard, it was a race to see who could be out the door the fastest.

On the porch they could see the buggy ambling down the pathway to them, little Carol coming into sight as she leaned over the buckboard to wave at them. Noelle made a broken sound, her hand flying to her open mouth as she realized that this was truly happening. Tears swam in her blue eyes, his own blurring his vision. Nicholas felt his own heart soar, his little girl ever more beautiful as she smiled broadly.

They both broke into a sprint at the same time, their feet slipping slightly on the melting snow as they clamored down the path. Their boots crunched on the ice as they went, their arms pumping and their breaths coming in rapid bursts. Nicholas' heart pushed against his chest, wanting to burst from his ribcage and soar on the winds of pure joy.

Noelle was making small whimpering sounds as she ran in front of him, her dress fluttering behind her, hair a trail of copper in the bright morning sun. Carol started yelling now, squealing in excitement like a little piglet instead of the chicken they'd just accused her of being.

The distance between them all felt like miles, unending miles that kept them from each other for much longer than was necessary. As his legs ate it up, he willed them to go faster, wanted the winter winds to scoop them up and carry them to each other.

The air rushed by his ears, the tips of his nose freezing in the frigid cold of winter. Carol shouted, jumped up and down on the buggy, screamed, squealed, and cried as they did. Nicholas' lips trembled as they came closer and closer and closer, inch by agonizing inch. It felt torturously slow, even though they were running as fast as their bodies allowed. Noelle was yelling now too, and a smile broke his face.

Sister Beatrice smiled as they came running, sharing in their joy and relief; but they paid her no heed when the buggy stopped, and Carol jumped from it. Her tiny legs flailed in the air for a moment, her white dress making an umbrella as she fell from the buggy.

She yipped and her hands hit the path a moment before she, too, started running. Barely on the ground and she was ambling toward them, the same desperation that overtook them, surging through her little body, forcing her legs to run faster than he thought possible. Tears streamed down her face, her blonde curls bouncing as she ran and ran and ran.

They had not seen her for what felt like months. Days without her laugh or her never-ending stories felt like decades. The absence of her light having left them in the dark with no light and no map to find their way again. But now she was back, and they would be a family again. Their little girl was back, and she was theirs and no one else's.

Carol reached Noelle first, jumping into his wife's arms a moment before he cascaded into them, crushing them in a bear hug. Snow and mud stained their clothes as they sank to their knees, breaths ragged, and cheeks wet as they finally got to hold each other again.

Relief crashed through them as they had crashed into each other, laughter and sniffles filling the air as their love did. Carol clutched at both of them, her tiny hands gripping at their clothes as if she could pull them into her very soul. Nicholas crushed them against his chest, folding them into the V of his legs as if he could shield them from everything that threatened to separate them ever again.

They were together again, and Nicholas could not hold back the sob that escaped him. Noelle looked up, cupping his cheek as she too sobbed and laughed, all at once. Love and devotion shone in her eyes, gratitude and absolute joy making them sparkle like snow in the sun.

Nicholas turned his face and kissed her palm, an unspoken promise shining in his own.

They were together. And they'd never be separated again. Never.

Chapter Thirty-Five

Noelle grasped Carol and Nicholas' hands tightly as they made their way to the church entrance. She lifted her chin defiantly, happiness making her chest fill with courage and her soul with light. She'd been on this happiness high for a week now, and she was not allowing anything to burst her bubble, not even the judgmental looks they received from the town gossips as they walked towards the church. Noelle had been nervous to attend at first, afraid of what people might think or say, especially since rumors had started circling regarding what had happened to them in the last few weeks when they'd lost Carol.

Noelle's heeled boots clicked off the sidewalk, as they stepped into the small courtyard of the sprawling white church. Carol wore her special red dress again, not one bit concerned that the holidays were over, and she was supposed to be returning to normal colors. Her blond curls were pinned up into a bun, wisps of hair falling around her pretty little face.

Nicholas matched his daughter in a red undercoat, winking at Noelle when she glanced over at him in appreciation. The man really knew how to wear that undercoat. Noelle was the odd one out, sporting a white dress and a black coat over the top, her black boots stark against the snow and the white of her dress. Her hair was pinned up similar to Carol's, but with half of it cascading down her back—just like Nicholas liked it. His frequent touching of her hair did not go unnoticed, either. He'd brushed his hand down her curls about five times in the span of two minutes.

Noelle and Nicholas smiled warmly at Pastor Sam and his wife when they arrived, their friends' eyes damp with emotion as they watched Carol amble off towards her friends. Katherine burst out crying almost immediately as Noelle hugged her, the woman squeezing her tightly as they shared a few whispered words and tears.

"I am so happy for you, Noelle," Katherine sniffled, wiping the underside of her eyes as they stepped apart. "My heart was absolutely broken for you when I heard what happened. I am so happy that you got her back."

Noelle squeezed her hands. "Me too, my dear friend. Me too."

Pastor Sam smiled broadly as Noelle greeted him, clasping her hand gently. They did not have time to speak as he stepped away, calling the congregation in for the start of the sermon. Noelle and Nicholas took their seat towards the back of the church, her husband staring down any fool who tried to look at Noelle in any manner that wasn't friendly. Sometime during the sermon, Noelle had to pinch his arm to get him to stop staring a hole in the back of a woman's head; she'd been the ringleader of the group that started a particularly nasty rumor about why Noelle and Nicholas had lost Carol. He hadn't looked in the least bit apologetic, and Noelle had had to bite back her laugh.

Pastor Sam spoke about the kindness of strangers, and how one kind act from someone might change the chain of events in another's life. He told the story of the Good Samaritan, and how we might be kinder and more caring towards those around us, because we never know what might be happening to them or if one word or act could change the course of their life forever.

Noelle couldn't help but think of her own life, how it might have ended differently for her if Pastor Sam had not encouraged Nicholas to look deeper than the surface of what she'd shown him—a little tale he only told her about the day before when they'd laid in bed that morning. How they might have never gotten Carol back if it hadn't been for Nicholas's effort, and Pastor Sam's kind words.

She thought of the truth behind what he was saying, how one act of kindness could hold so much power that it could make or break another person's character, or alter the way they might live their lives for the rest of it.

And while Noelle had not gotten the start to her life that she'd hoped; as she glanced over to her husband, and then down at their intertwined hands, where he rubbed the palms of hers, Noelle was grateful for the blessings God had sent her way through the middle of it. She had a loving and caring husband who would do anything for her.

A daughter who was perfect in every way, and would grow to be a wonderful young lady. A ranch that was flourishing thanks to the aforementioned husband, along with two new horses; one dapple for Carol and one Friesian to help Goliath with his burden of pulling the wagon and plow. And she was *happy.* Irrevocably, and unfathomably happy. So Noelle closed her eyes, sending a prayer to her all-powerful Lord, and said *thank you.*

***

Noelle and Katherine sat at the breakfast table in the kitchen of her and Sam's home, the pastor having changed from his official's clothes and into his casual wear. They gazed out the window, the children screaming and laughing with joy as they embarked on yet another make-believe adventure, and started a snowball fight that all of them knew would only have one victor, just as it always had—Jack. The boy, just two years older than Carol, at age 8, had a mean arm when it came to throwing snowballs; so much so, that his father had refrained from ever playing against him again after he'd knocked him out cold last year with a solid ball of compact snow.

Noelle watched as Carol cupped a heap of snow in her small hands, rolling and cupping the ice until it formed a solid round ball. She raised her eyebrows as Carol cocked her arm, aiming with the other hand stretched out in an 'L' shape, and threw it right into little Bethany's face.

She threw it hard enough that the impact of it made a dull thumping sound, the 6-year-old girl immediately bursting into tears at the force of it. Noelle gasped, jumping from her seat, ready to apologize. But it seemed there was no use. Katherine was still seated, clutching her stomach as she howled in laughter. Noelle stared in shock, maybe a bit of disbelief too.

Bethany entered the home via the front door that led into the kitchen, clutching her face as she scrambled to her mother. Her face was red where the ice had struck it, snot and tears running down her face as she sought comfort from her still-laughing mother.

Katherine bit her lip to keep the laugh from boiling over, pressing her child's head right into her chest as she shook with the force of it. Noelle put her own hand to her mouth, closing her eyes as they laughed at the poor child. She felt horrible, felt like the worst aunt in the world, but she had to admit that it was really very funny.

Katherine stroked her child's hair. "Now, now, Bethany. Carol didn't mean to hit you that hard."

Bethany surged up from her mother's chest, anger twisting her little face, "Yes, she did! They were all laughing at me, Mama!"

The child wailed again, and Noelle felt absolutely horrible. Katherine smiled softly, shaking her head. She rolled her eyes, patting Bethany's back until she was calm enough to attempt a conversation. Noelle pouted her lips in sympathy when the girl lifted her face again, those little cheeks blood red and her eyes puffy from the crying.

"Are you ready to go play again, my love?" Katherine asked the girl softly, smoothing strands of dark hair from her face. The girl nodded, rubbing at her eyes as she slid from her mother's lap. Bethany hesitated at the door, turned back to her mother in silent question. Her mother winked, gently shooing her out the door with a waving hand. The girl went reluctantly, armed with courage only a mother could provide. Noelle shook her head in wonder, Katherine winking at her when she noticed Noelle's incredulity.

"Just you wait, sugarplum," her friend said, sipping from her own cup of coffee. "That'll be you soon enough, soothing your child because Carol almost dented their face in with compact snow." Both women laughed.

Suddenly Noelle gasped. "Nicholas and I haven't even talked about kids yet. I'm not even sure if he wants any."

Katherine wiggled her eyebrows. "Oh trust me honey, he wants kids. He wants *hordes* of them."

Noelle's eyes widened and she sat forward in intrigue, whispering softly. "Really? How do you know?"

Katherine frowned as if Noelle had just said she sprouted a second head. "We've known him about as long as we've known you. He's always said he wants kids, and judging by the way he looks at you, he'd love to have thousands of them—with you."

Noelle looked towards the living room where she knew Nicholas and Sam were seated, as if she could see him through the wall. Katherine suddenly stood, grasped her coffee mug, and motioned for Noelle to join.

"We should probably leave the kids be for a little bit. We look like bored old women with nothing better to do than watch the neighborhood children in hopes they'll do something naughty so we can scold them," her friend said, as Noelle trailed after her, laughing.

Noelle took a seat next to Nicholas, her husband absentmindedly tucking her into his side as he slung an arm around the back of her seat, deep in conversation with their friend. They were talking about some inventor having created a sketch for the first ever *car*. She had no idea what it was, but apparently it was supposed to be the new big thing.

Katherine and Noelle busied themselves with their own conversation, leaving the men to their dreams and inventions. During it all, Noelle wondered if life could really get better than this. Her daughter was outside playing with her friends, Noelle was tucked against her husband who just could not stop touching her or her hair. Some part of him had to brush against her, or be pressed against her—whether it be a hand on her knee, his fingers twirling her hair, his arm slung across the back of her seats. Nicholas was always touching her in some way, never sated with proximity alone. Not that she was complaining.

Noelle loved every minute of every day with him, loved being near him and waking up next to him every morning. She loved having his scent wrap around her like a phantom blanket; a comfort when she had a bad day, or when she felt the dread that things were too good to be true and would soon fall apart, just as she feared. And when she felt that way, and his scent wasn't enough to alleviate that worry, he'd be there—flesh and blood—to hold her through it all.

Noelle realized that her days of sorrow and disappointment were over. That all of those years of despair and heartbreak had earned her this happiness. That she had suffered enough and been blessed with everything she'd ever dreamed of. Noelle Birch placed her hand on her husband's thigh, squeezing the muscle briefly as she continued her conversation with Katherine. A smile cut across her face when he placed his own hand on hers, and she knew everything would be alright, as long as he was with her. As long as her family was with her.

Epilogue

Copper Mountain, Colorado, 1886

Christmas day, one year later

Christmas afternoon, Nicholas and Noelle Birch stood in their very own kitchen, intertwined, his hands resting on her lower back and her arms on his shoulders as they swayed to the beat of imaginary music. Noelle smiled happily, gazing deep into her husband's eyes, her very pregnant belly prohibiting them from moving any closer. It had been a year since that fateful conversation with Katherine in her kitchen, and here she was, pregnant with one of the seemingly thousand babies Nicholas wanted to have with her.

They were patiently waiting for the chicken to finish roasting, and for their dear friends' arrival for Christmas Lunch—a tradition they decided to implement starting this year. Carol was upstairs in her room, loudly playing with her dolls and narrating what Noelle considered to be a very interesting drama; complete with a betrayal, and a secret crush that Carol hadn't decided if she wanted to reveal to her 'audience' yet.

"That child's imagination will mean her success someday," Nicholas said. "Mark my words. She'll be a writer before she's even finished school if she keeps it up."

Noelle nodded, glancing up at the ceiling as if she could see her daughter through the floorboards of her room. "An aspiring writer indeed, with the amount of tales trapped between those pretty little ears."

Nicholas rubbed her back gently. "Is there something we should get her to help that sort of gift along? Maybe some parchment and a pen?"

Noelle considered it, still swaying side to side with the love of her life. "I'm not really sure. I think we should—but when she's older and actually knows how to write. And when she won't break the pen."

They both laughed, reminiscing over the various things their daughter had broken in the last year. The girl didn't just have the gift of creativity, but also the gift of destruction.

"I think we just keep buying her books, help her expand her vocabulary, that sort of thing," Noelle finished, sighing with contentment as Nicholas rubbed a tender spot right in the middle of her lower back.

He hummed in agreement, his hands trailing up her arms to settle on the back of her neck, right where her shoulder and neck meet. He rubbed his thumbs gently into the tight spots.

"We'll see what she wants to do, and go from there. As long as she's happy, I'm happy."

Noelle smiled, her eyes closed in pure ecstasy as he carefully massaged the soreness from her body. "Such a good papa."

He hummed again and planted a soft kiss on her temple. Nicholas removed his hands from her neck, settling them on her hips as he bent down. He nuzzled her hair, and inhaled deeply,

"You always smell amazing, do you know that?"

Noelle opened her mouth to reply, but she was interrupted by a very disgusted Carol.

"EW! In the kitchen?" She yelled, covering her eyes. Her blonde hair was down to her waist now, the ends of it curled and beautiful. She wore a green dress, done with a red bow in her hair that she still couldn't get enough of, despite wearing it almost every single day. Her little teeth were exposed as she smiled, her covered eyes peeking through slightly separated fingers.

Nicholas stuck his tongue out at her and pulled Noelle in closer, planting thousands of kisses all over her face while Carol squealed in mock horror. He hooked her head in his elbow and dipped, placing his lips against hers and shook his head gently back and forth. Carol ran away, caught between laughter and screaming at the embarrassment of her parents actually *liking* each other.

Noelle stepped away from him when he brought them upright again, slapped him lightheartedly on the chest, and went to remove the chicken from the oven. Nicholas took the oven pan from her, and placed the heavy bird on the wooden counter closest to the dining area where they'd be eating in just about a half an hour. She put the casserole in right after, closing the oven door as Nicholas began preparing to carve the delicious roast chicken.

Noelle watched him work. While he always took care of everything without her having to ask, these days he took it even further; taking anything from her that was too heavy or too much work, would stress her out, or was remotely opposite to what he considered an acceptable amount of work for his pregnant wife. And while she appreciated him, and appreciated all he did for her, she would like to be active again. In fact. Noelle would very much like it if she were left alone long enough to do anything but rest, sit and knit, read, or nap for four hours every day—though she was human enough to admit that she was living her best life. She finally accepted that it was what she deserved, and what Nicholas had no problem giving her.

"You know I'm not incapable and that I'm just pregnant, right?" She asked him, sipping at the glass of water she'd— *he'd* retrieved for her awhile back. Nicholas glanced up from his cutting, his brown eyes boring into her as he glanced at very pregnant belly, and back at her eyes. He smiled crookedly, and made her heart flutter.

"Of course," he answered. "But why would you want to do it when you have a perfectly good-looking man to do it for you?"

Noelle rolled her eyes, "Well you have a point there. Just reminding you not to get used to this."

Nicholas chuckled. "Okay, honey. Whatever you say."

"I'm serious, Nicholas Birch," Noelle said. "I don't like sitting on my behind all day. As soon as this baby is born, it's back to business as usual."

Nicholas nodded, humming in mock agreement. He was more amused than compliant, which annoyed her to no end.

"You better take this seriously," she warned, leveling a finger at him. Nicholas winked, slicing the last of the chicken,

"As serious as a hangman's knot."

Noelle rolled her eyes again, smiling brightly as Carol sauntered into the kitchen, doll in hand. Noelle twirled one of Carol's blonde curls around her finger, beaming down at her daughter as she gazed around the kitchen.

"When's Jack gonna be here?" Carol whined, the same question she'd been asking since that morning, before either Nicholas or Noelle had fully awoken. Though a small figure in white, standing by their bed in the early dark hours of the morning, was just what they needed to solve the problem of sleepiness. Noelle glanced outside, the light suggesting it was close to noon, and the time Sam and his family would arrive.

"Soon, honeybee. They should be here any minute now."

Carol swayed on one foot, one of her hands clutched at the lip of the counter for balance. Her doll hung limply from the other hand, forgotten for the moment.

"Can we ride the horses to the lake?"

Nicholas shook his head immediately. "Sorry, honeybee, that's not going to happen. You guys can't be out there by yourselves alone."

Carol stuck her lower lip out in a pout. "But why?"

He turned and crouched, getting to her eye-level as he explained. "Because it's dangerous, honey. You could fall into the lake, or a bear could eat you, or..." His eyes went wide, his voice a low whisper. "The fairies might take you. And then how will we ever get you back?"

Carol sighed dramatically. "No they won't, Pa. They don't like red," she pointed to her bow, a very obnoxious *'duh, obviously'* look on her face as she stared her father down. He sighed.

"Sorry, honey. That's a definite no." He stood, returning to the chicken he had so dutifully carved up. Nicholas slid the knife under the bird, lifting the many pieces of sliced chicken flawlessly into the serving plate beside the pan, before he slid the knife out from under it. Noelle watched Carol's frown deepen, bracing herself for the meltdown that was about to happen in full force.

But Nicholas just winked. "Tell you what. When we're done with lunch, and Jack's gone home, we can go down to the lake together as a family. How does that sound?"

She watched her daughter contemplate the merits of this offer, watched her weigh the pros against those of taking her friend, Jack. Her frown dissipated and she nodded, not too thrilled but also not on the verge of a tantrum.

"Okay, Papa."

Nicholas smiled. "Good. Now go play in the living room and keep a lookout for our guests. We don't want to leave them waiting out in the cold, do we?"

Carol clamored off, Noelle caressing her head in passing. She glanced over at her husband, smirking.

"That was pretty impressive, Mr. Birch," she teased, and made her way over to him slyly and languidly, "You disarmed that loaded gun like an expert in your field."

"What can I say, sugar," he drawled, a grin spreading across his face. "I'm just that good."

Noelle laughed, throwing her head back with the action.

She tapped him playfully. "Keep it up and I'll give you ten more of these critters," she said, rubbing her belly.

Nicholas snorted. "Sounds like a plan."

They exchanged a quick kiss, breaking apart just as the doorbell rang and Carol announced the arrival of their guests.

Sam and Katherine stepped in, her friend looking as beautiful as ever, with a new baby tucked into the crook of her arm. The baby's name was Joseph; the newest addition to their family born in the early months of summer. He had fat little cheeks and neck rolls that looked like freshly raised bread dough—and Noelle thought he was cute enough to eat. She greeted her friend, placing a quick kiss on her cheek before she took the babe from her arms.

"He is beautiful, Katherine." Noelle cooed, and snuggled Joseph close to her. "Absolutely beautiful."

His mother smiled and gazed down at him with adoration. "He is, isn't he? Though I wish he wasn't—Sam already wants another."

Noelle's eyes widened as she looked towards their horde of children behind them. Katherine followed her line of sight, making an exaggerated face that made Noelle snicker. She ushered her friends inside, away from the cold and the illnesses that it brought with it. The kids stayed outside, Carol having joined them only a second before Noelle closed the door.

"Pastor Sam," she greeted, inclining her head as she balanced little Joseph on one hip, her hand on her belly. "Congratulations on the new baby."

He smiled warmly and squeezed her hand. "And to you too. When can we expect the little miracle?"

Noelle smiled. "Any day now. It shouldn't be too long."

"Wonderful," he exclaimed. "Then Joseph will have a friend to keep him company."

She nodded, following them into the dining area of the kitchen. Nicholas clasped Sam's hand in greeting, and placed a kiss on Katherine's cheek. He immediately took Joseph from Noelle's arms, cooing at the baby just as she had done a moment before. Noelle frowned.

"I had him first."

Nicholas stuck his tongue out. "Well I have him now."

"Now, now, children," Katherine chided as she plopped down on one of the dining table chairs. "Play nice. Everyone can have their turn holding the baby."

"Very funny," Noelle replied with a smirk, and took her own seat at the left side of the table, right next to the head.

Nicholas clapped his hands together, and cupped them over his mouth. "Children, time to eat!"

He moved back to the kitchen, carefully bringing one serving dish after another piled with food. Noelle's eyes stretched at the sheer *amount* of food they'd made. It was a true holiday feast.

The children came running through the front door, barely stopping to kick snow from their boots as they ambled towards the dining table. Jack sat beside his father on the right side of the table. Next to him sat Carol, and Katherine opposite, and then the rest of their hordes of children filed into their own seats scattered along the table. Little Joseph was sadly excluded from this event, having been laid on the sofa for a nap, with a stack of pillows to prevent him from falling off of it.

Nicholas at last took his seat at the head of the table, all of the food laid out splendidly. Every single piece of food looked scrumptious, and Noelle's mouth was watering at the sight. She almost begged Pastor Sam to make it a quick prayer so that she could sink into the meal Nicholas had so kindly prepared for them all.

They all joined hands, smiling warmly at once another before Pastor Sam prayed for them.

Nicholas piled food onto her plate before he served himself, just as Noelle served food onto Carol's plate. He gave her some of the roasted potatoes, roast chicken, sweet carrots, some green beans, and a slice from one of the freshly baked loafs she'd shoved in the oven this morning, before Nicholas had prepped everything else.

She smiled at him in gratitude, and dug in like she hadn't eaten in days. Since her pregnancy had started, she'd been nothing but *hungry*. The type of hunger that she hadn't even known existed. When her unborn child wasn't making her nauseous, they made her so incredibly hungry she felt like devouring one of the cows Nicholas had bought a few months ago.

The ranch had been flourishing, with Nicholas taking the time and effort to plant some corn, and buy a few cows, that they could either sell off or butcher themselves for a winter to eat. He even fixed the chicken coop she'd asked Henry *years* ago to fix; Noelle no longer had to chase after them in the mornings when she was barely awake enough to find her way outside. But out of all the things he'd done around the ranch, all the improvements and the effort, and the days spent tirelessly in the sun, she was probably the most thankful for him just being there.

She didn't need any of the other things he so graciously did for her without question or hesitation, she just needed him, and Carol, and their baby, and she'd be fine for the rest of her days.

Noelle shoveled the food into her mouth, accepting the giggles and wide eyes from the kids seated around her. She supposed she could put more effort into not eating like a bear after hibernation all winter, but the food was just so good, and she was just so hungry. She ate until her stomach was even more distended than before; gloriously full and almost to the point of bursting. Nicholas glanced over at her, shook his head at her satisfied smile, and continued eating with a smile of his own gracing that beautiful face.

Nicholas had started to grow a beard, one she wasn't entirely sure she loved or not. It was dark and thick, covering a large amount of his face and hiding that tiniest little dimple she just could never get enough of. When he'd first informed her of his idea to grow the thing, she'd naturally been opposed to it. But she had to admit, it was starting to grow on her.

Noelle cast a glance at the people around her, the full dining table and her friends that were laughing with her husband. She thought of the past year, and how it had been such a blissful dream compared to what she'd endured before she'd met Nicholas and adopted Carol. It felt like her life before had been nothing but a fever-induced dream, a nightmare she couldn't escape—until she did.

Nicholas smoothed his hand over her back, once again having to touch her as if to make sure she was still there. She leaned into his touch, hand rested on her belly as she gazed contently at her loved ones. Carol was down the table from her, deeply engaged in a conversation with Jack about goodness knows what.

Her hands were flailing as she explained something, Jack listening more intently than Noelle would have given him credit for. She had to give the boy his due, he was absolutely enamored with what Carol had to say as he chewed on his piece of chicken skin.

And while it was very cute, just the sight of him chewing the greasy piece of skin had her stomach roiling.

Noelle's face pulled into a scowl, her lips thin as she tried to stop the nausea from ruining her Christmas lunch. Nicholas, of course, took notice, and rubbed his thumb over her palm, something they'd discovered helped aid her nausea for some reason. She shook her head, her stomach roiling and roiling, and the muscles tightening to the point of pain. It was no longer nausea that had her uncomfortable, but the stabbing pain in her belly. It was hard to sit, so she stood and rubbed the side of her belly in an attempt to soothe the ache.

Nicholas frowned. "What is it, sweetheart?"

Another stabbing pain shot through her stomach, her entire belly contracting with the force of it. Noelle hissed, a breath escaping through her clenched teeth as she clutched at the back of her chair. Tiny droplets of sweat were now appearing on her brow.

"Nothing, I'm fine. It's just a stomach-ache," Noelle said. "I think I ate too quickly. Or I ate too much."

Nicholas' chair scraped on the floor as he stood, putting a hand on her back immediately. He rubbed his hand in circles on her upper back, soothing some of her pain right before another blindingly painful stabbing pain shot through her belly again.

Katherine shot up from her chair. "Noelle, I don't think it's the food." Katherine's voice was laced with a mixture of excitement and concern.

Noelle whimpered softly as another stabbing, burning pain emerged only minutes later. Again and again and again, until she was half-crouched, half-hanging onto the back of the chair, Nicholas' hands under her elbows to support her weight. Katherine had come to her side and placed both hands on the underside of her belly, where the muscles were feeling like they were on fire.

"Noelle, you're in labor. You're about to give birth, sweetie," Katherine exclaimed delightedly, which almost sent Noelle into overdrive.

"Is the baby coming?" Carol squealed. Katherine nodded, Sam already moving to remove all of the kids from the house. Nicholas was smiling broadly, but it quickly faded as Noelle started wailing.

Sweat was dripping from her in buckets now, her hair clinging to her forehead as she tried desperately to breathe through the pain. She smiled softly when Katherine's words sunk in, but that was quickly put to a stop when another contraction almost brought her to her knees. They ushered her up the stairs and to the main bedroom, Katherine instructing Nicholas to fetch some clean, boiled water and strips of cloth she could use.

"Come on, honey," her friend said gently. "Let's get you out of this dress and into something more... comfortable."

Noelle shook her head and ripped her arm from her friend's grasp. She laid her elbows on the side of the bed, taking just one moment to breathe through it. A groan slipped out as she exhaled, another wail following soon after. Katherine started unlacing the loose-fitted corset, careful not to pull too hard or put more pressure on her aching belly. Noelle smoothed sweat-slicked hair from her forehead, before bundling the sheets in her fists as another contraction made her want to hit somebody in the face. Specifically Nicholas, for no apparent reason.

She said as much out loud, to which Katherine responded with a laugh. "Oh that'll happen, sweetie. They put us in this position, so it's only fair."

Noelle huffed a laugh, sighing in relief when the corset finally loosened and fell to the floor. Katherine removed the dress, threw it over the back of the chair along with the corset, and helped her slip into her nightgown. After that, her friend removed all the covers from their bed, positioning the hordes of pillows so that she would be in a sitting position.

"Okay, honey, you can lay down now," Katherine said just as Nicholas returned with water and the rags she'd asked for. Noelle crawled onto the bed, one hand returning to clutch her belly as if that might stave off some of the pain. Her back hit the pillows, but it only worsened when she laid back. Noelle shook her head, motioning for Nicholas to help her stand up again.

He pulled her upright gently, grasping her smaller hand in his and didn't let go. She crouched in front of the bed again, her face smashed into the bed linens as she rode wave, after wave, after wave, of pain. She was sweating from everywhere now, and it was all she could do not to scream. Why had no one mentioned this to her? Why hadn't Katherine at least tried to make her understand just *how much pain* there would be. She glared at her friend, no longer wanting to punch just her husband.

"Do you want to do it this way?" Katherine asked, motioning towards her crouching position.

Noelle nodded. "It feels better." She gasped the words out, ending in another groan. Nicholas was perched next to her, soothing her with words of encouragement, soft-spoken words of devotion and love, and a hand on her back.

"Whatever you want, honey. You can do this your way," she said. "I've found that this position works best anyway."

She would know, she had close to what seemed like a thousand children. Noelle was thankful to have her here, especially considering her experience with all of the things pertaining to children and birth.

318

Katherine placed a damp cloth on her forehead, wiping at some of the sweat that stung her eyes. Noelle almost whimpered with gratitude, so incredibly blessed to be surrounded with those she loved. People that supported her and stood by her no matter what, friends that would stick by her side during Christmas day instead of returning home and leaving her and Nicholas alone to navigate what was about to happen. She was thankful for those around her, blessed and so incredibly thankful. Especially during this monumental and memorable experience.

Katherine smiled with joy. "You can start pushing, Noelle. It's time to meet your baby."

***

Sweat-slicked, exhausted, and unsure what part of her body hurt more, Noelle Birch gazed lovingly down at her first baby boy. Nicholas was perched on the edge of the bed beside her, arms slung over the top of her head, both of them tucked tightly into his side. He smiled down at his son, wonder and awe making his face light up in silent joy.

The little boy cooed and fussed, his gummy mouth opened in a whine. He had a full head of dark hair, beautiful pink skin, and the tiniest little hands she'd ever seen. He was barely bigger than a sack of flour, and he was absolutely perfect.

Nicholas leaned over and lightly grazed his forefinger over the boy's face, making soothing noises. Noelle looked up at him, exhausted but so incredibly happy she could burst out of her skin. Katherine had left moments ago to dispose of the rags and the bucket of blood-ridden water. Her friend had been nothing but supportive through the entire process, and talked her through everything she might have wanted to know or needed to know in order to not spiral out of control with nerves or fear.

Sam was downstairs with the children, only having called them inside from the cold when Noelle had calmed down. She was immensely grateful for both of them, taking control of the situation and making sure that Carol was taken care of while Noelle and Nicholas focused on this. She would be lying if she said it was an easy task, or that she hadn't been fearful for a moment. Giving birth had been the most challenging thing she'd done in her life, and even though it had hurt and had been the most exhausting thing she'd ever had to do, she would do it again and again and again.

There was nothing that could compare to the insurmountable love she'd felt once Nicholas had laid their son on her chest, still dirty and screaming, but beautiful, nonetheless. And theirs.

There was a knock at the door, both of them glancing toward it in anticipation as Carol's little blond head popped in. She held Katherine's hand as she entered the room, uncertainty painted over her entire face. Noelle's heart squeezed, and Nicholas, without a word, scooted over to make space for her right in between them. Her voice cracked as she asked,

"Do you want to meet your little brother, honeybee?"

Carol's face lit up like the sunrise on an early morning, eyes sparkling like the snow outside when the sun's rays shone upon it. She ambled over, careful not to disturb Noelle's body and hurt her, and climbed carefully onto the bed, right into the little space they'd reserved for her. Their daughter leaned over, smiling brightly as she finally laid eyes on her very first sibling.

Nicholas smiled broadly at the sight of her joy, meeting Noelle's eyes over the top of her head. She gazed up at him with adoration and devotion, made every single emotion she felt in that moment evident in her eyes, so that he might see and try to understand what this meant to her—what they meant to her.

This was all Noelle had ever wanted in her life. A home, a loving husband, hordes of children, and nothing but unconditional love. She had everything she had ever wanted or needed, and even more, all thanks to the man that sat at her side. He could have done what most husbands did and left the room when she pinched his forearm, when she screamed in his ears, or when she threatened him.

But he did not. He took it all in stride, allowed her to feel her emotions with no offense taken, and congratulated her on her strength afterward. Noelle was insurmountably in love with her husband, and by the heat in his gaze, she supposed he felt the same.

Carol leaned in closer and carefully caressed her brother's cheek with the tip of a finger. She giggled quietly. "He's so soft."

Noelle let out a laugh of her own. "He is, isn't he?"

She nodded, almost perched on Noelle's shoulder as she tried to scoot closer and closer and closer. Noelle didn't mind, though, as her daughter tried desperately to get as close to her little brother as possible. It was far better than Carol not wanting anything to do with him.

More knocks sounded at the door, along with some excited whispers as the Hastings family entered the room with Nicholas' permission. They filed into the spacious room, taking up so much space even though their bedroom was far from small.

Sam and Katherine kept the kids calm, reminding them of the delicacy of the little boy, and that Noelle's body would still be sore from the birth. They circled the bed, tiny faces smiling down at their little boy, some of the girls squealing with delight when he cooed again, and flailed his hands about.

Noelle adjusted her hold on him, hoisting him higher so that the eager little eyes might see him fully where he was wrapped in his blanket, beautifully small and innocent. All of them, even the boys, gasped when they saw his face fully, smiling at each other before they returned their gazes.

"He's so pretty!" Little Catriona exclaimed, and Bethany nodded, clapping her hands together in excitement.

Sam and Katherine scooted closer, peeking over Nicholas' shoulder at the bundle of joy. While Katherine had seen him just moments before, she still made kissing noises in his direction as if it were the first time she'd seen him. Sam held his tiny hand in his, the fingers wrapping around his finger tight enough that the man chuckled.

"He is absolutely beautiful, Noelle," Sam said, eyes damp as he gazed down at the little boy. "Extraordinary."

Nicholas smiled up at his friend. "It's a good thing you like him, then."

Katherine frowned. "How so?"

Noelle smiled sheepishly. "Well, we were hoping you would be their godparents…"

Sam looked ecstatic at the thought, but Katherine cast a glance around the room; to all of the of children they already had. Noelle bit back her giggle, pleading with her eyes until she finally sighed.

"Oh fine," her friend snapped, with no real heat. Nicholas laughed, and Carol frowned up at her godmother. Katherine met her eyes, frowning back as she folded her arms,

"You keep frowning like that, and I'll feed you to the chickens, little missy."

Carol huffed, but finally cracked a little smile when Katherine mimicked her.

Nicholas looked at Noelle again, cupping her cheek with love as he asked, "So what are we gonna call this little chicken?"

She glanced down at their son, at the full head of hair, the perfect little lips, and eyebrows. Noelle looked up, gazed deeply into the eyes of her husband, the love of her life, and said, "Gabriel."

THE END

Also, by Olivia Haywood

Thank you for reading "**Christmas Miracles and a Snowfall of Blessings**"!

I hope you enjoyed it! If you did, here you can also check out **my full Amazon Book Catalogue** at: https://go.oliviahaywood.com/bc-authorpage

Thank you for allowing me to keep doing what I love! ❤

Made in the USA
Monee, IL
07 December 2023

48441853R00184